UNTAMING LADY VIOLET

THE TAMING SERIES BOOK III

APRIL MORAN

UNTAMING LADY VIOLET

By
April Moran

For the shy violets in this world,
Don't let anything keep you from blooming wild.
And for James,
My love always.

CHAPTER 1

arby Meadows
Kent, England

LIFE AS A WALLFLOWER sometimes had its perks.

Wallflowers were forgettable. Unnoticeable. Invisible.

And Lady Violet Everstone had long ago decided that being invisible was a valuable commodity.

Today would be no different than any other, and once again, she was grateful her presence would go unnoticed.

With almost detached curiosity, she watched the man draw closer. His strides consumed the terrain, long legs never slowing as he marched with a single-minded purpose. Advancing across a hillside stained deep, emerald green, he glanced neither left nor right on his unwavering path.

Violet's heart gave a flutter of apprehension.

Was her imagination playing tricks or was he stalking straight toward her? Or more precisely, the tree she'd just recently climbed?

Violet almost lost her balance, trepidation morphing into

awkward clumsiness. With her free arm, she gripped the tree tighter, a dismayed cry escaping tightly pressed lips when one low-heeled shoe slipped free of her foot. Crafted of golden damask, it landed like a colorful leaf amongst the oak's exposed grayish-brown roots. She stared at the ground, horrified there was now tangible evidence of her presence.

Another quick check of the man's location dragged a groan of disbelief from deep in her chest.

Of all the meadows in England...

And of all the trees, his focus seemed narrowed on the one where she sat perched like a plump little partridge.

Blasted bad luck.

I'm safe up here. There is no reason to believe he will see me or my stupid slipper. And, I can do this before he comes any closer.

Violet's fingers scrambled over rough bark before finding purchase in the oak's grooves. With stocking-clad toes curling into the wood, and one hand clutching a branch above her head, she kept her precious bundle safe while moving away from the main trunk.

She stretched out the hand holding the crumpled bit of handkerchief, then stretched some more, and even more, until her arm ached and her toes cramped from digging into the tree's rough surface.

Just a... bit... further...

There!

Finally nestled within a cocoon fashioned of twigs, leaves, and bits of morning glory vine, the wee bird flopped disjointedly. Mouth yawning wide, it desperately chirped for food alongside two equally hungry siblings.

Violet tucked the bit of silk back into her bodice as the mama robin landed on the nest.

The bird's inquisitive eyes darted several times between Violet and the fledglings before deciding she could resume feeding her flock.

Violet watched, transfixed to see something so natural and primitive up close.

The chattering of a nearby squirrel jerked her back to awareness, a reminder that the discovery of her location was still possible. A course of action should be decided quickly.

Earlier, she'd scaled the enormous oak with stubborn determination, ignoring the possibility of a nasty tumble. Now, clutching the thinner overhead branch with both hands, Violet did not feel so brave. With her weight centered upon a limb, she froze in position like a circus performer toeing a tightwire.

Well, I would be very foolish to climb down now. And as long as I don't make the mistake of looking directly at the ground, I'll be fine.

Violet glanced down.

Her stomach flip-flopped as oxygen was suddenly in short supply. Deep, desperate gulps of air became essential to maintain her balance.

The ground could not possibly be so far away.

Or was it?

Oh, goodness. It truly was.

Her insides tumbled as if caught up in a maelstrom.

Violet carefully inched her feet sideways. When the thick trunk loomed before her, she embraced its solidness but found her arms would not wrap completely around its ancient girth.

That wasn't surprising as this particular oak was likely one of the largest at Darby Meadows. A perfect specimen of a climbing tree, it possessed numerous crooks and forks for one's feet and hands. Gnarled arms jutted in every direction, twisting upon themselves where they swept low along the ground. Bright with spring greenery, the thick foliage provided excellent concealment for curious squirrels and frantic mother robins.

And foolish girls such as herself.

It was from this vantage point that Violet accidentally discovered the ideal perspective for a commissioned painting of the Earl of Darby's sprawling manor house. Off in the distance, framed by forests and open green fields, it was a pastoral scene worthy of display in the Royal Gallery.

If only the earl's son would join her. He would certainly appreciate the stunning view and commit it to canvas.

But she wouldn't dare do something so imprudent as drawing his attention. He must never know she hovered in the branches high above him. If fortune were in her favor, that blasted errant slipper would remain undiscovered. The same went for the books stacked rather messily near the oak's base. And the woven basket containing grapes and cheese the cook so thoughtfully packed in case she grew hungry.

Watching the man emerge from the grove, Violet fervently swore she would never, *ever* climb anything higher than the steps to her own bed.

He halted where the widespread branches of the surrounding trees cast an edge of shadows on the ground. Violet wondered what he might do next. There was no reason for stopping here while tramping through the forest.

Why did he not continue on his way?

Thwap. Thwap. Thwap.

What a strange noise. Intermittent. Muffled. Out of place amongst the singing birds and the leaves which rustled every time the breeze picked up. Seconds ticked by until inquisitiveness got the better of Violet.

Her neck stretched as she tried for a better view through the canopy of leaves.

Is that a riding crop?

Crudely fashioned and thick as his wrist, it certainly resembled a crop. Violet frowned, having just watched him stalk across the meadows with no horse in tow and nothing in his hands.

In obvious agitation, the man slapped the object harder against his thigh. The noise rang even sharper. Violet winced.

Thwap!

Why, it wasn't a crop at all, but a stick. Something he must have picked up upon entering the strand of trees.

"Hell and damnation… If he thinks I'll be guilted or bullied into marriage, he'll find it a wasted effort."

The words were not muttered. They were forceful and clearly stated.

For eight long years, Violet had hung on this man's every utterance, lived for every careless smile, and the roughness of his tone was unfamiliar. It was a bit frightening if she were being honest, and Violet believed very much in honesty.

Shrinking back against the tree trunk, she frowned again while his words sunk in.

Marriage.

Concern chilled Violet's bones.

Had his father summoned him to Darby Meadows to issue that abhorrent ultimatum?

The earl must realize marriage was impossible for his only son, at least in the near future. After all, it was common knowledge the viscount currently suffered from a melancholy of rejection. An unfortunate by-blow of Grace Willsdown's marriage to Nicholas March, the Duke of Richeforte.

How could anyone believe the handsome viscount pacing so restlessly below might forget his broken heart so quickly?

Or so easily?

When he leveled a baleful glare back in the direction of the manor house, Violet sucked in a low breath. Tearing her gaze away from the hardened planes of the viscount's face was too difficult, so she settled herself against the trunk of the tree, content with observing him from this safe distance.

Her fingers twitched as they dug into the oak's bark.

Even angry, the man was incredibly handsome. Perhaps more so because of it. Violet could imagine the rich, chocolate-colored waves of his hair spilling over her palms, like reams of rough silk if she were to tug his head close to hers for a kiss.

It was one of her favorite fantasies.

"I can't believe Mother is pushing this issue. And Celia, the meddling traitor..."

The viscount again swatted the branch against his thigh.

Violet's gaze drifted helplessly over his impressive form as he turned the stick over and over in his palms. The viscount was an amazingly gifted artist, and his hands fascinated her. She couldn't stop looking at them. They were large and strong and so incredibly talented.

That gift was rarely shared with those outside his family. Violet counted herself lucky to be among the few to see his canvases.

The pieces he created were breathtaking slices of his inner thoughts. Violet felt voyeuristic gazing at them, wondering if it was a violation of his privacy the first time Celia showed her his studio.

Now, she dreamily wondered how it might feel to have the viscount's touch brush her skin. Would his fingers be warm and calloused from holding paintbrushes and bridle reins? Or cool and unblemished like Lord Gadley's?

Lord Gadley.

A fine tremor of distaste shimmied down Violet's spine. The man her parents would have her wed shared little in common with the viscount. Other than being of the male species and born of nobility, the two men were as different as night and day. Unfortunately, her parents had decided all solutions to their financial woes rested at Lord Gadley's feet.

Violet recalled her father's admonishment the morning she headed for Darby Meadows without them.

"Violet, it will be a stroke of luck on your part should you land Gadley. And a stroke of genius on mine. Remember our situation, young lady."

"Oh, do try harder, won't you, Violet? Won't you try to be charming and less like an overstuffed ottoman waiting for someone's

propped feet when next he sees you?" Her mother's tone echoed her father's long-suffering exasperation. *"It's said he prefers a girl with a bit of spirit, but your father has extolled the virtues of a quiet, dutiful wife. One must hope the lure of our family name overcomes the reality of gaining a pretty, but dull, wife in the bargain.*

Violet could only nod, eyes prickling with tears. She was always obedient when following her parents' wishes, although secretly she hoped Lord Gadley never offered for her hand. Her unsuitability on the Marriage Mart was a failing Violet faced daily. Landing a wealthy spouse was her responsibility. One her father reminded her of with increasing frequency over the last six months.

Only once did Violet dare question the need to marry at all.

Her mother's lips thinned while waving herself in an agitated manner using a red Chinese silk fan. The earl's face turned a shade identical to the fan. The awful color did not stop spreading until it reached the tips of his ears.

"It is what dutiful daughters do for their families." Father's manner was blustery and indignant. *"To further social standings. To repair old feuds. To gain financial freedom and repay debts."*

Repay debts. That part worried Violet the most. Those two words caused a lack of sleep over too many nights and left her acutely aware of her worth as a daughter.

Whether love was part and parcel or not, Violet must marry. Whether *she* wished it or not, she was a sacrifice.

The fact she did not want the man her parents selected was inconsequential.

Questioning their choice required courage she did not possess. Their motives remained a murky unknown and Violet felt queasy gaining further insight into her parents' actions. Perhaps her ignorance was for the better.

She'd not thought of Lord Gadley at all during this brief respite from London, at least until this very moment. Instead of worrying over unwanted engagements, she spent the past few days immersed in books, enjoying the springtime of the Kent countryside, and rising as early as she pleased for breakfast chocolate and crumpets.

How easy it was pretending her life was not on a collision course with fate. Until the viscount below her began cursing the institution of marriage, she had ignored it. His one-sided argument was a rude reminder that Violet's idyllic escape would soon be over.

Yes. Over. Along with any illusions of freedom. Lord Gadley would arrive at Darby Meadows. Father and Mother would follow. And an engagement would likely be announced shortly thereafter, provided she charmed the man into offering for her.

"Damn it all!"

The viscount's curse drew Violet's attention away from her depressing thoughts. When he raked a hand through the thick strands of his hair, she nearly sighed aloud at the romantically tragic figure he cast.

But then his pacing moved him out of eyesight.

Heart thumping fast, Violet leaned away from the tree so she could keep him in view.

Dark of countenance, with lightly bronzed skin and richly colored hair, the viscount was devilishly attractive. Women, young and old, swooned over the fact his eyes gleamed like aged mahogany. Famously witty and possessing an affable nature, his firm mouth curved often in a smile.

Many inside their social circle, and even those outside it, considered him an important friend. An influential lord. Although Violet had never attended one, it was said he hosted fabulous parties, unrivaled in generosity and rumored to be quite scandalous.

The viscount was also very... fit. Broad shoulders strained the seams of his afternoon coat, while muscular legs and thighs spoke of a fondness for the outdoors and physical activity. He was an excellent rider, enjoying a hands-on approach with his horses. Such athleticism contradicted the artistic side of his nature.

Heavens, his chest is wider than the burlwood desk in Father's study. And, oh yes, his hands...

Violet smiled dreamily at the wanton path her thoughts took. Should the viscount ever touch her, she imagined it would feel like raw silk brushing over her skin. Fine, but rough. Gentle, but sturdy. Those large hands of his would hold her firmly, and the viscount would...

"I'll not marry simply because it fits Father's vision for the future."

The stick cracking in half punctuated the viscount's fierce declaration. The pieces of wood were cast aside with a snarl of disgust and an oath so foul Violet let out a startled gasp.

She couldn't help it, for it was a very wicked word, although she had no idea of its true meaning.

And because he'd not suffered a loss of hearing since she'd seen him last, the involuntary sound did not go unnoticed.

Violet's heart pounded until she grew lightheaded.

Concealed by foliage, she pressed herself against the oak's thick but her lone slipper suddenly snagged on the rough bark.

A bit desperate, she gave her foot a little shake, then watched the shoe fly off her foot. It tumbled through the canopy of leaves and bounced harmlessly off the top of the viscount's head.

"Oh, no!"

Oh, no indeed.

Dark brown eyes, so dark with frustration and surprise they were nearly ebony in color, unerringly searched for the owner of that feminine voice. As if it might aid in concealment, Violet squeezed her own eyes shut, praying he could not see through the leaves where she cowered.

Another snarled oath slashed the air, and Violet's pulse sprinted, slowed, then raced again.

"You, there. *You!* What is your business? State it quickly!" His command barked out in militant fashion.

Violet's eyes flew open, clashing with the viscount's as he bent and retrieved her shoe, his gaze never wavering.

A crisp breeze rustled the leaves but had little to do with the shiver rushing down her spine.

Lord Tristan Buchanan, Viscount Longleigh, had found her.

CHAPTER 2

"*Come down.* Show yourself at once!"

Tristan's voice rang out in a staccato of clipped, hard notes.

Unforgiving.

Rigid.

In that moment, he was a far cry from the charming gentleman society knew so well.

"I warn you… trespassers are dealt with harshly here. Poachers even more so."

Poachers? Good lord. Violet never considered there might be men of nefarious character trespassing on Darby property.

She considered her options. Should she throw herself upon his mercy? Or remain cowering amongst the leaves until he gave up and went on his way? He did not know her identity, and there was little reason that should change.

Still, nauseating shyness overwhelmed Violet. *This* man's attention, sparse though it was, never failed to throw her emotions into a veritable whirlwind of panic. Countless times over the years he'd left her tongue-tied and blithering like a simpleton after simply bidding her good-day.

11

And now…

Oh, blast it all … my shoe actually struck him.

The viscount stood directly below the branch she stood balanced upon. Hands planted square on his hips, the errant shoe clenched in one large fist so it resembled a balled-up bit of fabric, he glared at her. Annoyance flowed off him in waves. Violet had a quick image of him stalking about as though he were a pirate on a marauding ship. Only a cutlass dangling from his side and a hat sporting an oversized, feather plume atop his head was required to complete the image in her mind

"I'm neither trespasser—" Violet's tongue tangled, impeding her speech in the worst way, "—nor poacher."

The sentence ended in a squeak.

Valiantly attempting bravery, she cleared her throat. Hopefully, she wouldn't sound too bloody terrified. "Lord Longleigh, it's-it's only me. Violet Everstone. Celia's friend. Remember?"

Tristan's stare was unblinking.

Mortified by his uncharacteristic silence, Violet cringed. She'd been Celia Buchanan's closest friend for years, yet the lady's brother scowled as if he really had stumbled across a trespassing stranger.

"Violet Everstone?" A muscle ticked in his tight jaw. "What the fu—" The words died in an abruptly strangled cough before he spoke again. "What in God's name are you doing up there?"

Edging into view so the viscount could see it was truly her, Violet's fingers dug into the tree bark. Picking at the coarse surface was ruining the perfect ovals of her fingernails. Mother would be displeased, as would Lord Gadley. He commented once how lovely her hands were, then seemed genuinely surprised he might actually like something about her.

The thought of his disappointment, along with her mother's, proved oddly invigorating. A small tingle of rebellion reminding her that she did not desire Gadley's approval. Not one bit.

However, if Tristan Buchanan decided he wanted them, Violet would climb to the moon and gather the stars.

"Must I ask my question again?" he barked.

Violet was startled so badly she was forced to clutch the tree if she had any hope of remaining in it.

"I can hear you perfectly well, my lord. There's no reason to shout as though you were a street hawker," she reprimanded in exasperation.

"Street hawker …." Tristan's mutter was incredulous before his tone became absolutely icy. "What, if you will permit my inquiring, are you doing up in a tree on my family's property?"

"I've good reason for my actions, my lord."

"I'm breathless with anticipation to hear it, Lady Violet."

She frowned down at him. "I would not be up here without purpose."

"And this required risking life and limb so you could hide like a frightened kitten?" His voice was deceptively flat, but a tiny spark of interest appeared in the velvety brown eyes trained so intently upon her.

Violet imagined flinging herself from the tree and happily drowning in the depths of his gaze.

Then those eyes sharpened in a predatory manner. Indeed, his entire body went on alert. As if searching for hidden dangers, his gaze swept the clearing's perimeter. "Are you up there of your own accord?"

Violet nodded then added, "Yes," when it seemed he expected a verbal response.

"Were you frightened into doing so? By man or beast?"

Puzzled, she shook her head. "No."

Tristan relaxed. Tipping his head back, he pinned her with yet another hard glare. "Then what is the reason for your current location?"

The viscount shifted his arms, crossing them over that impossibly wide chest. The movement stretched the black superfine cloth of the coat across his shoulders. From her vantage point, Violet could see his throat muscles contract when he swallowed.

She swallowed, too. Why did her face suddenly feel so dreadfully hot, like she suffered from fever?

Pressing a palm against one cheek, she tested her temperature in distracted curiosity. Then, reminded of her precarious position, she clutched the tree trunk again.

"I-I, uh, you see, it was a baby robin. The poor thing fell from the nest." Violet nodded toward the bundle of twigs which was barely visible through the abundance of green leaves. "The mother was quite frantic, so I decided there was no harm returning —"

"Come down this instant."

The words were not a veiled plea in the interest of safety but a command she should follow without question.

Ordinarily, Violet would have scrambled down as instructed. She would have obeyed the assertive tone of that husky voice without hesitation, but for some reason, she grew more still. Her body, while internally snapping to attention, refused to actually *move*.

Wasn't that just the strangest thing?

"Lady Violet, should I procure a saucer of milk as enticement?"

"What? I do not understand..." she stuttered. Why would he offer her milk, of all things?

"I'm told kittens love it." Tristan's manner shifted, becoming something silky and... wicked. "Will that bring you down? Or will you be lured by other means?"

Violet's lip pursed. He confused her. It was as if the viscount *wanted* a reason to make her obey his demand.

Silence stretched between them until she shifted her feet. The branch swayed in response.

Tristan moved closer. "You misunderstand me." There was

the impression he might prove dangerous should his commands go unheeded. His eyes narrowed slightly. "I'm not making a suggestion."

"It is you who misunderstands, Lord Longleigh. I've no wish to disobey you, but… You see, you must turn around," Violet explained.

Tristan's dark slashing eyebrows knit together in a vee of irritation.

"I cannot extricate myself while you watch," she sputtered with embarrassment. Did he have no comprehension of her dilemma? "It's quite improper."

"Improper." His full lips quirked. "Stuck midway up an English oak, and you are concerned for propriety? Despite the strangeness of this situation, I think I find you most amusing." He waved the slipper at her. "By chance, are you still wearing this one's mate? Let me see."

Violet quivered at the scandalous suggestion. Crippling shyness might shroud her like a morning mist, but it wasn't enough to silence her tongue.

"I'm *not* stuck."

She deliberately ignored the wicked directive to lift her skirts.

The viscount made a noise that might have been a snort.

"Well, I'm not." Violet's stubborn tone was quite foreign to her, the tilt of her chin even more so. She hoped she sounded very brave when she loftily instructed, "Turn around, my lord. I shall not come down otherwise."

"Oh, very well!" Tristan's hands rose in surrender as he whirled and presented his back. "When you fall, you may only blame yourself. Even with my reflexes, I doubt I'll catch you."

"I won't fall." Violet shimmied around the tree, strategically placing her feet in different crooks and crannies. "I've always thought this oak well suited for climbing, although this is my first attempt with such endeavors."

A wave of dizziness swept her and was fought back.

"Climbing up was much harder," she explained unnecessarily. This chatter was *not* normal for her, but Violet attributed it to nerves. After all, she'd never descended from a tree with a handsome viscount in such close proximity before.

He isn't peeking, is he? My position is most unladylike. Oh, I do hope he has not crushed my slipper too badly.

With a shake of her head, she gathered her courage while continuing her descent.

"I did not have use of both hands before, as you see I was holding the poor bird. Which means, Lord Longleigh, the chances of a tumble now are greatly reduced."

CHAPTER 3

$\mathcal{A}$ feminine cry of alarm was Tristan's only warning of impending disaster.

He spun just in time, dropping the slipper and catching Violet as she plummeted like a stone. Well, in truth, he only partially caught her. Mostly, he served as a breakpoint for her fall.

With a muffled *"Oof!"* they landed on the ground, cushioned by lush grass and loamy earth. By twisting his shoulders just so, Tristan maneuvered them so he absorbed the brunt of the crash.

Violet wound up sprawled across his stomach with her hips, her plush, graspable hips, nestled between his legs.

Indecently nestled between his legs.

Pressed intimately against his groin.

Grinding. *There.*

A rush of blood, hot and fluid, surged to that precise area. Tristan let out a tortured groan, and along with it came unmistakable panic.

His panic, not hers.

Lady Violet's gaze locked with his. Her eyes were wide. Shocked. And such an impossible shade of blue, they appeared stained purple. Tristan never realized that her eyes were such an intense color. They sparkled like precious jewels as she gaped unblinking at him. Thick and surprisingly dark eyelashes framed the crystal-clear depths.

Rare amethysts. The rarest shade of the deepest violet.

Her tongue darted out, bringing attention immediately to a spot of blood in the center of her lower lip. She licked the crimson drop away, and before he could help himself, another groan, this one constructed of pure lust, escaped him.

It was quickly buried beneath a layer of concern.

"You are hurt."

The words emerged as a growl, but it couldn't be helped. An abrupt desire to protect this delicately plump female over-whelmed Tristan.

Primal. Heated. Surprising.

And completely unwelcome.

Violet stared as though he uttered nothing but sheer gibber-ish. Well, in all fairness, maybe he had. His head felt scrambled enough.

"Your lip... it's cut," Tristan prompted. Fascinated, he watched the milky hue of her cheeks turn a shade of scarlet that almost eclipsed the color of her hair.

Speaking of which... Tendrils escaped what was probably once a tidy bun arranged by her maid that very morning. Now, it was a glorious mess. Curling wisps of rich, glossy, burnished red. A bright green oak leaf accented one upswept curl still held haphazardly within the hairpins.

Another rumble issued from deep in Tristan's throat. Violet had been Celia's friend for years, and he was just now seeing her. *Really* seeing her.

When the hell did she grow up?

"Oh." Violet touched a fingertip to the injury. "Is it? That-that was from before. Not from falling. I bit it, I think."

Her voice was so soft, so... so lyrical. And so different from moments ago when a bit of feistiness laced her words. This hesitancy he heard now? Tristan did not like it at all.

"You were far more impudent up in the tree." The corner of his lips twitched with a grin as he teased her. "Testing those claws from a safe distance, it seems. Now that has been erased, what shall the kitten do?"

A lacy scrap of a handkerchief was shoved between her breasts. It was a tempting valley, created by the modest neckline of the deep green dress she wore. Tristan considered taking the cloth and dabbing her lip, but in a flash of utter weakness, he did something entirely unexpected.

His index finger gently skated over the tiny wound in a soothing fashion until Violet's eyes fluttered half-shut. A new blood droplet swept across the plump flesh of her lip, staining it. Dazed, she watched as he slowly brought his finger to his own mouth and sucked it clean.

Electrifying jolts of abrupt awareness coursed between them. This—this was an awakening. An unfurling. A violent spring storm rolling over the meadows and everything in its path.

She was the thunder, low and distant while he was the lightning, intense and blinding. And this attraction between them roiled immediately to life.

Sweet. Heady. Dangerous.

With a strangled squeak, Violet scrambled away in a flurry of green velvet, hampered by the tangle of her skirts.

Knife-sharp pain lanced through Tristan, sizzling nerve endings and a few he never realized existed. Dislodging Violet's knee from his groin, he half rolled onto his side, hands fisted so he wouldn't clutch those parts now furiously throbbing.

On her feet at last, Violet stood just out of reach. His obvious distress concerned her, evidenced by the frantic wringing of her hands.

"I've crushed you, haven't I? Is it your arm? A rib? Tell me… what is broken? Perhaps you've suffered a head injury."

"A head injury?" With a grimace, Tristan pulled himself into a sitting position.

"Oh, dear. You do not remember a shoe landing on your head? This may be more serious than either of us realize. I shall seek help, but I cannot go in my bare feet. Speaking of my slipper, I do believe you are, um… sitting on it now."

Tristan sucked in another breath, willing the fuzziness in his head to dissipate. "It's neither my ribs nor my arm, for God's sake. And it's not a head injury, although not for lack of trying. You—"

He abruptly clamped his mouth shut. How did one inform a well-bred young lady that she'd kneed him in the ballocks? One couldn't, of course. Even if he'd licked the coppery-sweet tang of her blood from the tip of his finger just mere seconds ago, for God knew what reason, he couldn't be that bold.

Had he really done that? Tasted her as if he were some sort of animal and she were his latest catch?

St. Simon's Cross… what the hell am I thinking? She's my sister's dearest friend. I've known her since she was just a girl. His teeth ground. "An elbow to my stomach is the only damage. I'm fine."

Violet looked unconvinced, flushing such an alarming shade of pink, that Tristan worried she might actually faint.

"My slipper…" she squeaked out.

Rolling to his feet in one smooth motion, Tristan grasped Violet's elbow, steadying her when she swayed in alarm at his quickness. Eyes wide, she touched the center of his chest, the palm of her hand flat against his skin.

Imagining all the things he could do with Violet Everstone was turning him inside out. He sucked in a breath, his heart racing beneath her palm.

"You've turned a peculiar shade," Violet whispered, peeking

up at him. "Greenish. Like a gooseberry. I don't know what to do to help you."

"I'm quite all right, Lady Violet. Do not concern yourself."

"It is hardly inconsequential to have someone of my size land on you. You have my sincerest apologies." Her hand clenched his shirt as she regarded him anxiously. "Can you walk? Or should I return to the house and arrange for a cart to help in transporting you across the meadow?"

"Your size—" Tristan stared in astonishment, suddenly realizing Violet thought herself to be overweight.

Nothing could be further from the truth. While softly rounded in all the best places, those places a man expected to feel plump flesh between his fingers and beneath his palms, Violet hardly needed to worry about an overabundance of figure.

She was lush and feminine, the top of her head barely reaching the center of his chest. Everything about her made him feel strangely more masculine. Dear God, she even smelled delicious. Like lavender mixed with something delicately earthy. Vanilla, perhaps. Or bergamot.

Tristan frowned. "Rest assured, your size is *not* an issue. I daresay you weigh no more than a dormouse."

Violet's eyes lowered. Again, she licked her bottom lip. It was still bleeding, but just barely. Tristan reminded himself she *had* fallen from the tree. And the devil take it, now he knew how she tasted.

Easily holding her captive with a hand on her elbow, he asked, "Are you injured anywhere on your person?"

"Injured?" She repeated his question breathlessly. "No. I don't believe so."

Tristan ran his palms down her arms.

How lovely she would be captured on canvas. Damn if I wouldn't pay a king's ransom for the privilege of painting her.

An ordinary man might overlook the details his artist's heart and eye greedily noted. Devouring her features, he took in the heart-shaped face and daintily upturned nose. Eyebrows of dark auburn arched above thickly lashed, violet-hued eyes, giving her the appearance of a gentle doe. High cheekbones sat in pleasing proportion with the rest of her features, and a tiny dimple graced her right cheek whenever she smiled.

As far as Tristan could see, Violet possessed not a single freckle, unusual given the shade of her dark red hair. Smooth and unblemished, her skin was the color of ivory. And warm. So damned warm she didn't feel real. He half believed she would feel like cool marble beneath his hands.

Tristan abruptly sank to the ground. Delving beneath her skirts, he traced her ankles with gentle fingers. There were no swollen or tender areas, but she was now missing both slippers. He quickly assessed her tiny toes through silk stockings, smiling when a mortified gasp escaped her.

Violet stumbled back as far as he would allow.

Tristan's fingers circled around one trim ankle and tightened, keeping her prisoner.

"Lord Longleigh! This is completely unnecessary!"

Tristan chuckled. His hand lingered, brushing the fine bones in exploration. "I disagree. You appear quite shaken. How else should I determine your injuries?"

"I've no injuries!"

"I must make sure. After all, it's the very least I can do for such a dear friend of the family."

Violet gave him such a look, one teetering between horror and elation, that Tristan hesitated. That one look slammed him back to awareness.

Toying with her was amusing, but this little flirtation might be considered cruel by some. And pointless.

"It's turning cool, Lady Violet, and dusk approaches. You should return to the house." Coming to his feet, he scooped up her slipper. Its mate was found along with other items at the base of the tree.

While she slid the shoes on, Tristan turned away. He refused to look at the dainty feet and fine-boned ankles his hands had roamed all over under the pretext of checking for injuries.

"You will forgive me if I do not escort you?" he said, staring at the canopy of glossy oak leaves above them. "It's best not to court rumors."

"Yes, of course."

Her voice was hesitant again. Unsure and almost trembly.

Tristan hazarded a glance in her direction in time to catch her shaking out her skirts.

"There's no need for formality at Darby Meadows, especially when our families have known one another for ages. You and Celia are like sisters to each other so you may call me Tristan, if you like. I would be honored to use yours in return, if you are so inclined to grant that permission."

A flash of sadness lit Violet's eyes, but her sweet smile had his heart stuttering in its beat.

It was difficult not to wonder how her pretty mouth would feel molded beneath his own.

"I've no objection to you using my given name, Tristan." Violet took the picnic basket from his hands, nodding with approval when she saw he'd placed all of her books inside. "Will you attend supper tonight with everyone?"

"As I've only arrived, and with May Day festivities approaching, I won't disappoint my mother so soon. So, the answer is yes. I shall."

Tristan rarely disappointed his parents. Theirs was an uncommonly placid relationship, only recently marred by more recent disputes regarding his failure to pursue marriage.

"Surely, there are suitable women you could entertain as potential brides," Father remarked earlier that afternoon. "You are turning twenty-

seven years of age this year, Tristan, and it is high time you followed your friends' examples. It is your duty to carry on the Buchannan bloodline and provide the next Earl of Darby. Knowing my poor health this past winter, it is imperative you address this matter soon."

Tristan was admittedly concerned for Father's health. Shortness of breath and troubling chest pains had laid the man low since the previous autumn. Now, feeling somewhat better with the warmer weather, the Earl's attention re-focused on his legacy. Celia and Mother, curse them both, helpfully supplied a list of young women deemed eligible.

Privately, Tristan scoffed at his parents' opinions on his avowed state of bachelorhood.

He did not suffer from a broken heart.

Nor melancholy. Or dejection. Nor was he drowning his sorrows in a string of mistresses and nights made hazy from alcohol, although he certainly enjoyed the delights of both.

The *ton* was frantic to turn his failure in marrying Grace into something worthy of a Shakespearean turn. Gossip mills insisted he still pined for the new duchess. That he drank and caroused so he might forget his stolen love.

No one realized more than Tristan himself that a union with Grace would have sputtered and burned to a quick death. They were too much alike, headstrong and impulsive. And while Grace amused him with her cleverness and wild spirit, he had regarded her as a possession kept out of his reach.

Grace recognized that from the very beginning. She never treated him as anything other than a sibling for which Tristan was eternally grateful. It made the swirling rumors of a bitter rift between himself and Nicholas easier to ignore. After all, any lingering resentment had been dissolved over a bottle of brandy before Nicholas and Grace's nuptials even took place.

A carefree, pleasure-seeking bachelorhood where Tristan only worried for himself seemed the best path for him. He intended on keeping that status for as long as possible. Maybe even forever, regardless of his father's wishes and pleas to find a suitable wife.

It was why rationalizing the words spilling from his mouth proved especially troublesome.

"I'll have Mother seat me beside you for dinner. We'll continue this discussion on tempting reluctant creatures from trees and what is best served as an incentive."

Violet blushed but nodded in agreement. Before Tristan could utter another word, she turned and practically galloped down the hillside away from him.

The predator lurking within his soul reared its head.

What the devil was she running from?

Me?

Surely not.

She moved with such haste Tristan feared she might lose her slippers again and go tumbling head over heels down the gentle slope. Brow creased with perplexing interest, he watched until the green of her dress melted into the strand of woods beyond the open meadow.

What an odd little creature you are, Violet Everstone.

And if the lady wished to be chased...

He might change his mind and oblige her.

CHAPTER 4

Upon reaching the Rose Parlor, Violet plopped down in a carved rosewood chair. Deep in thought, she traced the intricate pattern of the cream brocade upholstery with a forefinger.

After that mad dash across the meadows, she was completely out of breath, her heart pounding as she recalled the viscount's words.

He would sit beside her at dinner. Engage in conversation. Laugh and smile with her while others watched. While people whispered and speculated.

Her anxiety steadily increased as she relived the unexpected encounter with Tristan. His body was so hard and muscular, yet when used as a cushion for her fall, she found herself perfectly content while scandalously sprawled across him.

Pressing a hand against her stomach, her insides tumbled topsy-turvy as she recalled how he smiled. Even though his voice was gruff, he had not seemed cross that a shoe landed on his head, followed by herself.

Thank goodness she'd been too impatient to don her

customary walking boots this afternoon. Had one of those struck the viscount, it most certainly would have left a knot.

"Twenty gold crowns."

Violet bolted upright. Celia Buchanan, the daughter of the Earl and Countess of Darby, trailed a finger across the door's paneled surface as she entered the room. Flashing a wide grin, she repeated herself, "Twenty gold crowns. To know who or what placed such a smile on your face, dear friend.

Violet blushed. "Don't be silly. I'm thinking of no one in partic—"

Celia held up a hand. "Ah-ha!" Shaking her head until dark, glossy curls bounced on her shoulders, she took a seat in a matching chair. "You were off on a wonderful adventure just now, in a faraway land of great pleasure and excitement. And, I wager it was not Lord Ghastly waltzing you about in circles."

Lips stretching into a thin line, Violet *humphed* in exasperation. "Had I realized the constant misuse of it, I would not have told you the creation of that nickname."

"But it's so perfect!" Celia sighed, dramatically. "Truly, it couldn't possibly be anything else."

"I shall forget myself and say it aloud in his presence one day." Violet bit her lip before remembering the slight injury. "My parents will disown me, of course."

"Of course." Celia nodded in calm agreement. "Then you'll come live with us here at Darby Meadows. And have all the freedom your heart desires."

"Unless you are of the male gender, no one is allowed that much liberty."

Celia's lips pursed at Violet's observation. "Don't be such a sourpuss. Not today. Not when the person you love most has finally arrived. The chance he will ask for your hand still exists."

Standing abruptly, Violet made her way to the bank of windows overlooking the north lawn. Leaning against the heavily carved frame of the sill, she watched the groundskeepers trimming the masses of white rose hedges in meticulous fashion.

Preparations were being made for the May Day celebration and the subsequent ball on the Darby estate in three weeks' time. Over the coming days, guests would trickle in, including her parents and the man they expected her to marry.

Even the Duke and Duchess of Richeforte would celebrate May Day at Darby Meadows. Returning from a honeymoon tour of the continent, they had sent word of their attendance before continuing on to Bellmar Abbey for the foaling season.

Violet's stomach hurt when she thought of Grace March.

"Your brother hardly realizes I'm alive, Celia. It's a foolish dream that he might ever consider me in a romantic sense. Besides, they say he is still in love with Grace. And I'm doomed to wed Lord Ghastly. I mean, Gadley."

"*They* have no inkling of what's going on," Celia answered brightly. "Oh, Violet. We both know Tristan was never *in* love with Grace. He only thought he was. He truly sees her now as he should have from the very beginning. As a sister."

"Well, he certainly did not love Grace as one would a sister a few months ago." Violet traced a wormwood trail in the windowsill with her fingernail. "The moment he laid eyes on her, he was enamored. I witnessed it myself at every turn. And it was painful to see."

"You witnessed infatuation. Nothing more. Had it been *true* love, my dear brother would have ceased consorting with his various mistresses. He would not have been able to think of anyone or anything other than Grace, and that was certainly not the case. Tristan saw her as someone unlike any other girl in his orbit. A conquest, an oddity he could admire, but one he would never understand." Coming up beside her, Celia reached out and tucked a flame-hued strand of hair behind Violet's ear. "You see, Grace and the duke understand each other. They are perfectly matched and *that* was fate. Two wild at heart creatures that found love and contentment at last. Tristan would never have that with her."

"No other woman will ever measure up to Tristan's idea of her perfection." Violet did not bother stemming the tears that sprang to her eyes. "You cannot tell me he does not regret losing her."

Tristan might behave in a carefree manner, creating a façade of merriment and good humor after being rejected so cruelly, but surely, he was suffering.

"He could not lose her when he never had her to begin with, dear. Now, Father has reminded Tristan he must become serious about marriage. And Violet, with every ounce of my soul, I believe you are meant to be together. You knew it the moment you saw him. Now, we need Tristan to realize it, too. Before it's too late and another captures his attention."

A tiny shiver raced through Violet, remembering the first time she saw Tristan.

It was inside the Darby Meadows conservatory eight years before. Chasing Celia in a madcap attempt to retrieve a hair ribbon, Violet skidded down a gravel path and found a dark-haired, dark-eyed viscount instead. That particular day was rainy and cold, but her heart exploded with sunlight when she saw the smile curving his lips.

Having just turned eighteen, the viscount had come home from Cambridge. Upon his arrival, frustrated perhaps by the boring monotony of his travels, Tristan escaped to the conservatory. Seated on a stone bench, he busily sketched one of the potted lemon trees by the fountain in the building's center. A jewel-toned butterfly perched on one of the blossoms, its wings slowly fluttering.

When Celia asked why he chased butterflies instead of choosing a steed for the fox chase scheduled the next day, Tristan's firm, full lips tugged upward. Violet lingered in the background, staring unabashedly at the handsome viscount.

"Does the horse I choose matter all that much?" He had replied with good-natured affection for his younger sibling. "Little fiend, you will undoubtedly out-ride me."

With Celia's assistance, Violet haunted the viscount's footsteps like a tiny ghost for nearly two weeks that particular spring. The girls spent hours discussing every look or smile Tristan haphazardly tossed Violet's way.

Celia had not minded when her new twelve-year-old friend fell instantly in love with her older brother. And she never shied from expressing her insights on matters that oddly enough almost always came true.

That year, when goodbyes were being said, Celia clasped her friend's tiny hands within her own and said something that forever changed Violet.

"Don't worry, sweet little Violet. He will see you one day..." A *faraway light sparkled in Celia's dark brown eyes. "My brother may search, but he will not find happiness with anyone else."*

How Celia was so certain of that fact, Violet did not know.

Because for the past eight years, she remained invisible. Tristan never acknowledged her existence with anything other than a respectful distance.

Until today.

Today was different. Violet's heart fluttered as she recalled her boldness.

She was different today in the woods. Today, she actually *conversed* with the man. Laughed with him. Felt his body against her own.

Which made her wonder...

Why did he do something so strange? Why did he taste the blood from my lips? And was that truly hunger I saw in his eyes or wishful hope on my part?

"I wanted your name placed on the list of eligible young women, but Mother would not allow it." Celia did not conceal the irritation in her tone. "She says it would violate the trust

Lord Everstone has placed in my father when they act as your chaperones. It is complete poppycock. Oh, Violet! I don't care what your parents say. You will *not* marry Gadley! It shall be tragic if you do."

Violet half-turned from the window, gazing solemnly at her dearest friend.

"Have you been kissed many times, Celia?"

Her head tilting with the odd question, Celia grinned. "More times than is proper, I'm afraid. I've decided it will be much easier choosing a husband if there is some sort of measurement to determine suitability. Why do you ask?"

Violet blushed under the scrutiny. "If a man has the chance to kiss you, but chooses not to do so, would you consider that an indication of disinterest? I ask out of curiosity. In case I find myself in a similar situation and the gentleman does not ..." Her words trailed off in embarrassment.

"I can't imagine a man with such willpower exists, Violet. When the moment arises, you will find yourself kissed with such thoroughness it shall astound you," Celia replied honestly. "You are the very essence of temptation, my dear. Few men can resist that once they are made aware of it."

WITH AN HOUR of free time before dinner, Celia insisted that Violet join her in the main salon. A variety of activities were planned for the guests, including card games such as whist or vingt-et-un.

More scandalous sport would take place as well, provided no one's parents or chaperone ruined the fun. Many of these involved females either being kissed or surreptitiously fondled under the guise of harmless amusement.

Violet had never played such games before. The outrageous ones, that is. Wiping damp palms along the side of her dark, lavender-hued gown, she prayed for the nerve to actually participate.

Surely, Celia was only joking about the kissing ones. Those could get out of hand. Reputations could be put at risk. Lives ruined.

Which reminded Violet of the rather daring cut of her new gown. Tugging at the bodice, she frowned. Even in the darkened hallway, the uppermost swells of her exposed bosom proved distracting. Her mother's motives in allowing this particular dress begged questioning but Violet suspected its intent was enticing William Gadley into offering for her hand.

"It's more likely I'll be mistaken for a Covenant Garden doxie," Violet muttered.

She thought wearing such a garment was best undertaken without her parents' hovering scrutiny and William's cold perusal to make her even more nervous. But she was wrong. This exercise in confidence was vaguely uncomfortable.

Too much of her flesh was showing. Too much of herself that would draw attention. She jerked at the bodice again.

It wasn't too late to change her gown although Bridgette, her maid, would certainly protest. She'd declared Violet as lovely as any woman attending this year's May Day gathering. All the men would clamor for her attention, the maid predicted with a while placing the final touches on her mistress's coiffure.

Violet's lungs squeezed tight with the sudden burst of panic tumbling over her. She whirled about, blindly intent on returning to the safety of her room's four walls.

The collision knocked her backward. Landing on her rear end, the thick carpet cushioned her fall.

Propping herself up on her elbows, Violet stared up at the unmovable block of stone she'd crashed into.

Tristan extended a hand.

"I'm beginning to think you have ulterior motives, Lady Violet."

In the dim light of the corridor, the viscount appeared awfully tall. Like a giant in a fairy tale. An incredibly handsome giant with twinkling dark eyes.

"What?" she replied stupidly.

"It's not the first time I've assisted you. While the role of hero is unfamiliar, it is not unpleasant. In fact, I rather think I like it."

His words slowly registered, and when he bent at the waist with the obvious intent of lifting her up, Violet knocked his hands away with a scowl.

Tristan only shrugged at her refusal of help, watching while she floundered like a turtle flipped on its back.

It wasn't gracefully done, not with the gown's full skirts and the very real threat of her breasts springing free of the tight bodice, but somehow, Violet got up from the floor under her own power.

Ignoring Tristan's appreciative regard of her bosom, she made a show of dusting her hands lightly against the ruched edges of the low neckline, subtly checking that all remained in place. Her scowl never wavered.

"The first occasion was a result of you sulking beneath a tree. Now, you are lurking in dark hallways." Violet's voice was weighted by embarrassment and a dash of indignation. "Why were you sneaking behind me anyway?"

"Why did you abruptly change course?"

"I was returning to my room, if you must know," she bit out with long-suffering patience.

"Hmm," was all Tristan said.

Under his perusal, something odd welled inside Violet. Anger, yes, but also awareness. Tristan was looking at her in a certain way. A way her mother would most certainly deem inappropriate.

His eyes consumed her in the same manner as when she laid sprawled across his chest under that oak tree.

Arching a brow as she'd seen Celia do on countless occasions, Violet pressed him. "Well? Why are you sneaking about?"

Tristan's gaze sparkled with sudden bemusement. "Sharpening your claws on me, kitten? I don't mind at all."

The interested spark in the coffee-colored depths of his eyes sent a ripple of confused excitement cascading down Violet's spine. Why did Tristan's attentiveness seem to grow with her timid insolence?

Her chin tilted. "I don't know what you mean. And don't call me that. It's improper."

The man had the audacity to grin, teeth flashing white while deliberately ignoring her command. "I'm curious, kitten. Would you care to discover what it truly means to be improper?"

"Do you intend on answering every question with a question? It's quite tedious." Violet hoped she didn't sound as flustered as she felt. The viscount was mixing her all up inside. Scrambling her thoughts until she could only think of him kissing her right there in the darkened hall.

"All right." Tristan threw up his hands in mock surrender. "I concede the battle for the moment. To answer your initial question, have you forgotten my bedchamber is located down the hall? Just a bit further past your own, in fact. Before I could make my presence known, you whirled about, barreling head-first into my chest. So, you see, my dear Lady Violet, my intentions were completely innocent. At least at first."

"And now?" Violet's eyes narrowed with suspicion, helplessly drawn to his chest. He had mentioned it, after all. And it was such a nice chest. All warm and hard, with swells of muscles and ridges she'd already felt with her own two hands.

"Oh, I'm full of wicked thoughts. Overcome by them," Tristan cheerfully replied. "And eagerly willing to demonstrate a few of my favorites."

CHAPTER 5

I'm doing it again. Teasing her. Flirting. This will not end well. I know this. So, why continue this madness? And why do I find it so enjoyable that my actions disturb her?

Violet's lips once again pursed together. The gesture did not detract from her loveliness. Indeed, it called undue attention to the lush beauty of her mouth. Tristan wanted to trace the upper curve of that plump flesh with his tongue. Pull it between his teeth and test its suppleness. Would she melt, easily molded to his liking, or would this newfound sauciness stiffen her resistance?

The tang of her blood still lingered in his mouth. It was difficult believing he'd done something so audacious and out of character.

But not for all the gold in London would Tristan erase that moment. That moment when Violet's eyes darkened to the hazy purplish color of a winter morning sky, her lips parting the slightest bit for more.

"Such efforts would be a waste of your time, Lord Longleigh," Violet said primly. "And speaking of time, you keep me from an appointment in the Emerald Parlor."

Instead of pressing her against the wall and taking her mouth to explore its flavor without the stain of blood, Tristan moved away. Hands clasped behind his back, he smiled when she added a few more discreet steps between them. "And who awaits you in the Emerald Parlor?"

"Your sister, if you must know. And I had hoped to change my dress before you barreled into me, but now there's not enough time."

She appeared vaguely distraught but did not elaborate further.

With a sigh of defeat, Tristan let his fingers curl around her elbow. He maneuvered her until he could see the garment better.

"Your gown is quite lovely." His eyes strayed to the bodice where twin mounds of creamy flesh tested the stitching of the lavender fabric. "Why change it?"

A different answer must have teetered on the tip of her tongue, but she swallowed it with a pained expression.

"You would not understand my reasons," she replied in a suddenly morose fashion.

"Probably not. 'Who is't that can read a woman?'" With gentle urging, Tristan pulled her into step alongside him. "Come, I'll escort you to the parlor myself."

As if against her better judgment, Violet smiled. "Do you quote Shakespeare often?"

"If and when it suits me. Do you enjoy Shakespeare?"

"Should I say yes, I will be considered not only a wallflower but a bluestocking as well."

Tristan grinned, his head dipping close to hers. "I would never. You are too lovely for such characterizations."

"While you are so free with compliments one might doubt your sincerity. Especially in this case, my lord."

Tristan's brows knitted. "Never doubt my honesty, Lady

Violet. I would gladly sing praises of your beauty aloud if scandal's broad brush would spare you in the aftermath."

To his utter delight, Violet blushed, the rosy tinge spreading across her face and further until the swells of her breasts were the same hue. That gorgeous color would likely saturate every inch of her pale skin.

Tristan could envision nothing lovelier than Lady Violet Everstone bared for him. Soft, warm, willing and eager, waiting for his hands and mouth to discover all her vulnerable parts and turn them the same shade of delectable pink.

As they descended the marble steps of the main staircase, Violet remained silent.

"Does the thought of scandal worry you, Lady Violet?" Tristan chuckled. "I swear I shall be on my best behavior during dinner."

"Perhaps you shouldn't sit—"

Before Violet finished the sentence, there was an interruption behind them.

"Longleigh, is that you?"

Tristan paused and Violet half-turned, her hand resting on the balustrade.

To his great irritation, it was Henry Bowman. The gentleman was pleasant enough, although he possessed a reputation of playing rather fast and loose with his mistresses. Lately, it was said he was on the hunt for a wife.

If he decided a pursuit of Violet was warranted, the man would need to address the size of his estates. It was rumored Lord Everstone searched for deep pockets when it came to the selection of a husband for his daughter. Lord William Gadley fit those requirements handily. Bowman hardly stood a chance.

"Bowman." Tristan nodded as the man drew closer.

"Are you on your way to the Emerald Parlor?" Bowman inquired of Tristan, sketching a quick bow. "If so, there is no hope for other gentlemen in attendance."

Not waiting on Tristan's response, Bowman turned his full attention to Violet.

"Lord Henry Bowman, my lady." Bowing over Violet's hand, he gallantly kissed her gloved fingertips.

"We've met before, Lord Bowman." With a pained smile, Violet tugged her hand free. "Most recently in London. At Lord William Gadley's townhouse on Chelsea Court."

Tristan ground his teeth. If the man would bloody look at Violet's face instead of her breasts, perhaps he'd recognize her.

Bowman's pale blue eyes finally lifted. "Gadley's… oh, yes. I believe I recall the occasion."

"This is Lady Violet Everstone, the Earl of Everstone's daughter," Tristan offered when it became apparent Bowman did not remember her at all.

A calculating expression crossed Bowman's handsome features, but it was gone so quickly Tristan could not discern the meaning of it.

"Of course. Please, forgive my forgetfulness. I blame it on the tediousness of the long journey from London. I only arrived a short time ago and have yet to recover my bearings." Bowman smiled in an engaging way that made Tristan's fists clench. "If by chance you are headed to the Emerald Parlor, Lady Violet, it would be my honor to accompany you."

"I am already escorting the lady." Tristan reached for Violet's hand, tucking it under his arm. Tilting his head, he regarded her curiously. "I was under the impression you were meeting my sister alone in the Emerald Parlor?"

"I never said we would be alone," she replied as they resumed descending the staircase.

"Several of us are converging there," Bowman provided from the stair treads behind them. "Your delightful sister sent word that a variety of games have been arranged for everyone's amusement. Very thoughtful of her."

"What manner of games?" Tristan did not bother hiding his suspicion.

Reaching the grand foyer, Bowman drew even with them. "Just a bit of sport to pass the time, I'm sure. You should join us, Longleigh."

Violet extricated herself from Tristan's grip and sidled a few inches away. "The viscount must think such things are trivial amusements. I'm sure he has other matters requiring his attention."

Bowman smoothed light brown hair with the palm of his hand. "An evening spent in the company of beautiful women is never trivial. Besides, Longleigh is known for his enjoyment of those pleasures and much more."

A lazy grin hid Tristan's increasing aggravation with Henry Bowman. "I relish a great variety of games. Hide and seek is a personal favorite. Even as an adult, I find it exhilarating, if one has a worthy opponent."

Violet gaped at Tristan, struck speechless by the brash reminder of their time in the forest. Bowman shifted his feet, eyes darting between the two of them in an effort to determine what he'd stumbled into.

"Violet! There you are!" Celia rushed across the foyer's wide expanse. "I was just coming to look for you. The others have already gathered, and… Oh, my heavens." She drew up short, an expression of shock gracing her lovely features. "Your dress, darling. It's stunning. You are stunning."

Violet's hand fluttered over the bodice of her gown while Tristan was struck with the strangest urge to knock it away. He wanted to whisper words of encouragement in her tiny shell of an ear.

Words of reassurance.

This shy flower should be told how beautiful she was. Someone must show her how she could use that beauty. It was a bargaining tool when it came to men such as himself and granted power over weaker ones like Henry Bowman.

"Your brother was escorting me there now," Violet said softly.

"Was he now?" Celia shot Tristan an indecipherable look.

"I was," he drawled. "Celia, dear, I believe I'll join your little group."

"No," his sister insisted firmly. "No, you won't, Tristan. Father and several gentlemen have gathered on the north terrace for a brandy. I'm sure their company will be more to your liking."

"And I'm sure I'd rather see firsthand what sort of trouble you're brewing."

"Oh! You are impossible!" Celia stomped a tiny foot, causing Violet to jump in surprise and Henry Bowman to cover a smile with his fist. "I won't allow it, Longleigh. I won't! Violet is rarely allowed freedom, and you will ruin everything before there's even a chance for a tiny bit of fun."

Violet flushed such a deep shade of red, Tristan felt a surge of pity. *Is she under that tight of a leash? Do her parents manage her that closely?* She was a frequent visitor of their family while growing up, but admittedly, she'd not come around as often over the past two years.

Thinking on it now, shortly after Grace Willsdown arrived as his father's ward, Violet's time at Darby Meadows dramatically decreased.

He was inserting himself into matters concerning Violet when he had no standing for it. He wasn't her brother, nor her betrothed. Or even a distant relative. What right did he have placing himself in her path? Especially when it came to harmless parlor games and whatever amusements young people devised?

None.

But still…

Tristan couldn't let her go without offering some type of protection.

"If you will excuse us for a brief moment, I must ask Lady Violet something requiring a bit of privacy."

"I don't mind, Longleigh," Bowman agreed, both hands going up in surrender when Tristan shot him a heated glare.

"I'm relieved to hear that, Bowman. Not that I sought your consent."

Turning toward Celia, Tristan found her regarding him with narrowed eyes.

"If it will keep you from the Emerald Parlor..." she clarified, and Tristan huffed in exasperation at his younger sibling's persistence.

Giving Celia a terse nod of agreement, Tristan took Violet by the elbow and pulled her several steps away. Puzzlement lit her amethyst-hued eyes as she waited for him to speak.

Tristan began, then closed his mouth. There was a way of saying what he wished to say, a way of stating it tactfully. But damned if he knew it.

"Violet, will you give me a truthful answer?"

"Of course." She smiled, the tiny dimple in her cheek begging that he dip his tongue into it. "I'm a very honest person."

"You may not wish to give me what I want."

"I will. I promise." She leaned toward him. "What is it?"

"Have you been kissed before? Kissed by a man who would devour you?" To his own ears, his voice was hard. Gruff. Vibrating with the unmistakable truth he wanted to be that man.

Glancing down, he saw his own fingers unconsciously caressing the fabric covering her elbow.

With a low growl, Tristan turned them so his body shielded Violet's shocked face from his sister's bemusement, Bowman's curiosity, and the faint interest of other guests trickling into the foyer. "Have you?" he prodded.

Violet swayed. Just the tiniest bit, but that in itself was an answer. Tristan's blood nearly ignited within his veins.

"No," she admitted softly, eyes wide and hazy with innocent arousal.

It took everything inside Tristan to keep from snatching her up against him and rectifying that abomination—*no, it's a blessing*— right there on the spot. Only by gritting his teeth to the point of pain did he gain control of himself.

When he dared look at her again, the possessiveness of his irrational demand astounded even him.

"Your first kiss is mine. You will save it for me. And when I want it, you will surrender it without question."

CHAPTER 6

The entire evening dissolved into something Violet could only categorize as slightly bizarre.

It began with Tristan monopolizing her attention at dinner. Unconcerned with the whispers the seating arrangements stirred, he blithely disregarded the stares while keeping her engaged in conversation.

At one point, he leaned close and murmured a bit of advice. "Ignore them as I do. They will gossip, regardless."

Violet nodded, concentrating on not cutting off her own pinkie finger while slicing the roasted beef on her plate. It was very hard ignoring Tristan's warm breath in her ear. It was as though a fire had suddenly roared into life along her nerve endings. She felt alive. More than alive.

The viscount's devotion was both terrifying and exhilarating. Even the puzzled glances cast their way by Tristan's parents could not diminish the heady pleasure of it. Seated directly across the table, Celia grinned in obvious delight every time she caught Violet's eye.

Following dinner, Tristan escorted Violet back to the Emerald Parlor, holding her arm when she would have filed with the others into the elegantly appointed room. Other than a round of introductions, very little had taken place in the hour prior to dining. Those returning now chattered amongst themselves, agreeing the evening would prove a lively one.

"Shall I stay?" Tristan asked, his brow raised.

"Of course not." However, Violet secretly wished he would. "There is no harm in a few silly games. And Celia is here."

Tristan's eyes darkened. Violet could not discern what he was thinking, but something about the tight set of his jaw made her stomach flutter. Like it was filled to the brim with butterflies. She thought perhaps he was unhappy leaving her there, a thought reinforced when he glared at the men entering the parlor.

A great deal more gentlemen were in attendance than before, Violet noted nervously.

Tristan tipped her chin with a forefinger, bringing her attention back to him. "Remember what I said, Violet."

He did not elaborate. There was no need. She'd thought of little else but his fierce demand from the moment he uttered it. He knew the power it held over her, sure of her compliance to the point of arrogance.

Violet nodded, and Tristan spun on his heel, leaving her there on the parlor threshold.

An hour later, Violet trembled, prepared to bolt from the room.

"Don't go, darling," Celia pleaded. "We'll find another..."

"Why must we change games simply because one person is too frightened of the outcome?" Lady Fiona Blackerby stated coolly, looking for support from other participants.

"Violet is one of the bravest girls on earth." Celia squeezed Violet's waist tight, her chin tipping upward as Fiona rolled her eyes. "But I'll not make her play if she doesn't want to, Fiona. Besides, I don't like this game anyway. We shouldn't play it at all."

"She wouldn't play Kiss the Four Corners. And now she balks at Squeak, Piggy Squeak?" Fiona tossed one perfectly curled lock of hair over her shoulder. Shooting Violet a hostile glare, she said, "One would think you've never played games outside the nursery before. It's all harmless fun, my dear."

"Permitting a man to… to… kiss and grope you?" Violet countered. The ferocity of her response surprised even Celia, judging by the raised eyebrows. "And not just one, but a multitude."

"If there was just one participant, it wouldn't be much of a game, now would it?" Someone chuckled. "It's all very sporting."

Others murmured similar thoughts aloud.

"How is it sport?" Violet demanded.

"So, there is a bit of fire beneath that meek exterior." A gentleman standing disturbingly close laughed softly. A thread of excitement, mingled with something resembling admiration, laced his tone.

"It's how the game is played," Fiona snapped, as it became apparent Violet was the epicenter of male attention. "I understand your reluctance, considering your size, but if you won't sit in the player's lap and…"

"And be pawed and humiliated while making ridiculous noises? Risk being compromised while looking incredibly foolish?" Violet's voice shook as Fiona's taunt found its mark.

Violet decided it couldn't be helped. It was just that she was so very *angry*. With herself. With these men. And women. And even Celia, whose dark eyes flashed with pained regret even while she attempted dissuading others from this ridiculous game.

Fiona merely smiled, smoothing a hand down the front of her dress. She truly was a beautiful girl. Tall, willowy, and blessed with champagne blonde hair and a complexion rivaling fresh cream. She was the perfect counterpoint to Tristan's darkness, her appearance so similar to the new Duchess of Richeforte that it almost certainly warranted Tristan's attention. At least twice during dinner, his eyes strayed in the lady's direction before he focused on Violet with a most charming smile.

Fiona Blackerby was everything Violet was not. Most notably, she would serve beautifully as an obvious substitute for Tristan's lost love.

Violet's chest expanded with unimaginable hurt. Maybe a little indignation that she'd been invisible for so long. Resentment that she'd allowed it.

"Violet." Celia sounded a bit panicked. Perhaps because this evening of harmless parlor games was quickly disintegrating into something else. Or perhaps because she did not recognize the heat in Violet's tone. Nor the spark in her eyes when their gazes locked.

"It's all right, Celia. I'm rather exhausted, so I believe I'll retire for the evening."

The chorus of strident male disagreement brought Violet up short.

How... astonishing. She heard mention of Longleigh followed by a bit of laughter from the gentlemen. Looking about the room, she found several men rather blatantly appraising her form. Unconsciously, she sucked in a breath to flatten her stomach and straightened her spine then cursed herself for caring about their opinion.

"It's past your bedtime, I'm sure," Fiona urgently piped up.

"Oh, do hush, Fiona!" Celia snapped. "Your jealousy is most unbecoming."

"Jealousy!" Fiona cried. "Many gentlemen seek me out. More than I can count. More than this wallflower..."

"Pity, that." Violet's head tilted as she regarded the other girl, her voice lowering into something husky and determined. "To be so desperate you would give up everything rather than hold close to something which should be fought hard to win. I cannot and will not offer myself so freely. A gentleman must prove himself worthy of a favor. And if I am a wallflower because of this, then I suppose it is what I am and I must bloom alone."

Fiona scowled while Celia's eyes glimmered with unmistakable pride. Others regarded Violet with a curious mixture of discomfort and interest. Bowman maneuvered through the field of gentlemen, steadily pressing closer until he stood directly behind her.

"You are a prude," Fiona finally sputtered.

Violet's lips tugged upward with a tiny smile, the dimple in her cheek peeking out.

"Perhaps I am." Her voice still quavered the tiniest bit; anyone listening carefully would recognize her trepidation. "But that will not be decided by these games. Nor by men who have not earned the right to discover if true or not."

TRISTAN STOOD QUIETLY, having slipped into the parlor just a few moments before. He had no idea what the current disagreement between the two women consisted of but Violet just amplified the tension. She issued a direct challenge no man could possibly ignore. It was a blatant invitation for pursuit.

The girl was either truly, woefully innocent, or she was a consummate flirt intent on enticing every man in her orbit. Regardless, she would prove a popular mark for gentlemen seeking sport.

His fists clenched at the thought.

Tristan studied Lady Fiona Blackerby. Her name was recently deemed acceptable for inclusion on the list Mother and Celia had devised. Although she resembled Grace March in coloring, with her blonde hair and fair complexion, upon closer inspection, one could see how little the lady held in common with the new Duchess of Richeforte. Grace's sweet spirit spilled out of every pore. Lady Fiona, in stark contrast, possessed a hollowness of character which could not be concealed.

She'd also earned herself a comparison with Violet. Fiona could never hope to overcome such a challenge. It was unfair to expect it. With her quiet loveliness and pureness of soul, Violet was a burning light in a cavern of unending darkness. Tristan did not understand why he was drawn to her, but there was no denying the pull he felt.

It almost explained his presence here now. He watched Violet from a distance, drinking in the very sight of a girl he'd never really thought much about before their chance encounter in the forest.

Annoyance tipped something dangerous inside Tristan when Bowman placed a solicitous hand on Violet's elbow.

"Lady Violet, it would be a pleasure to offer my services as escort, should you truly intend on retiring for the evening."

Flouncing away in a show of aggravated temper, Fiona caught sight of Tristan near the parlor entrance. Her delight had all eyes swiveling in his direction.

"Longleigh!" Fiona exclaimed in a breathless exhale of syrupy sweetness. "You came after all! How wonderful!" Hurrying across the room as quickly as her heeled slippers would allow, Fiona slipped her hand into the crook of Tristan's arm, beaming up at him. "It's so frightfully boring here. Have you come to take me for that stroll around the gardens?"

Celia crossed her arms in obvious irritation, but Violet's reaction disturbed Tristan the most. A flash of something similar to betrayal bloomed in her eyes before it was quickly shuttered. Bending her head toward Bowman, she murmured something indistinct. The man's eyes lit up like twin bonfires.

St. Simon's Cross.

Tristan could not in all honesty dispute Fiona's misinterpretation of his actions. He had encountered the young woman upon leaving Violet in the parlor the first time, and in a state of distraction, he mentioned returning at some point in the evening.

Was it his fault Fiona believed he'd come for her instead of the auburn-haired, violet-eyed little cat casting surreptitious glances at him that very moment?

Tristan allowed Fiona the claim of his arm until they reached the main group. Using a maneuver that the Duke of Richeforte had taught him long ago, he slipped from her grasp. Her pouting huff of dismay was ignored.

"I shall happily escort you to your quarters, Lady Violet," Tristan said, giving Violet a hard, warning look. He didn't trust Henry Bowman within five yards of her, and certainly not isolated from view in a darkened corridor.

Violet's lips curved in that oddly endearing bow shape. For God's sake, how he wanted to trace those lips with the tip of his tongue. He'd kiss her slowly at first. Learn everything about her. Her pressure points. The tender spots.

How would she respond when he pulled that plump bottom lip of hers between his teeth, tugging slightly before his tongue slid deep into the recess of her mouth?

She would taste like ripe fruit. Peaches, maybe. Or red, juicy grapes just off the vine and bursting...

"No, thank you, my lord," Violet said softly.

Her refusal startled Tristan out of his decadent thoughts. A bit woozy from the erotic path his mind galloped down, he still recognized the firmness of her tone. It left no doubt as to her intent.

"I shall stay and play a few games after all." Violet flashed a smile at Henry Bowman, and the man's chest inflated by double its previous size. "I'm suddenly not as tired as I thought."

CHAPTER 7

$\mathcal{V}$iolet owed Celia a debt of gratitude.

Twenty minutes into a new game involving a silly concoction of kissing a candlestick or something equally foolish, Celia clapped her hands, squealing at her partner.

"Have you not seen the Chinese lanterns Father purchased for the terrace? They are absolutely splendid. They light up the lawns so delightfully. You can almost see the very edges of the garden."

It was a subtle way of drawing the activities to a close when it seemed Violet's involvement was inevitable. With Lord Henry Bowman glued to her side, waiting for the moment he would win a kiss, Violet could not thank her friend enough.

It was reckless, throwing herself back into the mix after such an impassioned speech against the games themselves. But seeing Tristan and the girl hanging on his arm had sparked Violet's temper. That unexpected emotion swayed her decision to stay, just so she could see what the viscount would do.

Tristan hovered on the outskirts of the lively group, dark and scowling, ignoring Fiona and her grip. Indeed, he disregarded all her enticements, and Violet overheard one gentleman comment how contradictory Tristan's behavior was. After all, the viscount was normally quite jovial… quick to engage in any activity which would gain a kiss or two from a pretty girl. And even more, if rumors held any truth at all.

"Yes. A visit to the terraces is a fine idea. I, for one, could do with a bit of fresh air," Tristan muttered, shooting Henry a burning glance when the man once again grasped Violet's elbow.

Violet calmly met Tristan's glare when his eyes found hers.

Why is he so angry? Fiona can scarcely keep her hands off him.

Excited chatter filled the room as the occupants filed out.

Violet subtly extricated herself from Henry's grip. "If you will excuse me a moment, Lord Bowman."

"Don't you wish to see the gardens by lantern light?" He sounded almost plaintive, although his eyes retained a calculating light. Just beyond him, Violet saw Tristan's hands clench into what could only be considered fists.

"I must retrieve a wrap. The night air will be chilly and—"

Henry waved a dismissive hand. "There are servants for that."

"Yes, but I have a particular one in mind. It shall be quicker if I get it."

"I'll accompany you, of course."

Violet's heart plummeted. Bowman was certainly proving to be a persistent fellow.

"Oh, no. That is not necessary," she stammered.

"Go with the others, Bowman."

Tristan's softly uttered command sounded like the crack of a whip.

Henry might have considered staging a protest, but the arch of Tristan's dark brow convinced him otherwise. Suddenly understanding he was treading upon claimed ground, Henry picked up his snifter of brandy and exited the room without a backward glance.

Which left only Fiona to contend with.

"Do run along, Violet. Longleigh and I shall catch up. There is something we, ah, must discuss." Favoring Tristan with a simpering smile, Fiona snuggled closer, hugging his arm tight against her breast.

Tristan watched the girl as one would an interesting bug making its way across a window ledge. For a moment, he said nothing, then very softly, he made his preference known.

"Lady Fiona, I suggest you join the others."

Fiona stared at Tristan until her surprise began a slow melt into outrage.

"Don't be cruel, darling. Do you worry the little wallflower will spread gossip about us?" she snapped before catching herself. Sweetening her tone, her eyelashes fluttered. "She won't tell a soul. Will you, Vi—"

"Stop." The viscount's voice did not raise, nor did he sound particularly angry, but it had the similar effect of Fiona slamming into a brick wall at high speed.

Violet watched in horrified fascination as the other girl's mouth clamped shut as directed.

Tristan spoke quietly, but firmly.

"I feel a certain responsibility for the guests in my father's home, so you can understand why I will not allow anyone the license of referring to Lady Violet as a wallflower. Or employing the use of any other term that could be construed in a derogatory manner. One may not like the results of my displeasure if these instructions are ignored. Is this perfectly clear, Lady Fiona?"

He waited for Fiona's tight nod and, once satisfied, waved a hand in her direction. Like a sultan dismissing an unfaithful or wearisome subject. "Excellent. See that you do not forget my warning. And please, tell others how disappointed I shall be if I hear of it again. You may go now. Close the door behind you."

Violet swallowed the lump in her throat as Fiona stomped to the door. Although the girl most certainly thought very hard about it, she refrained from slamming the portal behind her when she exited.

Hearing the soft click of the latch, Violet sagged against the nearest wall, her legs wobbling. Her eyes met Tristan's, lips twisting in a half-smile of pained regret.

"So much for not feeding the rumor mill, Longleigh. You've served up a virtual feast with your actions."

Tristan poured himself another dram of whiskey. With the languid grace of a jungle cat, all sleekness and dark power, he moved toward her.

One could become entranced watching the viscount's nonchalant actions. There was little point in running when he'd already pounced and had a victim by the throat. Taking a sip from the glass, he ran a careful, steady finger down the side of Violet's neck, his mouth curving upward.

Violet blinked. When did he get so close? And why did her breath suddenly feel as though it were being squeezed inside her chest?

"What do you mean, kitten?" Tristan asked softly, stroking the same path down her throat again and again until Violet nearly threw her head back and begged him to do *something*. Anything. She didn't know precisely what, but she suspected he did. Tristan's eyes, deep and full of fathomless secrets, were now the same dark shade she'd seen in the forest earlier that afternoon.

"Rumors. You told me you had no wish for them, but now you've created a whirlwind. And, I asked you not to call me that." Her voice trembled. She hated that it trembled. She wanted to be strong. To stand up to him. To withstand him and his brand of seduction. Because for a shy, inexperienced wallflower, the promise of it was a cruel lie.

"Kitten? I can't seem to help myself." He drank from the glass again before setting it down so he could mesh his fingers with hers. Very slowly, he drew her closer until their bodies were nearly touching. "You're soft like a kitten. You scratch and hiss at me, ineffectively of course. I wager if I touched you, very gently, and in the right place, you would purr for me. You would nestle against me, seeking the stroke of my hand. Wouldn't you?"

Tristan's words wove a spell of such delight, such darkness and pleasure, that Violet felt lightheaded.

Would she purr? Would she melt for him? Give him anything he asked for? Regardless of the scandal?

His reputation would ruin hers... devastate any chance for a respectable marriage. With Gadley or any other gentleman foolish enough to offer for her. And while Longleigh's ego would certainly be stoked with the conquest of another woman, Violet knew her heart would fall behind him in tatters.

"Did you love her very much?"

The words tumbled into the air between them.

Tristan's hands dropped away from her. His mouth tightened into a hard line, but his eyes remained soft.

"I thought at the time I did. I believed she was meant to be mine. It's complicated."

Violet pressed on. "Do you still love her?"

"Of course, I do. Just not... not in the manner you think. Grace is like a sister to me. She always was, even when I refused to see it."

"Even before she married the duke?" Violet tilted her head, trying hard to understand. He was so single-minded in his pursuit of Grace. She could not comprehend the gap between the type of infatuation Tristan exhibited before and the sisterly affection he claimed now.

Tristan raked a hand through his hair. "What Nicholas and Grace have is far beyond anything I ever witnessed. The love they share is…"

Biting his lip, he glanced away, having no words which could adequately describe the relationship between Grace and her new husband.

Violet smiled. "If it resembles anything like that of the Earl and Countess of Ravenswood, or the Earl and Countess of Bentley, then perhaps I do understand. What they have is enviable, isn't it?"

"Yes. And, one shouldn't assume something so magical is commonplace. Better to have a more realistic expectation of marriage, I think. After all, not everyone is meant to find their true love."

Tears shimmered in Violet's eyes when she thought of her likely union with William Gadley.

How she wished now she'd never fallen in love with Tristan. Wished that she had never experienced the blinding warmth of his smile. Or the abrupt, confusing whirlwind of his attention. Better to crush this dream of becoming his wife while her head was still somewhat clear.

"What an incredibly sad thing to say," Violet replied slowly. "You don't really believe that, do you?"

"There are too many disappointed people in this world to think otherwise," he replied flatly.

"True love is always possible," she retorted.

"Really? Will true love compel you to accept Gadley's proposal?"

"I will accept because I must." When his eyes bored into hers, Violet's gaze skittered away. "Love will have little to do with it, but I will never stop believing in its existence."

After a nerve-racking silence, Tristan's head dipped forward.

The tiny movement reminded Violet she still leaned against

the wall. He had her pinned against it, and for a second, her heart raced with a crazy apprehension.

But Tristan only sighed against her neck, as if her words released something he'd been afraid to let go. Perhaps it was relief he'd not been so foolish to fall in love. Even if it wasn't true love.

Violet's heart melted, even while she steeled herself against him.

How awful the past few months must have been for him. He'd been rejected by someone he'd believed was the woman of his dreams, watched his closest friend marry her instead, then listened as gossips discussed the details of the whole affair over and over. All while retaining his composure, his humor, and his relationships with those involved.

Violet's free arm embraced the viscount, patting his back in awkward gestures of hidden comfort. Nonsensical murmurs slipped from her lips with no focus on actual words.

Tristan. Tristan. She'd loved him for so long. Now, her heart felt it would burst as her senses filled with him.

The heavy weight of his body pressed hers, the clean, tantalizing scent of wintergreen forests, spice, and leather emanating from him.

The width of his shoulders was massive under her palm. Her hand smoothed and stroked the muscled strength stretched so tight beneath the fine broadcloth.

With a quick intake of breath Tristan's head nestled deeper into the crook of her neck.

Violet froze even as the warmth of his breath on her skin burned her. A strumming urgency coursed between them, linking their souls as if forged of silver chains. Her hand drifted until it rested on the back of his neck, and she sighed as her fingers sifted through the waves of his hair.

Slowly, as if afraid of breaking the spell between them, Tristan's head lifted until his cheek almost touched her own.

Violet held her breath, certain he held his too. For a long moment, they remained in that position, cheek to cheek, mouths aligned horizontally, neither inhaling nor exhaling.

It almost seemed he was waiting for her…

An inexplicable force pulled Violet. Controlled by hidden strings, her head turned slightly, meeting his lips in the softest, sweetest brush of a kiss.

Tristan issued a ragged sigh in response. Rather than push her away, his arms snaked around her waist and tightened.

"That doesn't count as a first kiss, Violet," he rumbled.

Violet's soul soared high, then plummeted to earth, shattering into a billion pieces. She couldn't do this. Not when he'd been so desperately in love with another woman just months ago. Not when he might only be using her as a means of forgetting his disappointment.

She couldn't do this when she'd been so desperately in love with him for so very long. The agony that would come from being claimed by Tristan Buchanan would be devastating. Worse than if she was never claimed as his.

It would be worse than anything she could ever imagine.

"I'm sorry. I-I can't stay. Not like this." She tried disentangling herself from the tight circle of his arms; however, Tristan increased the pressure required to keep her in place. His deep brown eyes searched hers until Violet faltered, uncertain she should trust what she glimpsed in that moment.

Desire. Puzzlement. Conflict.

"Please," she murmured, and he finally relaxed his grip. Not enough that she could escape, but enough that she wasn't afraid to stay where she was.

"Must you go?" he queried, keeping her stare captive. "Or is that something you feel compelled to say so I'm kept at arm's length? It won't work. For reasons I cannot fathom, I am drawn to you."

Violet wanted nothing more than to nestle within the warm,

steel cage of his arms. By sheer willpower alone, she remained upright. "It is improper to be here like this. If someone came through that door..."

"It was improper fifteen minutes ago," Tristan interrupted with a crooked smile. "A few minutes more won't matter now, I'm afraid."

"But they could, Tristan. Anyone could come searching for me. For you. For both of us. You practically demanded Lady Fiona leave us here alone." Violet succeeded in tearing herself away while Tristan's eyes narrowed in thought. "What do you think she has done as a result? She is surely telling everyone we are cosseted here together. Unsupervised. If someone caught us like this, caught us... kissing... it would be ruinous. And while that may not mean anything to you, it does to me. You—we could be forced to wed."

Violet placed some distance between their bodies. And a few pieces of furniture as well. The grin Tristan flashed acknowledging her actions was ignored, but her anger, and she recognized the strange feeling as anger now, could not be denied. Anger and excitement.

"Married? For a single kiss?" Tristan scoffed. "What strange notions they put in young girls' heads in these misguided efforts of keeping them pure." He allowed her escape with a shrug of nonchalance. They both knew he could easily recapture her if he wished it. "If that were the case, then why were the entire lot of you playing those ridiculous parlor games? Everyone knows what they are about. Besides, if kisses required marriage, my sister would already be someone's wife several times over. Holy matrimony isn't so easily accomplished, my dear. And I should know."

Even as he said that, the doorknob to the parlor was turning, a distinctly feminine voice calling out first Tristan's name, then Violet's.

Celia's head poked through the opening between the door

and the jamb. Her eyes widened almost comically, noting the space yawning between Violet and Tristan.

Scowling as if disappointed she'd not caught them in a passionate embrace, she hurriedly swung the door open wide.

"Are you two coming out into the terrace or not?" Celia's gaze darted from Violet to Tristan. "And what's this about my being someone's wife?"

CHAPTER 8

$\mathcal{A}$fter Celia interrupted their peculiar conversation, Violet wasted little time in retreating. Murmuring a rather paltry excuse, she fled the parlor, leaving Tristan to dodge Celia's pointed questions. Questions he had no intention of answering.

Tristan rose early the next morning, determined to put the previous evening behind him. Determined he would keep his distance from Violet for the remainder of his time at Darby Meadows.

As soon as the May Day Affair is over, I'm off to Longleigh Woods. Staying here is a recipe for disaster.

Stalking down the path leading to the stables, he recalled Violet's agitation the night before. During her escape, she'd not spared him a second glance and Tristan couldn't blame her. He'd made a terrible mess of things.

Thinking which of his father's geldings he would saddle, he rounded a bend in the path and found the object of his dreams striding along the same walkway.

"Of all the damned luck..." Tristan bit off the curse.

There was the hope she never caught sight of him, but the

crunch of his boots on the path's gravel alerted her of his presence.

Violet glanced over her shoulder, a small sound of distress escaping at the sight of him. But she halted, waiting on the path until he caught up.

"Good morning, Lord Longleigh." Her smile was wan and somewhat exasperated.

Tristan fought back a surge of arousal.

I nearly devoured you last night. Your hips were against mine yesterday afternoon. I woke at dawn with your name on my lips, my own hand gripping my cock. Fantasizing that it was your innocent fingers stroking me. And still, you call me by my formal title?

How could she look so beautiful this early in the morning? It wasn't fair she appeared somewhat well-rested when he'd tossed and turned all night, mind overflowing with all manner of debauched plans for the lovely Lady Violet.

And it wasn't fair there was no chance a single one of those would ever come true.

She must have forgone the services of her maid and dressed herself. Her morning gown was a lovely peach moiré silk, simple in design with delicate ivory buttons pulling the bodice closed. Left unbound, her hair was a banner of dark auburn flames, the soft waves reaching the curve of her waist. A matching silk ribbon pulled it all away from her face.

Tristan could hardly tear his gaze away from the beauty of those tresses. He wanted a chunk of it wrapped tight around his fist while he brought their mouths together for a scorching kiss. He'd use those soft curls as a silken tether. Tug them until her spine formed a lovely arch, and with one hand spanning her perfect heart-shaped buttocks, he'd anchor her in place while he slid inside her…

"Good morning, Violet."

She frowned, obviously dismayed he was using her given name.

Turning toward the stables, Violet began walking once more, the delicate scent of her lavender and vanilla perfume drifting on the morning air. She seemed determined to place some distance between them, as was he. He just couldn't let her go so soon.

"What are you doing up and about so early?" He noticed she carried a bit of cloth but couldn't see what it contained.

"I've business in the stables." Seeing where his gaze drifted, Violet clutched the tiny bundle tighter.

"Will you ride this morning?"

Her lips firmed. "I will not."

"I'll accompany you, if you do not wish to take a groom. I'm going anyway, so— "

"I do not ride, my lord."

"Of course, you do," Tristan insisted.

"I haven't ridden in a long while." Violet shot him a faintly accusing look, as though he was expected to know this bit of information. "There was an… incident, you see. Horses frighten me."

Tristan stared at her. He and Celia were expert riders; he couldn't imagine anyone being afraid of a horse.

"Oh? What happened?"

He knew by the way her chin tilted Violet would not share that information.

"It is of no matter now." Her steps quickened.

Changing tactics, Tristan motioned at the cloth in her hand. "What do you have there?"

Her eyes shyly darted to meet his. "You're quite curious this morning."

"Some say inquisitiveness is one of my finest qualities," he smirked. "My persistence even more so."

"Surpassed only by your vanity, apparently," Violet huffed and resumed marching briskly.

Tristan grinned and, with a shrug of his shoulders, fell into step beside her. Silently, they continued until they reached the stables. A few stable boys bustled about the dim interior, gathering items for their morning chores.

"Enjoy your ride, my lord." Violet nodded in dismissal as she moved down an aisle leading toward the rear of the building.

Where the devil is she going?

Tristan watched her hurry away, torn between letting her go or following so his curiosity could be satisfied.

Stepping to the stall of a gelding he often rode when he did not bring his own to Darby Meadows, he stroked the bay's muzzle, deep in thought.

What business did Violet have here in the stables of all places, this early in the morning? And what did she have wrapped so tightly in that piece of cloth? A treat for one of the horses? One of the groomsmen or a stable boy? If she didn't ride, there was no reason she should be here.

Why was she being so secretive?

More importantly, why did he care?

With a sigh, Tristan straightened his coat.

"Well, there's nothing for it. I'm off to pursue a vexing redhead." He smoothed a hand over the gelding's neck in an apologetic farewell. "Perhaps we'll get that ride in later, boy."

In a matter of moments, he caught up with his selected prey. There was a small courtyard at the back of the stable building and upon reaching the doors, Tristan slammed to a halt.

He couldn't be sure what he was witnessing. Neither could Violet, for she stood immobile, the morning sun creating a halo around her.

They both stared at the scene before them.

"You're goin' in this bloody bucket if it's the last thing I do on this earth, you spawn of Satan. *Owww!* You blasted creature!"

Mister Pope, Darby Meadows' head groomsman, sat on a low bench, a metal pail between his knees. His shirtsleeves were rolled up and towels lay spread around haphazardly. Latched onto his forearm, claws digging deep into the flesh, was a dark grey bundle of fur roughly the size of a lady's slipper. It snarled and hissed, and each time Mister Pope unlatched its claws from one area of skin, it found another unprotected patch to attack.

Mister Pope screeched again. "*Bloody hell!* In you go, with my arm or not!"

Before Tristan could demand what was going on, Violet took matters into her own hands.

In one smooth motion, she dropped the mysterious bundle and snatched up a pitchfork leaning against the last stall. Then, like an avenging angel of fire and brimstone, she rushed toward Mister Pope.

"Stop! Whatever you are doing to that poor kitten, stop! You're killing it! Oh, you heartless monster!"

"Violet! Wait!" Tristan shook off his dazed astonishment. "Wait!"

Startled by the well-dressed young lady brandishing a pitchfork and crying murder, Mister Pope jumped up from the bench. The pail overturned, sending soapy water across the courtyard bricks.

Pope's grip never loosened on the kitten. Or perhaps, its grasp never loosened on him.

"Violet!" Tristan reached her before the tines of the pitchfork found their mark. Wrapping an arm about her waist, he lifted Violet off her feet while ripping the weapon from her fists. It was tossed aside with a loud clatter.

"Mercy! Mercy, milady!" Pope scrambled back, knocking the bench over in the process. Ungodly caterwauling from the kitten accompanied his panicked pleas.

Slipping and sliding in the suds, the poor man tripped over the bench, falling with a thud on his backside.

"Let me go!" Violet wailed, grabbing Tristan's hand where it pushed against her belly. She was crushed tight against him. "He means to drown the poor thing... Oh! He's hurting it. Can't you hear it screaming? Let me go, blast you!"

Tristan jerked her harder to him, his mouth against her ear as she struggled.

"Settle yourself, Violet. Right *now*. I'll get to the bottom of this, but if you cannot calm yourself, I shall take you into an empty stall and do it for you the only way I know how. Do you understand?"

"Please, go help it..." In an absolute panic, she continued pushing at his hands until Tristan nipped her ear.

At her shocked gasp of breath, Tristan murmured low in the silence, "*Settle. Down.* Take a deep breath, now. That's it. Easy. Shh. Easy, now. As long as I'm here, no one will dare hurt or kill anything. I swear to you. I swear. Do you believe me?" When Violet gave a slight nod, slumping almost defeatedly in his arms, Tristan's lips brushed her temple in a fleeting caress. "Good girl. Now, I'm setting you down so we may determine what this is all about."

Violet's answer was a hiccup of a sob.

Tristan lowered her to the ground, curling his hand in hers. Pope watched warily, covered in soapy water and streaks of dirt. The kitten emitted a low, grumbling meow. It sounded as if it was in excruciating pain, but Tristan could see how carefully the man held the tiny thing.

"Mister Pope, explain yourself if you can. And for the moment, I'll keep Lady Violet from running you through with a pitchfork."

CHAPTER 9

$\mathcal{V}$iolet clutched Tristan's hand tight.

Had she truly almost accosted a man with a pitchfork? Like a savage?

Hesitantly, she touched her earlobe with trembling fingers. It stung just a little. How odd that the viscount's action both grounded her and inflamed her. She trembled, ashamed of her actions, grateful Tristan stopped her, but still overwhelmed with concern for the tiny kitten.

"It fell into a coal bucket," Pope began earnestly. "A bath seemed the trick, but the little bugger—"

"Careful, man," Tristan interrupted with a tilt of his chin toward Violet.

"Pardon, milord. I mean, the wee thing didn't take too kindly to the notion of a bath." Pope wrapped a towel around the kitten so he could finally pry it off his arm. "I wasn't trying to hurt it. Honest. Oh, milady, you can't think I'd do such a thing, do you?"

Violet's face flushed. For the past several days, she had provided scraps from the kitchen for a mama cat who'd just given birth; Mister Pope proved kind and gentle during those visits. He let her sit in the empty stall where the cat was kept so

Violet could feed the scraps. He even checked on her occasionally, making her feel safe amongst all the huge, scary horses with their dangerous hooves and enormous bodies.

How *could* she think he might ever harm a helpless kitten?

"I'm so very sorry, Mister Pope," Violet said miserably. "It is inexcusable I thought the worst when there was no basis for it. Please forgive me. You've been nothing but kind to me and to those kittens and their mother. Where do you suppose this one has come from? It's much larger than the others. And much more vocal."

"Aye, that it is. I think it might be a stowaway, ridin' in on someone's coach," Mister Pope said. He held the kitten out to Tristan who accepted it with a raised eyebrow of disbelief. "It's not one of Darby Meadows' rat killers, I can vouch for that. And still covered in coal dust, so a bath is still in order." The man set the bench to rights, handing the bucket to a stable lad with instructions that it be refilled with soapy water.

The kitten continued growling, but wrapped within a towel, it was not as dangerous an opponent.

"Let Mister Pope try this once more. Then we shall decide what shall be done with the disagreeable thing," Tristan said with a smile for Violet.

WHILE MISTER POPE bathed the kitten with Tristan's supervision, Violet delivered the scraps to the mother cat. A pile of straw provided a cozy bed, but she had added a bit of cloth as well to protect the delicate kittens from the straw's needle-like ends.

After watching the cat eat all the bits of stewed chicken, and petting the soft babies, Violet returned to the courtyard where the stowaway kitten was now freshly cleaned.

Both men were fairly soaked, and Tristan scowled as Violet

drew closer. He held the kitten wrapped in a clean, dry towel. Its tiny head peeked out of the white cloth, and Violet was surprised to see its coat was a dark, orangish tabby. It had been so completely coated in coal dust before there was no discerning its true color.

Tristan thrust the bundle toward her.

"Here. Take it."

The cat let loose a screech of displeased indignation while hovering midair.

"Oh, you poor thing," Violet crooned, taking the kitten from Tristan. She scratched it between the ears, rewarded with a subdued growl that faded after a few moments.

"It's a boy, if that makes a difference, milady," Mister Pope said.

"Is it?" Violet's head bent, and the kitten stared back with startling green eyes. Her heart melted. "Will he have a home?"

"He'll live in the stables with the rest of the cats, and we'll hope for the best, him being such a wee thing." The head groomsmen cleaned up the items used for the bath. "Excuse me, your Lordship, I'll be seeing to my other duties this morning. Milady." He executed a respectable bow then disappeared into the stables.

The kitten rumbled out another aggravated growl along with an open-mouthed meow of protest when Violet tucked it closer to her body.

"Whatever you are thinking, I heartily advise against it," Tristan said calmly.

"You can't possibly know what I'm thinking." Violet rubbed the kitten's ears until the angry snarls slowly morphed into a reluctant purr.

"You want to keep it," Tristan sighed. "Bad idea. I'm afraid that beast is half-wild."

"He is not. He needs someone to care for him. He has no mother, and he's too young to fend for himself in the midst of the other barn cats. They'll hurt him." Violet lifted her gaze. "He needs a name."

"'Demon' comes to mind," came Tristan's dry response.

"He's as orange as a carrot. What do you think of that for a name? Carrot?"

Bemused, Tristan shook his head. Taking her arm, he pulled Violet into the shadows against the outer walls of the stable where there was a little more privacy.

"I think he should be tossed out with the bathwater, if you honestly want to know my thoughts. How will you explain your new pet to your parents?"

Violet shrugged her shoulders. "They will likely not even notice. And if they do, I-I think I don't care." The kitten, exhausted from its ordeal or perhaps soothed by Violet's gentle caresses, was dozing off. His tiny whiskers quivered when Violet shifted him into a more comfortable position.

Tristan said nothing, merely watching her until Violet looked up at him quizzically.

"What is it, my lord?"

Perplexed by the train of his own thoughts, he frowned. "I do not know. It's just that… one moment, you are the girl I barely remember from all these years past. Shy, quiet, and perfectly content to remain in the background. The next, you would defy your parents to keep a half-rabid hellcat after you attack my defenseless employee with a pitchfork. A girl who would change her gown so no one sees her beauty, but challenges every man in my family's drawing room to discover for themselves whether she is a prude or not. These contradictions are driving me half-mad, if you must know the whole of it."

"I am only myself, Longleigh," Violet breathed.

But how could she truly respond when there was a world of truth behind his statement? She was a different person with him. A paradox that confused and muddled her own thoughts.

Tristan had the distinct ability to make her feel both invincible and vulnerable. Strong, but weak. Desired, and yet unwanted. It was a dizzying combination of emotions.

"Yes. Just yourself. I think I like you just that way. Fierce and innocent, but still the temptress. My sweet, wild Violet." Tristan smiled faintly, tipping her chin skyward with a forefinger. His dark brown eyes searched hers. "I wonder. If I asked for that first kiss right now, would you give it to me or skewer me with a pitchfork?"

Violet swallowed hard. Would she let him kiss her? It was best to place distance between them. No good would ever come of allowing this man to toy with her heart or her emotions.

He seemed to know her struggle because his mouth quirked when she hesitated in answering him. But it was no use. She was irrevocably drawn to Tristan, and she could no more turn from him than a hungry beggar from a bowl of soup.

Slowly, Violet nodded her head.

"A kiss would prove less fatal," she said.

"That all depends on you, sweetheart. I've the feeling you could do a great deal of damage, no matter the weapon you choose."

The golden flecks in Tristan's eyes glinted with something dangerous, calling to a piece of Violet's soul buried deep beneath countless layers of respectability and demure behavior.

"Ask me to kiss you, Violet."

"What?" She pretended she'd not heard him correctly. God, anyone could walk outside into the courtyard and find them against the wall, deep in the shadows. It would be ruinous, even if they were doing nothing more than sharing a conversation.

Tristan's eyes narrowed. "You heard me. Ask me, kitten. And know when you do, I will take from you without hesitation. Without mercy. With complete and utter ruthlessness. As I swore I would."

Violet was sure her hunger for him shone like a beacon. Sweat beaded in the valley between her breasts despite the coolness of the spring morning. The purr of the kitten in her arms faded away, and her heartbeat pounded like a drum in her ears. Her eyes locked with his until it seemed she was drowning in vats of rich, melted chocolate. So sinful, so deep, and so thick she would never escape.

"I-I, Tristan—" This kiss would ruin her forever. She would never forget it. Never forget him.

She couldn't do it for that reason.

And yet, she *must* do it.

"Violet." Tristan's tone remained calm and smooth, his finger never leaving its place beneath her chin, keeping it tilted so there was no choice but to stare into his eyes. "Ask me."

And Violet surrendered, toppling like a Saxon fortress overtaken by bloodthirsty Vikings.

"Please," she choked out. "Kiss me. Be the first. Show me what your lips feel like on mine...."

Tristan's eyes glowed like that of a panther finally snagging its prey.

Violet sagged against the wall, suddenly alarmed. "The way you are looking at me right now..."

He stepped even closer, and there was no mistaking the starved light in his gaze. "How is that, Violet? How am I looking at you?"

"Feral. Hungry." Her voice dropped to a whisper. "Like you... you might swallow me whole."

"I am. Hungry, that is. And I *will* devour you if given the chance."

When he leaned down, Violet held her breath, certain he would attack her mouth, take her so roughly that the very air would be stolen from her lungs. A whimper escaped her, but she couldn't say if it was a sound borne of eagerness or apprehension.

Tristan smiled slightly but instead of claiming with savageness, his lips brushed across hers.

Violet let his gentleness soak in. His lips were so soft. Pillow-like, but insistent at the same time. Firm. Inescapable.

Tristan kissed her again, letting her feel his lips across the full surface of her own before he exerted more pressure.

Beneath the tenderness, Violet sensed his restraint. He was holding back. For her.

She moaned in her throat with the realization, parted her lips in invitation, and that was what Tristan seemed to be waiting for.

Growling in triumph, his tongue traced the seam of her lips, parting them so he could dip inside. Violet gasped in shocked delight as he kissed her with violent sweetness. Over and over, his tongue swept through her mouth, delving and retreating in languid, yet fevered exploration as if he possessed all the time in the world.

He tasted like mint, and the only part of her body he touched other than her mouth was the finger which still lifted her chin. It was all he needed to control her.

Violet trembled. She was lightheaded, knees buckling, and while gripping Tristan's coat sleeve with her free hand, a low rumbling sound built around them. It slowly escalated into a screeching howl that sounded otherworldly.

Tristan tore his mouth away, swearing beneath his breath.

"Goddamn little beast…"

Easing back, his gaze dropped to the kitten cuddled against Violet's chest. Its ears were laid flat, eyes large and round, and the noise it emitted became a disgruntled growl, interspersed with little hisses of displeasure aimed at Tristan.

"I think you frighten him," Violet explained breathlessly. She stroked the cat's head in an effort to calm it. And to calm herself. Her heart was galloping like racehorses turned loose on a fresh track.

"Do I?"

Violet smiled. "Yes, I believe so. Poor little thing. I'd best get him to the house and settled in my room."

Giving Tristan an apologetic nod, she moved around his large form and stepped into the morning sunshine. She did her best acting as though that kiss had not irrevocably altered her forever. "Enjoy your ride, Longleigh."

Hurrying away, she did not glance behind to see if he followed or simply watched her exit.

Regardless, she felt the heat of his gaze on her backside until she rounded a corner. Only then did she take a deep breath of relief.

CHAPTER 10

*L*eaning against one of the pillars defining the drawing room, Tristan watched Celia sweet-talk her way into a game of whist where the prize was whatever the winner demanded.

She was a regular spit-fire, his sister. Too smart and too sassy for her own good.

That very nature of hers was both appealing and off-putting to the opposite sex. As such, he kept a close eye on her whenever they were in close proximity. Her fiery spirit needed reining in occasionally. Briefly, he thought of the times Grace Willsdown eclipsed Celia when it came to their wild antics. The memories made him smile.

But Grace was Richeforte's now. Tristan had long ago come to terms with that fact. There had never been any real hope Grace would be his, not once she and Nicholas discovered one another. Those two.... It was damn eerie how in tune they were —to the point their union could only be called fate.

Tristan's gaze slid over to Violet. She sat quietly at the pianoforte, plucking out soft notes to music he didn't recognize. He wondered if she knew how to play or if the simple tune was a concession to societal mores which demanded a young woman play a musical instrument of some sort.

In the midst of the room's loud gaiety, she kept to herself, which in itself drew attention. Tristan wasn't the only one who noticed her quiet beauty or her contentment in being alone. Satisfied with loitering on the edges, she watched the other women in an almost clinical fashion as they reveled in the spotlight male adoration provided.

Tristan didn't want anyone to discover the fire Violet hid from everyone else. Didn't want another man to unearth the complex treasure buried beneath the creamy complexion and that pile of gorgeous auburn hair. He was slowly coming to realize she was a girl with terrible power. The power to ignite the passion of any man she came in contact with. The power to make a man forget his will was his own.

The damnable thing was Violet appeared blissfully unaware of her effect on others. She floated through the maze of men and dazzling women like an amethyst-eyed fairy. Untouchable and intriguing, and yet, there was something achingly vulnerable about her.

It needled Tristan. Poking and prodding as telling him someone should shelter and protect her. Take care of her. Grant her every wish and desire and make her smile with contentment every day of her life.

She would make men dance a merry tune if she ever embraced her potential.

If he were a man searching for a wife, he'd be wary of such a girl. Tristan wasn't in the market for a bride, but recognizing Violet's shyness incited a need to help her navigate through the world. She was much too beautiful for any man to run roughshod over. And too sweet to accept her parents treating her as a commodity. Given a push in the right direction, she might actually discover a bit of power. A minuscule amount perhaps, but enough that she could have an opinion over her own future.

Besides, it might be interesting to watch Violet come into her own. It would prove a distracting activity during his time at Darby Meadows, despite any misgivings he held on becoming too involved. She would benefit from his interaction, after all, becoming better equipped to handle men like William Gadley and Henry Bowman. Men interested in taking advantage of her.

Seeing his attention was fixed on her and had not swayed, Violet gave Tristan a tiny smile. Fingers gliding lightly over the keys, she continued playing, her gaze fixed with his as if inviting his company.

Tristan pushed away from the column. He should sit beside her before someone else decided that was a capital idea.

Sliding onto the bench, he grinned when her fingers faltered the tiniest bit.

So, he *did* affect her.

When she'd slipped past him after sharing their explosive kiss, Tristan almost doubted himself. She seemed too at ease for a first kiss. Too calm. Too... reserved. It perplexed him that all he could think of since that kiss was how Violet Everstone tasted like sugared peaches. And how he wished he could trace the tiny cleft in her chin with his tongue before moving on to more intriguing areas of her person.

"Do you play?" Violet asked, her elegant hands stilling.

"No. Never had the propensity for it." He edged closer and experimentally touched a key. "I do enjoy hearing you play, however."

She bit her bottom lip, containing a grin. "I play as well as I sing. Which is to say, abysmally."

"I find that hard to believe."

"You wisely made yourself absent on the occasions Celia and I performed for our parents when we were young." She shrugged. "Lucky for you."

"You must have other talents," Tristan offered. "Tell me some of the things you like to do."

"A woman is not supposed to highlight her own interests." Violet half turned toward him, her eyes sparkling. "But, as you've asked me directly, it will not harm anything to say I do enjoy reading. Although, I suppose that is not really a talent. I am fairly accomplished at writing poetry. And I do have a head for numbers. My father despises that fact. He thinks it is completely inappropriate that a female possesses such knowledge."

Tristan's head tilted, his dark eyes studying her. "That skill will stand you well once you are managing your own household."

"Do you think so? I doubt Lord Gadley will appreciate it. His views are distressingly similar to my father's. And those of my mother." Violet sighed, unhappiness flitting across her features like a brief raincloud.

Tristan's heart clenched.

"Perhaps Gadley will change his mind and choose another to become his wife." His words were cavalier, but he felt anything but nonchalant. To think of that man dictating anything this lovely girl might do in the future left Tristan feeling slightly nauseated. With his cold, clinical reputation, it was highly probable Gadley would smash Violet's gentle spirit to bits.

Tristan could not imagine a worse prospect for a spouse, with the exception of himself, of course. Her parents must be mad to even consider the man as an ideal husband.

Violet regarded Tristan, remaining silent in light of his statement. He could see in her eyes she had no hope of Gadley suddenly becoming a sensitive, caring human spouse.

Tristan quickly changed the subject, afraid of where things were leading.

"How is your new pet doing? Settled in?"

A quick smile transformed Violet's features. Her adorably

pert nose crinkled. "Bridgette, my maid, has declared him a minion of the underworld. I cannot blame her. Carrot hid beneath the bed then attacked her skirts when she walked past. It was quite unexpected and resulted in a little scratch on her ankle while he was caught upon the fabric. But the skin was not broken, and he meowed quite mournfully in response to her terrified scream. He was very sorry, after all."

Tristan unsuccessfully smothered a laugh. "Such behavior is to be expected from a half-wild creature."

"He's quite intelligent. Bridgette set up a pan filled with sand, and he's learned that is where he should do his business. He's such a smart rascal, but prone to mischief. Already, he's ruined one lace shawl."

"If you insist on keeping him, my dear, I imagine he will destroy a few more of your belongings."

Violet giggled. "I will introduce you again, now that he's had a proper meal and a warm bed to sleep in. You will see he's quite charming. It makes it easier to overlook his shortcomings."

Tristan leaned forward, remembering how this girl's lush form felt pressed against his own body. She tasted as warm and decadent as a strawberry tart. He wanted another sample. "I despise cats, but for you, I shall endeavor to make friends with the beast."

"Violet, darling, come play a hand or two of whist with Lord Harvey and me." Celia slid into the open space upon the bench, placing Violet in the middle of the Buchanan siblings. Leaning past her friend, she gave her brother a mischievous grin. "You may join us, Tristan, if you don't mind losing."

"I trounce you at whist every time," he drawled with an indulgent smile.

"Only because I allow it. Your pride being such a fragile thing, I don't dare crush it," Celia teased. "Besides, you would face off against Violet. And she would have no qualms destroying your ego. She may look forward to it, actually."

"Oh, I would certainly not go so far as that." Violet blushed furiously, and Tristan reveled in the way her face glowed pink.

"I'm game if you are, Lady Violet," Tristan said, taking her elbow. "And I look forward to your efforts in crushing my… um, ego."

"WE MUST SET THE WAGERS," Celia claimed as they settled about the table. "Harvey, you should go first."

Lord Harvey grinned wolfishly. "Your hand for every waltz the night of the May Day Ball."

"Greedy, but I agree to your terms." Celia appeared bored by the man's request. Rolling her eyes, she nodded at her brother. "Tristan?"

Tristan rolled the whiskey so it glided up the sides of the tumbler he held. His eyes, dark and wicked, gleamed as he considered Violet. She squirmed a little under the intense scrutiny. "To paint Lady Violet's portrait is my fervent wish."

A scandalized gasp went up around the group of onlookers. Fiona Blackerby appeared as if she might explode with jealousy. Henry Bowman puffed up in righteous outrage, and Celia, bless her little misguided, matchmaker's heart, grinned with sheer delight.

But Tristan didn't care about any of that. He was already thinking ahead to the moment he had Violet under his paintbrush.

"Seems rather risqué a wager," Bowman sputtered from the sidelines.

"Daring, actually. Provided the lady agrees," Tristan murmured, his gaze never leaving Violet. She was blushing again, but she also looked determined not to let him intimidate her. It was strangely endearing.

"It's an excellent wager. In fact, I shall adopt it, Tristan. I heartily agree if you should win the game, you must paint our Violet's portrait." Celia clapped her hands in obvious glee. "How lucky for you, Violet! Not many are privy to Tristan's talent, or can say they are on the receiving end."

Violet looked vaguely distressed but smoothed her features back into an expression of blandness.

"Then I, too, shall base my wager upon Longleigh's skills as an artist."

"Oh?" Tristan's eyebrow rose high in surprise. Violet was exhibiting far more bravado than he expected. It was quite scandalous that he suggested painting her, an innocent, unwed girl. To her credit, she was taking it in stride. Perhaps, she *wanted* to be painted.

The very idea nearly made his hands shake with anticipation.

I'll position her on the floor so those lovely, amethyst eyes are looking directly up at me. A lock of that gorgeous auburn hair curling over one bare, ivory shoulder, her arm resting languidly on a plump ottoman. I want her to look as though she's been thoroughly kissed and is unable to stand from the lust I've stirred within her...

"I should like a painting of Carrot, if you please." She gave Tristan a shyly apologetic smile, unaware she was shattering his vision of their session. "I-I'm afraid it might be all I have of remembering him if I am forced to give him up."

"Oh, what fun this shall be!" Celia exclaimed. "Let us begin at once. I cannot imagine how you would entice a cat to sit for a portraiture, but if Violet wins, it will be the first time Tristan has ever painted one. He simply loathes the creatures, after all."

"Are you sure of your wager, Violet?" Tristan asked with a slight frown. He ignored his sister.

"Most certainly." Cocking her head, she stared at him, appearing surer than she had a right to be. "Are you?"

Tristan took a sip of whiskey, tipping the glass at Violet in mock salute. "I've never been more convinced of a decision in all my life."

Lord Harvey dealt the cards and the first game began in earnest.

Tristan, despite his best effort, lost the initial hand. It was expected when Violet commanded all of his attention. Her every move fascinated him. The way she bit her bottom lip in concentration. The manner in which she fanned the cards just so in her delicate hand. The devilish sparkle in her eyes when she won the first trick. All entrancing and arousing and so infuriating he wished they were someplace private for games of another sort.

"Congratulations, Lady Violet," Lord Harvey said with an admiring laugh. "A lucky turn for you."

"Thank you, sir," she replied modestly. "Shall we continue playing?"

"Best of three, my dear. It would be only fair," Tristan barked in a tight voice. Damn, he should pay more attention to the game if he hoped to win the prize. Could he get away with asking her to wear a shoulder revealing gown for his painting?

Of course, he could. He'd insist upon it. The difference in shading between her skin and hair would be a masterpiece. Because if any woman should be immortalized on canvas, it was this girl. Damn, if she didn't exude light. And yet, the light seemed determined to find its way back to her. She glowed with a creamy luminosity he found difficult to look away from. Couldn't everyone see it? Or was it only his artist's eye devouring such perfection?

"All right," Violet agreed, dropping her gaze from his heated one. Fumbling with the cards, she managed to deal them without incident.

The next hand was squarely won by Tristan. Celia crowed with triumph before giving Violet an apologetic embrace.

"So sorry, dear," Celia grinned at her best friend. "I am, however, quite excited to see your portraiture."

Violet grit her teeth and smiled. "There are still games to be played. And Carrot will prove excellent subject matter for the viscount's impressive talent."

Tristan's derisive snort was disregarded.

The next few hands passed in quick procession, and by the end, the crowd was stunned into silence by the precise brutality of the winner.

"I shall defer to your expertise on location for Carrot's painting, my lord." Violet stood from the table. "But I do prefer an outdoor setting as I've always admired your use of color when it comes to landscapes."

Tristan gathered the cards in one hand. Exactly how had he lost so quickly and so thoroughly to the shy, little redhead? She'd massacred them all in short order after he'd won the one and only hand. Her skill was amazing.

"Of course," he muttered. Unused to losing, he couldn't manage more than that.

"Tristan, I warned you she would crush your ego. Don't be angry that you lost." A note of anxiety threaded Celia's tone. She stood, linking arms with Violet while speaking to her in a low voice. "Darling, you might have shown him *some* mercy."

Tristan waved his hand in dismissal of his sister's concern. "I'm merely thinking of a perfect spot to capture the little beast on canvas. Congratulations, Lady Violet, on your masterful play."

"Here, here!" Lord Harvey exclaimed. "Never seen a trouncing so quickly done. I don't even mind losing when the opponent displays such obvious skill."

"Because of your generous spirit, Lord Harvey, I shall grant you at least three waltzes," Celia smiled, releasing Violet so she could lay a hand on the man's forearm. "A cheerful loser is indeed a rarity."

"I believe I shall take a turn around the terrace before retiring for the evening. I should check on Carrot anyway. He's a very mischievous thing when left to his own devices for too long." Violet gathered up her fan and shawl.

"I'll escort you, Lady Violet. Have a look at my newest muse. Get an idea of colors and inspiration." Tristan rose to his full height, tossing back the dregs of whiskey still lingering in the glass. His eyebrow rose when Violet's apprehension became apparent in the way her grip tightened on the delicate fan. He thought he heard one of the piece's thin ribs crack from being held so tight in her fist. "I should at least attempt making friends with the subject if I am to paint him in a realistic fashion."

"Yes, yes, of course," Violet stammered. "That would be best, I suppose. I would hate if he were to scratch you."

"I wouldn't mind." Tristan smiled, knowing the meaning behind his words was quite clear when Violet tugged her bottom lip between her teeth in disconcerted awareness. "It wouldn't be the first time I've been scratched by a hostile kitten."

CHAPTER 11

$\mathcal{V}$iolet did not care it was rude. She strode ahead of the viscount as fast as her skirts allowed.

Oh! If this insufferable man does not cease referring to me as a... as a kitten...I may slap any sense he possesses clean out of his egotistical head!

She did not stop until she reached the furthest end of the terrace where wide stone steps led down to the crisply manicured hedge garden. Gravel paths spread like tentacles through the boxwood evergreens, punctuated by iron lampposts flickering with oil-fueled flames and carved marble benches. The Chinese lanterns were unlit tonight, leaving the garden in a mysterious blend of dark shadows and pools of light.

The angles of the house concealed this portion of the terrace from view should anyone venture outside, and there were no windows here. It was an unexpected spot of privacy, and Violet gratefully took advantage of it.

Setting her ruined fan and shawl down on the terrace wall's broad, waist-high surface, she leaned over the edge and sucked in a deep breath. But it did not help calm her volatile emotions.

Different noises permeated the evening. Crickets chirping merrily under the cover of darkness. The cry of a bird in a nearby tree, confused by the inky black sky, and the breeze ruffling the leaves of nearby trees. The faint sounds of music and guests enjoying themselves in the Earl of Darby's elegant parlor.

But the one sound assailing her ears, the one sending shivers of apprehension up her spine and turning her mouth dry, was that of Tristan's measured footsteps as he unhurriedly stalked her.

And, *dear God,* was the man actually *whistling?*

Whirling, she faced him, hands clenched tight at her sides.

Tristan stood within arm's length of her, hands tucked in his coat pockets. He let out a low, admiring whistle before those full, pillowy-soft and somehow hard at the same time lips— *damn her own memory of their exact, confusing texture*—curved upward in a wicked grin.

"Go away," Violet demanded. An irrational order, considering this was his family's home.

"Sorry. Can't do that."

She nearly stomped a foot at his softly drawled refusal, then blurted, "Why are you following me?"

"Why are you so angry? Is it because you want me to paint you instead of that damned cat?"

"You are insufferable," Violet shot back. "Egotistical. Unmannerly. And obtuse."

"Don't forget talented."

She stared at him in stunned disbelief. "What?"

Tristan moved closer, trailing a forefinger along her arm until it reached the upper edge of her glove. A galaxy of stars swirled in the depths of his glittering eyes. His teeth flashed white again. "You said I possessed talents as an artist, so obviously, you have some admiration for my skill." His dark gaze captured hers. "Now, tell me why you are truly angry."

"You—you cannot continue referring to me as a kitten. It's scandalous," she finally managed. "You must stop."

Tristan appeared vastly entertained by her demand. "You are a kitten. Scratching, hissing, and clawing. I mean it as a compliment."

"Do. Not. Call me that again. I'm warning you."

"Warning me?" Genuinely amused, Tristan chuckled. "Eventually, you will learn to get what you want in a more subtle manner, but right now, you are nothing more than a feisty, snarling kitten."

Violet's hand flew before she could stop it. The loud crack of her palm connecting with his cheek joined the other nighttime noises. She gasped in shock at the boldness of her own actions, then cried out in alarm when Tristan's arm snaked about her waist and hauled her up against him.

"That's it, sweetheart. Didn't that feel good?" His breath landed hot on her face, laced with mint and the sweet sharpness of the whiskey he sipped while playing whist. He smelled like a *man.* Like arousal, traces of leather and bergamot and spicy things shy, inexperienced wallflowers like herself could not possibly understand.

"Slap me again," he urged in a husky murmur, watching her closely. "Put me in my place because I've dared touch you. My arm shouldn't be around you like this. I shouldn't have you molded to my body. You're so sweet and warm. Goddamn, Violet... I feel you in ways you can't begin to fathom. Your breasts rising and falling against my chest as you struggle to catch your breath. The heat of you scorching me through our clothes."

He brushed his nose alongside hers and breathed deep. "Your pulse thumping against my fingertips wherever I touch you. The silky smoothness of your skin. I smell your perfume, and I know what florals created it. I see your mouth trembling in terror because you *want* my kiss but think it's wrong that you do. I see and feel *everything* about you, Violet Everstone. Everything. And I'm telling you to slap me again because I do not possess the right to know these things."

"I don't understand!" Violet shuddered within the circle of his arms. "Why do you antagonize me so cruelly, then demand such things? I'm sorry I struck you. I'm sorry— "

"Christ above," Tristan swore under his breath. His expression turned so fierce he looked like a marauding pirate intent on ravishing her. "I'll untame you if it's the last thing I do. If it ruins me or both of us, I don't care. For your own good, I'm giving you a reason to do as I say."

"Untame me?" she whispered in confusion. "What are you talking about? "

Tristan's mouth swooped down, covering hers. Cutting off words and breath and rational thinking. This kiss wasn't gentle, or hesitant, or patient. It was soul-stealing. Hard. Demanding. Consuming.

Glorious.

Violet moaned into his mouth as the pressure increased. His tongue delved past the barrier of her teeth. Like a flame, it whipped the inside of her mouth, tangling with her own tongue, branding and igniting every bit of her until Violet felt like a flame, too. Tristan did not just kiss her. He devoured her. And she let him feast because she was starving for him as well.

No longer content with being stationary, his hands roamed her restrained curves as if on a treasure hunt. From the indentation of her waist, up her sides to the ticklish hollow under her arms, then around to her shoulder blades and the curve of her spine. He explored every fabric-covered inch with greedy fingers before moving back to the delicate framework of her exposed collarbone.

With the precision of a scalpel, Tristan's fingers traced the line of bone from one side to the other. They dipped into the well of her throat and brushed over her rapid pulse, stroking softly as if painting her. Then those artist fingers drifted down. Down to the undercurve of her breasts where the flesh caught within the cage of the corset molded to the palm of his hand.

The manmade contraption yielded to force as Violet arched her back, desperately offering more if he would only take it.

So, he did. His fingers boldly dipped inside her bodice, breaching lace and silk and whalebone until they gained the prize. Bare skin. The upper swell of creamy flesh. Then… an aching, pebbled nipple squeezed between thumb and forefinger with such exquisite purpose that Violet's entire being melted in astonished surrender.

Had he not braced her against the terrace wall, leaning her backward so her body was offered like a feast for the gods, she might have slipped to the floor. But Tristan had her skillfully trapped, one knee pressed between her legs, the other bracing her from the side. With a hand down the front of her dress, his other curved into a grip on her shoulder blade, providing support even as he made her tumble to pieces.

"Will you strike me now?" he breathed, tearing his mouth from hers finally, staring down at her as though she were the only creature worth seeing in the entire universe. His fingers pinched her again, twisting the hardened nub of her nipple until fireworks exploded somewhere inside her. "Will you make me stop?"

"I-I cannot." Violet's hands buried in the thick velvet of his hair. It was soft and luxurious, sliding through her fingers like sheaths of expensive fabric.

Tristan groaned in defeat. His head fell forward, his mouth latching onto her neck, kissing and biting the slender column until a blissful euphoria overtook Violet.

She couldn't stop him. Didn't want to stop him. Why would she when he was doing such marvelous things with his mouth and teeth? Why wouldn't she want those lips of his exploring where he pleased? Nibbling and claiming the pieces already conquered with his fingers?

"You are a goddamn witch, Violet. And I'll burn in hell because I can't stop thinking about the things I'll do to you," Tristan murmured, blazing a trail of fiery kisses across the exposed expanse of her décolletage. "Even when you become another man's wife, I'll still remember how sweet you tasted on my lips."

The words sliced through the hazy, dreamy web of desire drowning Violet.

Another man's wife.

She shuddered. Bile rose and ebbed in her throat, evidence of her own disgust for her weakness.

Yes, one day she would belong to someone else. Not Tristan Buchanan, Viscount Longleigh. No, she would never be his. He didn't care enough about any woman to attach himself for a lifetime of matrimony. The only exception being that of Grace Willsdown before Nicholas March snatched her away and claimed her as his.

Tristan certainly did not care about *her*. Violet served as a distraction. An amusement keeping his boredom at bay while he was trapped at his parents' estate.

A chill washed over Violet, scattering goosebumps across her skin. Tristan kissed her neck, her chest, her shoulders, unaware she'd sobered with his muttered statement. He still believed she lay cradled within the palm of his hand, ready to grant him all he desired for the price of a kiss.

"Stop," she said in a low voice.

She was nearly betrothed to another man, and yet, she kissed Tristan with fully engaged passion. What manner of woman was she? How could he make her abandon her own morals so easily? So quickly? This careless, heartless, cavalier man possessed a dangerous power.

He could make her forget who she was.

And who was she?

Quiet, sensible, rational Violet.

At least, that's who she used to be... and it was who she could pretend to be if Viscount Longleigh would keep his distance.

"Convince me that I must," he returned, biting her shoulder with sharp teeth before lavishing the spot with a hot, open-mouthed kiss.

Violet pushed his chest with balled fists, eyes swimming in tears. A desperate sob of humiliation escaped her throat when Tristan leaned back, sweeping her body head to toe with a scalding look. Then his face softened with something suspiciously tender, and his mouth lowered toward hers again.

This time, Violet delivered a slap so vicious her palm stung as if a bee had settled its stinger in its center. "Damn you, stop!"

His dark brown eyes widened. "You really mean that." Immediately, he stepped back. Sliding his hand out from the bodice of her dress, he repaired her clothing with careful attention until she was decent once again.

Did he even notice how she trembled with his touch?

Perhaps her fury amused him.

The imprint of her hand on his cheek glowed in the moonlit darkness. Tristan rubbed it with a rueful grin. "My little wild Violet finally made an appearance. Thank God."

Without his leg pressing intimately between her thighs, his hands no longer exploring her curves, and his mouth not ravishing hers, Violet could think clearly. Rationally. And what she realized was beyond disturbing.

"You play games, Longleigh. You toy with me because it amuses you, and this is how you keep women at a distance." Her voice caught before she steeled herself. "I've allowed it because of my affection for you, but as you point out, I shall be some-one's wife one day. Not yours, but someone's. For that fact alone, you will stay away from me."

Pushing past him, Violet gathered her shawl and fan off the terrace wall. She was several paces away when a mocking whistle swung her around in disbelief.

Tristan whistled a second time. The low, incinerating sound made Violet's blood heat slowly like a teapot set to boil. Her eyes narrowed.

Hands casually tucked into his coat pockets, grinning as if her fierce declaration merely served as the evening's entertainment, Tristan rocked on his heels. "What of the wager? It was a game fairly played, and you were the victor, after all. I won't be swayed from paying my debt."

Violet's teeth clenched, anger biting away the edges of her despair. "Don't you realize I counted cards to win those games? Your portraiture be damned. I'd rather fingerpaint Carrot myself than subject him to your presence."

Whirling on her heel, Violet left Tristan staring after her in astonishment at the admission of subterfuge. She half expected to feel his hard grip on her elbow before she escaped, but he allowed her to flee.

The pang of disappointment stabbing her heart when he let her go infuriated her more than it should have.

CHAPTER 12

Rhythmic purring woke Violet.

Opening her eyes, she watched as the tiny kitten yawned before settling himself into a bundle of fur with front paws tucked neatly beneath his chest. His perch on the extra pillow placed him at eye level with Violet.

Carrot's green eyes were little slits of contentment, the rumbling from his chest loud in the morning quiet. Laying on her side, Violet softly stroked the cat's orange tabby fur, smiling when the purring increased in velocity.

"Cheeky thing. You were meant to sleep on the little bed I made for you in the corner."

Carrot merely blinked, unconcerned with Violet's admonishment.

"And now you've stolen a spot on my pillow, little thief." She rubbed Carrot's ears until his eyes closed in blissful appreciation.

Violet's thoughts turned to Tristan as the kitten dozed off, and the prior evening's events pushed to the forefront. The man appeared both amused and perplexed when she'd left him behind on the terrace.

But her own feelings regarding the entire incident greatly perplexed her. The flood of emotions. The desire suffusing her bloodstream. The sharp zing of excitement shooting through every nerve ending she possessed when he kissed her.

Her body's involuntary reactions were alarming. How could Tristan's fingers wreak such havoc? How could his mouth, his lips, ignite a fiery longing for more?

Thinking of such things made her restless. Achy. Confused.

With guarded hesitancy, Violet cupped her own breast in the same manner Tristan handled her. Brushing a thumb over her nipple, she mused that although the resulting tingle set her stomach aflutter, it could not match the dizzying rush of pleasure experienced when Tristan touched her.

Biting her lip at the very wickedness of her actions, she lightly pinched the aching bud, again mimicking Tristan's actions.

From the flesh squeezed between thumb and forefinger, a bolt of lightning shot to the space between her thighs.

Violet whimpered, snatching her hand away as if her breast were a dangerous trap.

At the small sound of distress, Carrot's eyes slit open. Unfurling, he stretched lazily, touching his nose to Violet's with a questioning meow.

"That man is the very devil," Violet muttered aloud. Rolling to her back, she stared at the ceiling.

Carrot meowed again, rousing himself for an exploratory journey of the hills and valleys created by the bed coverings. He pounced, pinning imaginary prey beneath tiny paws while biting the coverlet with an adorable growl.

The kitten's antics distracted Violet from further thoughts of Tristan. She indulged her new pet's playfulness, trailing the ribbon from the bodice of her nightdress and laughing when Carrot attacked it with feisty vigor.

"How fierce you are," she admonished, tugging the ribbon from his sharp claws.

Carrot prepared to leap again, eyes bright with excitement and focused on the strip of fabric.

An unexpected tapping on the bedchamber door distracted both the cat and Violet.

Scrambling off the bed, Carrot took up residence beneath a chifforobe.

Only Bridgette would venture to her room at such an early hour, and the maid would not bother with the formality of knocking. But perhaps she'd fallen ill and another servant had overtaken her duties.

"Come in," she called out, but the person on the other side of the door merely rapped the wood again.

"One moment." Violet sighed. Rising from the bed, she donned a robe laid across the foot of the mattress. Knotting it tightly at her waist, she looked about for the matching slippers only they were nowhere to be seen.

Naughty kitten, she decided with pursed lips. Most likely, the missing footwear sat tucked beneath a piece of furniture. Carrot did like to carry things off as if they were fresh kill and he a great hunter.

Bare toes curled in protest at the chill of the hardwood floor when she stepped off the lush rug. At a tiptoeing run, she reached the door and flung it open.

"Good morning." Tristan's brow arched high, his gaze quickly covering every inch of Violet's body. Those chocolate-hued eyes lingered on her exposed feet and the lower region of her ankles, his lips twitching with a ghost of a smile.

Violet clutched the neck of her robe; the other hand remained on the door to keep it from swinging open completely. "What are you doing here?"

Tristan's eyes darkened, becoming twin pools of rich velvet that simultaneously caressed any exposed skin and ripped away her flimsy robe all at the same time. Violet shuddered, horrified that the idea of Tristan taking what he wanted at that very moment was somehow intriguing.

As if she could shut off those disturbing thoughts, she inched the door closed the slightest bit. Tugging her bottom lip between her teeth, she waited for his answer.

Tristan swore softly beneath his breath. His gaze shifted to focus on a point somewhere over her right shoulder.

"I hoped your maid would answer the door." His jaw clenched as his eyes remained averted. "Here. It is for the beast."

He thrust something at her, and Violet instinctively let go of the door to accept the offering.

It was a tiny collar. Small and delicately made from soft, butter-like leather, it had a small buckle crafted of gleaming brass.

"It's a curb strap I pulled from a yearling's first bridle." His voice was gruff. "With a ribbon as a leash, you can safely take him outside."

"Walk a cat?" Violet murmured, acutely aware of Tristan's gaze drifting down until it landed where she clutched the collar below the lower curve of her breasts. "Whoever heard of such a thing?"

Tristan chuckled, a low rumbling sound that constricted Violet's stomach in the strangest way. "It can be done. I believe the trick is beginning while he is young. Easier to handle and to teach."

"Thank you." Standing awkwardly, shifting from one bare foot to the other, she waited for Tristan to say more.

"It will certainly prove useful while painting my subject. Provided you accept my apologies for my behavior last evening and allow me to fulfill my debt," he finally said.

"I accept your apology," Violet agreed softly. "However—"

Tristan's jaw tensed even more. "Of course, you accept. Even when you shouldn't."

Tilting her chin, Violet glared at him. "Why offer an apology you don't mean? I don't understand you."

"I don't understand myself either," Tristan growled. He appeared so genuinely confused by his own behavior that Violet almost felt sorry for him.

Almost.

"Thank you for the collar." Her tone rivaled the chill in the room. The bit of leather was placed on a marble-topped stand beside the door. "However, I stand by my decision that the wager is forgiven, so you don't— "

Violet felt something soft brush against her ankles. It was gone in a flash, accompanied by the skitter of tiny nails seeking purchase upon hardwood floors.

"Oh!" Violet exclaimed as the kitten bolted between Tristan's legs. "Don't let him into the hall!"

Her momentum propelled her forward. Intent on following Carrot's escape route, she dove between Tristan's knees, then found herself trapped there. Now, her head was stuck in a very compromising position and her backside positioned even more so.

Tristan stumbled forward. Without thinking, he braced himself using both hands on Violet's shoulder blades until their position resembled an odd childhood game of leapfrog.

"What the devil— "

"Don't just stand there, Longleigh!" Violet swore. It seemed expedient she should scramble the rest of the way through the viscount's widened stance rather than back out and start over.

Tristan grunted with exasperation, shoving himself away just as Violet squealed, "Help me catch him!"

She continued crawling on her hands and knees, finding it mildly satisfying when Tristan also dropped to the floor, reaching toward the animal with an extended hand.

Carrot was not impressed by their combined efforts at

entrapment. Giving a ferocious hiss, he pressed forward in a renewed dash for freedom.

Tristan had him by the scruff of the neck before the kitten reached the shadowed underbelly of a carved walnut cabinet in the hallway.

"Aha! Caught you, you devil."

Carrot snarled in a half-screech, half-growl, twisting wildly.

"Son of —!" Rising to his feet, Tristan held the kitten in one hand while tugging Violet up with the other. "Little bugger scratched me."

"Let's get him back inside my room." Violet inhaled because Tristan's hand, so hot and hard on the upper part of her arm, did dangerous things to her ability to breathe. "I'll close the door so he cannot escape again."

Tristan muttered something but followed her instructions.

The kitten scampered away the moment he was placed on the floor, and Violet turned her attention to the viscount.

"Let's see the extent of the damage," she said, taking his hand in hers and holding it so the morning light illuminated his fingers. The scratch to his forefinger's cuticle was fairly deep. "Oh, you are bleeding." The examination continued for a few moments longer, her fingers gliding over his, coasting gently across the wound.

His hand was so much larger than hers. So strong and calloused. The faintest aroma of linseed oil teased her nostrils, and Violet wondered if he had laid paint to canvas that very morning.

"It is nothing to be concerned over."

Startled by the abruptness in his voice, Violet met Tristan's dark gaze. "I just wish to—"

He pulled his hand away, retreating until his back hit the paneled wall beside the door.

"This seems to be a consistent occurrence. We find ourselves alone under various circumstances. And there's little reluctance on your part to avoid said encounters." His full lips quirked upward. "I think perhaps you enjoy my attention."

"That's preposterous," Violet sputtered. "An inflated ego is a dangerous thing, my lord, and your theory is flawed."

"If you say so."

Violet's eyes narrowed. "I only wanted to help you. You should leave now."

Tristan's eyes drifted over her form, touching on the spot where her robe gaped open. Acutely aware of the heated, longing in his gaze, Violet clutched the edges of the garment tighter until the material wrinkled in her grip.

The moment stretched out, tense and awkward, until he finally smiled.

"Of course," he said. "No matter the innocence of the situation, it would mean ruin for us both if we are discovered."

Discomfited by the husky note of his voice, which hinted at all things decidedly beyond innocence, Violet moved past him. Her fingers curved around the doorknob just as Tristan swept an arm around her waist. He hauled her back against him until their bodies were flush with each other.

"Forget our wager if you wish but I'll have your promise I may paint that little beast." His murmur tickled her ear. "Consider it a gift."

"I don't think it is wise..."

"Promise me, Violet," he cut her off, his arm tightening while his other hand drifted down until it rested lightly on the curve of her hip. "It will please me to do this for you."

Violet knew the rejection of his apology disturbed him more than he wanted her to know. Nodding her consent, she saw relief flash in his eyes before his dark lashes swept down. That unexpected glimpse of vulnerability lurking inside Tristan Buchanan twisted her heart.

But far worse, it made resisting him nearly impossible.

CHAPTER 13

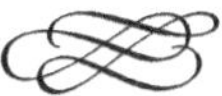

Tristan rested his shoulders against the wall and rubbed his eyes.

What madness possessed him to go to her room? Worse, what insanity made him enter?

"You're a fool. That's what you are. A fool," he mumbled angrily.

"Agreed, dear brother."

Tristan's head came up with a snap.

Celia stood outside her own doorway just down the hall, dressed for an early morning ride. Her maroon riding habit with gold trim was flattering, but the frown directed toward him was disapproving.

"Nothing untoward happened," Tristan said flatly.

"How can one be sure?"

"Because I said so."

Celia waved a hand. "Not good enough. Tristan, you simply cannot trifle with Violet in the manner you do other women. Don't you understand?" Fierce protectiveness loomed in her tone. "You may be experiencing a temporary fascination, but she will soon be engaged to another and your actions are bound to be considered scandalous. If Father knew what I just witnessed, he would—"

"Don't remind me. I know how eager he is to see me wed. He'd welcome any chance to tie me to a suitable bride." Tristan almost snarled the words then was immediately sorry when Celia bit her lip.

"He really has been ill, Tristan. And he has decided marriage is what you need to find contentment. After the situation with Grace, can't you see why he hopes you will find love?"

Tristan sighed. With an arm around his sister's shoulder, he gave a little squeeze and smiled apologetically. "I do understand. And I'm sorry for my tone, Celia. Only, I've no wish to be forced into marriage any more than you do. Father is concerned for his legacy, but my life should not be sacrificed for that." He kissed her temple. "I'll marry when I please. Whom I please. At this moment, that does not include anyone on the list you and Mother have concocted. And it does not involve Violet Everstone. Oddly enough, I hope I may help her avoid the state of matrimony as well. I cannot think of a more unsuitable husband than Lord Gadley. Other than myself, of course."

"Lord Ghastly," Celia corrected automatically.

"What's that?"

"Oh." Celia shook her head. "Just something of a joke between myself and Violet. Forget I said that."

Tristan's head tilted, but he allowed her comment to pass. "I'd appreciate if you kept this incident to yourself, but if you must know, I was merely apologizing for something I said last night. While renewing my offer of painting her cat, the beast tried escaping her room."

"I believe you, Tristan." Celia glanced toward Violet's door, a sad smile curving her lips. "Just remember, brother. Violet's heart is a tender one. If you have no intention of offering for her, then you must keep your distance. She wouldn't survive you, and you know that."

LATER THAT MORNING, Tristan pondered Celia's words upon returning to the third-floor salon. It was the space used for his artwork when he was in residence at Darby Meadows, and his parents agreeably kept it looked after.

With a corner location, it nearly always had perfect lighting; the soft magic of early morning, the sunshine-bright clarity of mid-afternoon, and the dreamy glow of dusk. It was such a special space he always had some project in progress whenever he visited. True, there was a large, well-appointed studio in his own home at Longleigh Woods, but for some reason, it could never match the magic of his childhood one.

He studied the canvas he'd started two days before. It was a rough outline of a massive oak with a stack of books and a picnic basket at its base. A horizon of rolling fields and fences was already sketched in; those details he would concentrate on at a later date. Right now, he wanted to put to canvas the figure of the woman who disrupted his sleep and possessed eyes the color of violets.

Celia's admonishment that he should keep his distance stung him more than he expected. Did she honestly think he would intentionally hurt Violet? He would never do such a thing. Cruelty was not one of his pleasures, after all. It was easier avoiding entanglement in the first place, his droll humor easing the pains a lady might experience from rejection.

Picking up a bit of charcoal, Tristan thoughtfully brushed lines onto the taut canvas. A lush, womanly form quickly emerged, and from there, he drew the pert upturn of his muse's nose in profile. He imagined her locks unbound, flowing over her shoulder as she slumped against the oak, a kitten in her lap and her attention fixed on the horizon. The scene flowed from the window inside his mind to the medium's surface.

And while he sketched, Tristan considered if he should try

harder to stay away from Violet or continue the unorthodox plan of gently pushing her to discover her own strength. It was encouraging she'd bantered with him that very morning, her initial apprehension melting away as he carefully teased her. She forgot her shyness when he pushed and prodded her, and Tristan liked the bit of fire sparking her amethyst-colored eyes to life.

The morning slid into afternoon, but instead of joining the other guests, Tristan enjoyed a glass of brandy and continued working. The piece was coming together rather quickly, which he attributed to sheer inspiration.

When a knock sounded on the salon door, Tristan threw an oilcloth over the canvas. He wasn't ready for anyone to see his work, at least not yet. And besides, he wasn't really sure what he would do with it once it was finished. It might find a home in his private collection, or he could gift it to Violet as a gesture of goodwill. He just wasn't sure at the moment.

He expected that a servant would be standing in the hall, perhaps sent by his mother as a reminder he was missing afternoon tea, but Violet stood there instead.

Carrot was cuddled in her arms, and around his neck was the collar Tristan had given her that morning. The kitten's demeanor was one of complacency; a long, braided strip of green velvet tethered him to Violet.

"I've come to apologize for my less than gracious acceptance of your gift this morning, and to show how well Carrot has taken to wearing his collar." Violet's smile was shy, her gaze darting past him as she looked around the salon.

"You shouldn't have come here," Tristan rumbled, then found himself wishing he could bite his own tongue off when her features registered disappointment.

"Of course, I shouldn't have. You-you are right, Longleigh. I just wanted to properly thank you," Violet turned to leave. "My pardons. I hope I haven't disturbed you overmuch."

Tristan touched her arm. "I did not mean you should go." She tensed beneath his fingertips, but he knew it wasn't from fear. "And I'm glad the collar fits so well."

Violet's grip tightened on Carrot's makeshift leash. "He was not easily convinced he should wear it. An offering of smoked salmon was all that could sway him." Again, she tried looking past him, her curiosity apparent.

"Would you like to look around?" Stepping back, Tristan swung the door wide. "I don't mind."

Violet's eyes glowed in pleased surprise. "I've bothered you enough…"

"It is no bother at all, I assure you."

She glided past, and Tristan's heart clenched. Violet would never have exhibited such boldness in the past. Were his efforts already taking root? After all, she warned him about keeping his distance only now to seek him out. That surely accounted for something.

Keeping the kitten in her arms, she stopped in the center of the room by a large round table holding extra brushes, pigment powders in glass tubes, a decanter of brandy, and fruit. When she slowly rotated, it appeared all the light in the room gravitated to her instantly; the sunlight, the glow from a small lamp on the corner desk, the light coming from the sconces by the door. All of it seeking Violet.

"It is as I remember."

Tristan's eyebrow lifted. "You've been in here before?"

She set the kitten down. "Celia brought me. She said you've never minded family seeing your work. I suppose she thought I was included in that category." Her cheeks flushed pink. "It was an invasion of your privacy, I know, but I could not resist even back then. Your paintings are so beautiful."

Deliberately leaving the door open, Tristan came closer. Picking up a new palette knife, he ran a thumb over its flat surface. "When were you last in this salon? Was I here at Darby Meadows?"

It was difficult concealing his overwhelming interest in the answer. All he'd dreamed of the past few nights was Violet in this exact space. Posing for him. Her body ready for direction and placement. The rose-colored day gown sliding off bare, ivory-hued shoulders and pooling at her feet. Her hair spilling free of the simple braid she wore now to tumble in a heavy mass of auburn red he could wrap around his fist.

The blood in his veins churned like the sea in a storm, stirred by the mental images his brain conjured up.

Violet leaned over, examining the detail on a nearly finished painting of a group of last year's foals. "It was just before Celia and I began our first season. Nearly three years ago." She glanced in his direction, her expression indecipherable. "I believe at the time you were in London with the Duke of Richeforte. He was only an earl back then."

That would have been around the time Grace's mother passed away and she'd come to stay with them. Tristan had made a point of being at Darby Meadows quite frequently as a result, persistent in the foolish chase of his father's new ward. He wished now he'd heeded Celia's advice, listened when she warned that Grace's fondness for him would never be more than sisterly.

Pursuing Grace meant Violet's intentional absence from Darby Meadows, and that made Tristan irrationally sad.

"Did you have a favorite painting?" His voice was scratchy. A quick gulp of brandy remedied the condition, however.

Violet laughed softly as Carrot batted at dust motes floating in the sunshine. "You'll find no critic in me, Longleigh. I'm woefully unsophisticated in such matters. Every painting of yours is my favorite."

"You are to call me Tristan, remember?"

"I remember very well. It's just things have… changed."

"Have they?" Tristan countered, still holding the palette knife.

She moved on to peruse a different painting leaning against the wall but glancing at the one hidden under the oilcloth. "Do you have a favorite?"

Tristan shrugged, refusing to answer at the moment. It wouldn't be wise to reveal that his current project, one he'd been working on since the day she'd fallen from the tree and into his lap, was his favorite. "Come closer, kitten."

Violet regarded him as though debating the wisdom of obeying his directive, but in the end, she did as he asked.

Taking her by the hand, Tristan untangled the leash from her fingers so Carrot could roam free through the studio. The kitten gave an obligatory hiss before jumping onto one of the wide window sills. After a few moments of exploration, he stretched out in the streaming sunlight and dozed off.

"I haven't painted my favorite yet," Tristan finally answered. "The subject refused to sit for me."

Violet's head tilted. "How disappointing for you."

"Very," Tristan agreed, pulling her lush body to him with a crooked smile. "Perhaps I could change her mind with the right persuasion. Shall I show you?"

oming to Tristan's salon was a mistake, but Violet could not keep away. Something about this man extinguished all the common sense she supposedly possessed.

And the punishment for that lack of self-control required she must listen while Tristan described painting his muse if given the chance. Of course, only a formal portraiture of the new duchess was possible now, and only with her husband's permission.

No doubt Tristan was very disappointed by this.

Caught in the viscount's grip, Violet's fingers trembled. When he turned her so she faced the western bank of windows, her body trembled as well.

"First, I would position my subject so the softest light illuminated her. I've found dawn's light and the hour before dusk to be the most flattering. It imparts a glow to the skin. Wait here, my dear."

Tristan left for a moment, clearing the table behind her of objects until all that remained was the decanter of brandy, his glass, and a crystal bowl containing peaches, apples, and dark purple grapes. He then dragged the table into a pool of the late afternoon light.

Tugging Violet by the arm, he led her to the piece of furniture. His chocolate brown eyes were serious now, intense and dark and oddly mesmerizing as his palm smoothed its way down her shoulder to her elbow.

"I would arrange her hair. Her arms. Her legs. All so the beauty I see comes through in the brushstrokes on the canvas." Tristan's voice dropped low, his fingers closing around her wrist and lifting so her arm raised above her head. His other hand drifted up, a forefinger landing on the underside of her chin, tilting it until Violet had no choice but to meet his gaze. "I would uncover a light no one has ever seen. And I would guard it with a jealous passion. Because if I uncover it, it would belong only to me. Is my subject brave beneath her brittle façade? Brave enough to let me paint her as I wish?"

"Her husband would never allow it," Violet whispered. That was true enough. She could not imagine the Duke of Richeforte would ever allow such a painting of Grace. Nicholas was outrageously possessive of his wife.

Tristan briefly smiled, leaving the impression he found Violet's words an amusing challenge. Dropping his hands to her waist, he quickly lifted her up onto the table, ignoring her stifled gasp of surprise.

"This would be only for my eyes. To appease me during a lifetime of frustrated bachelorhood. Here, lie on your side, with this arm cradling your head and the other draped across your stomach."

For some insane reason, Violet allowed herself to be positioned as he desired. Her heart raced like a thousand wild horses as Tristan moved her limbs. There would be consequences if someone saw her inside his studio, sprawled upon the table like a wanton creature. It was madness, for sure. And a recipe for disaster.

But there was magic in Tristan's voice, and in his hands, too. He had her as he liked, across the furniture, the brandy glass near the hand on her belly, the decanter placed within reach of the arm propped beneath her head. The bowl of fruit hid the junction of her thighs, and Tristan silently encouraged her to shift until her hip and one leg exaggerated the pose into something unbearably seductive.

The reclining position made her breasts swell against the edges of her gown's bodice. A sharp twinge of excitement electrified Violet when Tristan's gaze lingered in that area before sliding over the rest of her body in a heated caress.

For a gut-wrenching moment, she worried of appearing overly plump. The wayward thought vanished as quickly as it appeared when Tristan reached out almost hesitantly.

With a hand that shook the tiniest bit, he slipped her shoes from her feet. He twitched her skirts into place. The thick braid of her hair was arranged, draped like a silken rope over her shoulder.

"Now, look straight at me, little kitten. And do not move."

In a flash, Tristan had a sketch pad and charcoal in hand. His arm flew with almost maniacal energy while her image was committed to paper. As he worked, a simmering undercurrent swirled, a thunderstorm Violet was unsure either one of them could ignore.

She certainly could not ignore it. How could she when her breath was growing labored? Her breasts felt heavier, the tips incredibly sensitive where the chemise and corset rubbed the flesh almost painfully. Tristan studied her, eyes burning darker and becoming more dangerous by the second, his full, bottom lip captured between his teeth, and the space between her thighs tingled with bewitching awareness.

The silence stretched and swelled with a life of its own until Violet thought she might snap in two from the tension.

But she said not a word, afraid she would break the spell if she dared speak aloud. When a self-conscious twinge of doubt raised its head again, reminding her she was not the svelte, golden woman the viscount had pursued in the past, Violet closed her eyes and refused to listen.

"You are so goddamn beautiful, Violet. Do you even know that?" Tristan finally muttered. "Do you know what I would give to have you truly posing for me as I've dreamed? I would have you laid across this table without a stitch of clothing. Nothing to distract from the beauty of your skin and how it both reflects and absorbs the light. I've never seen anything like it. I'm obsessed with it, if you must know, and damned if I can determine a path to what I want without ruining you to obtain it."

Violet's eyes fluttered open. She stared at Tristan in surprise, as motionless as a deer caught by a panther and afraid of being ripped apart.

With a heavy sigh, he laid the sketch pad aside and leaned forward, trailing a finger over her cheek.

"If I painted you this way, just like this, I would name it 'A Feast of Violets'. Do you know why?"

Violet shook her head, afraid to look away from the intensity of his stare, hypnotized by the dark, craven need she glimpsed inside him. Was that for her? Did the Viscount Longleigh really desire her? Or was she a convenient substitute for the woman he'd loved and lost to his closest friend?

"Because I would devour you. Completely. Unequivocally. Every piece of you, every morsel would belong to me."

His finger left her cheek, traveling down the column of her neck to the line of her collarbone. With deceptive gentleness, he traced the fine bone.

"All of this beauty would be mine." His hand moved lower, passing over the swell of her breast then down her side to the indentation of her waist.

Violet sucked in a hard breath. "I would be no one's."

"Stated with such conviction." He laughed, slowly sweeping a hand over the lush curve of her hip. It was greatly exaggerated by her position, but when she attempted moving her leg, he immediately stopped her. "Stay as you are. I have not finished sketching."

"I'm merely a test subject, Longleigh." Her voice came out wobbly and unsure. What *exactly* was she? Even she couldn't say for certain.

"You are so much more than that." Tristan's head tilted while his hand crept along the vicinity of her ankles and breached an unspoken boundary zone. "I'd say you are the epitome of a muse, my prickly little Violet." A finger trailed higher, tracing the anatomy of a kneecap, burning her flesh and bone through the flimsy silk stocking.

Moving behind her, Tristan picked something up. There was a faint metallic ring as he tapped it against the table.

It was the palette knife he'd held earlier. Violet swallowed hard, wondering what in the world he might do.

While still leisurely exploring beneath her skirts, Tristan used the instrument to count the carved ivory rosebuds marching in a delicate line from the nape of her neck to her waist. He flicked each button as if in contemplation of slicing them free. Violet shuddered at the thought of being naked before him.

Naked and at his mercy.

"Does this alarm you, kitten?"

Honesty would serve her best. "A little."

His hand slowed in stroking the back of her knee, and Violet was glad she could not see his countenance. Would there be pity in his eyes? Contempt for her lack of sophistication? He probably played these sorts of games with every silly woman who chased him.

Poor, shy Violet. So frightened of everything. Even the very person she wants more than anyone or anything in this world.

Clenching her teeth in a sudden burst of temper, she uttered very calmly, "I worry someone might see. We left the door open."

Would Tristan snatch her up from the table, pat her on the head, and send her on her way? Her stomach actually clenched when his hand eased away from her leg. The palate knife pressed harder until she felt the dull, flat edge of the tool through the fabric of her dress.

The eddying coolness of air alerted her when Tristan stepped back. A quick glance over her shoulder revealed the viscount striding toward the open door. He toed it shut, an expression crossing his features one could only characterize as savage triumph.

Violet was truly worried then.

Because that look promised sinful pleasures beyond comprehension that both terrified and thrilled her.

CHAPTER 15

"Lie on your back."

Tristan removed all the remaining items from the table, watching closely as Violet settled herself. A pool of sunlight drenched her, so she shouldn't have been chilled, but a series of fine tremors shook her just the same.

The table was almost the size of a small bed; only her feet hung off the end. Not knowing what she should do with her arms, she crisscrossed them over her chest. Instead of looking at Tristan, she stared at the ceiling.

His chuckle immediately drew her gaze.

"Don't worry, Violet. I've no intention of offering you up as a sacrifice."

Violet smiled despite herself. "I imagine that would create quite a mess. And would be rather difficult explaining to your housekeeper."

Drawing a finger across her cheek, Tristan replied softly, "How you surprise me. Only you would take my words at face value and make light of them."

Setting the palate knife aside, he took her arms, stretching them above her head.

Curiosity sawed at Violet's nerves.

What would Tristan do with her? It was all so mystifying and stomach-wrenching. Women simpered like besotted fools behind raised fans whenever he strolled past; the bolder ones pursued him. This might be her only chance at uncovering the mysteries of the viscount's appeal.

You are one of those besotted fools, you know. The only difference being he never acknowledged your existence before now.

With a clench of her teeth, Violet resolutely ignored her inner voice, as well as the trickle of unease.

Tristan's hand drifted from her face, down her throat, dipping in the hollow at its center, then further until his fingers finally brushed the upper swells of her breasts. Violet swallowed.

"I'm frightening you," he murmured, almost sounding apologetic.

"No."

"No? Perhaps there is a core of steel beneath all that innocence. But still, something concerns you, I think. Other than the threat of imminent ruination." A sly grin dispelled the seriousness of his statement. He was toying with her, using that dark wit of his like a weapon.

Charm and disarm. Tristan was an absolute master in utilizing this particular strategy. Lord knew she was not immune to its effect.

Violet hesitated before deciding that honesty would serve her best. Besides, she could not hide with Tristan's gaze boring into hers. The razor-like sharpness of his eyes prevented escape from all her insecurities.

"I do not resemble your customary female conquests, Longleigh."

"No," Tristan breathed, his hand moving to the section of dress covering her belly. "You certainly do not."

Violet automatically sucked in, a feeble attempt at flattening her belly. "I do wish I were tall and willowy and slender of figure. Men prefer women to be so…"

Tristan's hand halted in its unnerving exploration, his head tilting. "We do?"

"Yes. Women should be pleasing of figure and countenance. I must work harder at accomplishing both."

"Stop. Don't dare utter another word." A muscle in Tristan's square jaw ticked. "Whoever spouted such nonsense should dance from the gallows at Newgate."

Violet bit her lip. "My parents have said …"

"Your parents are damned fools," Tristan said abruptly. Taking Violet by the hand, he tugged her upright into a sitting position on the edge of the table. Cradling her face, he tilted her head back. "Listen to me, Violet, and listen well. You are perfect just as you are."

When Violet tried looking away, Tristan wouldn't allow it. "Beautiful. Sweet. Kind. Soft. Lush. Desirable." His head bent until his lips brushed hers. "Touching you has become a need I cannot ignore."

Violet's heart tightened. Was this truly happening? She was so used to being overlooked by those around her. To be the focus of Tristan's interest seemed stolen from a dream she would never dare admit aloud.

"It is the same for me, Tristan." Her breath caught when his eyes flashed with her shy words. "I cannot think of anything other than you. How you make me feel when you kiss me. It is so improper, and yet I can't help but hope …"

With leisurely intent, Tristan cut off the impromptu confession. Taking full possession of Violet's mouth, he swallowed her moan of scandalized delight. He nibbled and sucked at her lips and tongue until she squirmed closer to him.

"Open your legs for me, kitten. Open, and I'll give you a glimpse of paradise." Tristan's words slid in a seductive whisper along the curve of her ear. "Are you as soft as I've dreamed? Let me feel you on my fingertips. Let me touch you as I wish..."

Violet did not hesitate with indecision. Tristan asked. She complied. Her legs separated as far as her skirts would allow.

"There's my brave, beautiful girl," he crooned between greedy but somehow lazy kisses. "Hold tight to me. And do not let go."

Was the world whirling away in slow motion? It seemed as if time was standing still while Violet spun in reckless abandonment. Every sensation was amplified, every nuance of her being so intensely attuned to Tristan it was overwhelming.

She smelled his cologne, sharp and woodsy. Felt the muscles of his shoulders flex and undulate when her fingernails dug slightly into the flesh. There was the roughness of his fingertips rasping over the edge of her stockings, the way his hand tightened and pressed harder when she silently granted permission that he could go even further.

And there was the minute exhale of wonderment that escaped Tristan's lips when he encountered bare skin. He skimmed past the opening of her drawers to spear through the patch of curls. Parting her, he slowly traced the petals of her sex with silky-rough fingers.

"Christ," he muttered as though greatly pained. "You are exactly as I imagined. Soft as velvet. Warm. And sweet. So damned sweet."

Euphoria swept through Violet; a wave of pleasure so intense she thought she might faint. His fingers touched her so gently and yet so precisely. The expertise disturbed her for a momentary flash of clarity then was blessedly gone.

She would mindlessly enjoy this. Without thought or guilt. Giving herself up to the sensations was a necessary indulgence. She prayed he would not stop what he was doing. The careful nature of his caresses was intoxicating, and he handled her as if she were a rare, fragile piece of artwork.

Somewhere in the distance, perhaps thousands of miles away, Violet heard a rousing chorus of dogs barking. They did not intrude on her world, however. No, in this little corner of Darby Meadows, the outside world was kept at bay.

It was a lie she told herself, even when Tristan's hand faltered, then the exquisite exploration he had embarked upon was easing away.

"No..." The murmur of protest passed her lips, quickly silenced by a brush of Tristan's mouth.

"Do not fret..." he soothed, but there was reluctance in his tone; a resignation tempered by the reality of having no other choice but to draw back. His hand left her, slipping out from beneath her skirts, fingertips trailing the skin of her thigh as though gathering a memory he could savor in private at a later time.

The barking dogs sounded closer. Louder. From the windowsill, Carrot hissed then meowed in agitation. A moment later, the kitten jumped down from the ledge, knocking over one of the smaller paintings in the process.

The clatter snapped Violet to her senses. She recognized the estate's hounds as the source of the barking. The small pack of dogs usually roamed the grounds, alerting footmen and servants of approaching guests.

Brow furrowed, Tristan helped Violet off the table and then ducked beneath it to retrieve the kitten. Handing the end of Carrot's leash to her, he then peered out the window to survey the sprawling courtyard below.

"We have a newly arrived guest." His tone carried a strangled quality when he glanced back at Violet. She stared at him, swaying unsteadily as the memory of his hand sweeping over her flesh seared her.

"Oh?" she managed to say, even as her knees threatened to give way. *Guests? What do I care? Tristan touched me, and it's the most marvelous thing I've ever experienced.*

"Lord Gadley has arrived." Tristan's features were schooled into a mask of indifference. "And no one could be more disappointed than I am."

CHAPTER 16

"Your parents shall arrive within the week, Lady Violet." William frowned at the sight of an orangish tuft of fur on Violet's skirts. Seeing where his eyes had fallen, she flushed and immediately plucked it away. Then, unsure what to do with the offending stuff, she simply closed her palm around it, letting her arm hang by her side.

"Yes, of course," Violet murmured. She obediently remained at her "maybe" fiancé's side.

Tristan clasped his hands behind his back, fighting the urge to rip Violet away from Lord Gadley and the hold he had of her elbow. Christ, the man was more odious than he remembered.

"What news of London, Gadley?" Henry Bowman asked, jovially. "Boodles must-have new play on the books. Details, my dear man. We need details."

"Not a suitable subject with ladies present, Lord Bowman," Lord Darby admonished, approaching the group where they stood in the grand entry hall.

"My apologies, ladies. Don't know what I was thinking, other than curiosity got the best of me. I do enjoy a good wager." Henry's apology was both contrite and yet unabashed. He winked at Violet, and Tristan grit his teeth.

Must he watch every eligible bachelor visiting Darby Woods flirt with his little wallflower?

"There's a time and place for such things," the earl responded, leaning heavily on his cane.

Tristan thought his father appeared paler than when he'd last seen him at supper the night before. His mother cast Tristan a concerned glance before greeting their newest guest.

"Welcome, Lord Gadley. If your valet will supervise the servants on carrying the baggage to your room, perhaps you would appreciate a brandy or other refreshments after your long journey from London." Lady Darby gestured toward Tristan. "Longleigh can accompany you to the main salon, if you like."

William released Violet's elbow so he could withdraw a hinged snuff box from a hidden pocket on the inside of his coat. Popping the ornately enameled case open, he took two pinches of tobacco and leisurely inhaled them before answering his host. Violet, meanwhile, gazed at him with barely concealed distaste.

"That would be delightful, Lady Darby. It's said your salon is one of the finest in all of England." William turned to Tristan with a smug grin. "Longleigh has never extended an invite, but I'm pleased to be here regardless. If you'll lead the way, Longleigh." He glanced at Violet. "We must have a private conversation, my dear. Later, of course, once I've settled in."

Tristan's eyes narrowed. God's blood, the man was truly loathsome.

Catching Violet's gaze, Tristan gave her a small smile. Unable to help himself, he rubbed his fingers together. A trace residue of her silky arousal still lingered there.

It was hedonistic, of course, but he reveled in that fact. He'd give his fortune to be in his studio at that precise moment with

Violet still at his mercy. He would make her shatter into a thousand pieces if granted a second opportunity.

His thoughts must have shown plainly, for Violet immediately blushed bright pink and tore her gaze away from his.

"Yes, lead the way, Longleigh. I believe we could all use a drink." Bowman laughed heartily, bowing toward Tristan's father. "Lord Darby, it is rumored your brandy selection rivals that of the Duke of Richeforte. Having only sampled yours, I am unable to present an unbiased comparison. Richeforte should bring a bottle or two so that a proper assessment may take place."

"Perhaps he will," the earl replied absently to Bowman. "But with a pretty new wife, such trivial things may be far from his mind." He watched Tristan's reaction with a curious expression on his features.

Tristan did not miss the way Violet bit her bottom lip with his father's off-the-cuff statement. The plump bit of flesh turned scarlet when she released it. If he had his way, he would soothe her with a kiss and the reminder he had no interest at all in the new Duchess of Richeforte.

"Will you join us, Father?" Tristan inquired, turning to the earl.

"Another time, son." Darby dismissed Tristan with a wave of his hand, then turned to smile at Violet. "Violet, dear, I do hope you are enjoying your stay here. I was just saying to Lady Darby it's been too long since you came to visit us. You are always welcome here, regardless of the season or event."

What an odd thing for his father to say. Tristan puzzled over it as Lord Darby gave him a hard stare. "Tristan, join me in my study in an hour's time."

Whatever the earl wished to discuss, Tristan was fairly certain it revolved around Violet and the attention he'd shown her the past week.

And that definitely set his nerves on edge.

~

OTHERS ACCOMPANIED them to the main salon; the arrival of new guests warranted a welcome round of beverages. A lively mix of both men and women soon filled the space.

Violet deftly avoided William. Each time he reached for her, she slid out of reach. Tristan found her evasiveness quite fascinating.

"Ugh," Celia sighed, taking up a spot beside Tristan. "I'd forgotten how disagreeable that man is. And I don't know what's gotten into him. In the past, he's scarcely shown her any attention at all, but now? Now, he seems obsessed with touching her every chance he gets. Poor Violet. I imagine it feels similar to pursuit by a reptile of some sort. Although, I suppose I should refrain from voicing my criticism. The man will probably be her husband soon enough."

Tristan clenched the glass in his hand tighter with his sister's words. He did not need that reminder.

Gadley's sudden interest in staking his claim was not so puzzling if one understood men's predictable reaction to perceived threats. Obviously, the smug and infamously emotionless man had deduced Henry Bowman wasn't the only gentleman interested in the shy redhead. Other men were now sniffing around her skirts as well.

Tristan included himself in that group.

"If only someone with a richer purse and an agreeable personality offered for Violet. Lord Everstone would surely consider an alternative." Celia stared into the pale depths of the glass of lemonade a servant handed her. "But then again, perhaps he would not. For a year, Violet has been dangled in front of Gadley as if she were a golden carrot. He links his name to the esteemed Everstone crest, and in return, the earl receives a generous settlement for the rights to his daughter. It's an unfair exchange, I think, with Violet coming out on the short end of things. He's not shown a whit of interest in her all this time, and now..."

Across the room, William swallowed the dregs of his third brandy. Setting the glass down, he successfully snagged Violet's elbow when she was distracted by Lady Fiona's entrance. Drawing her aside from the other guests, he spoke rather sternly while she listened with a blank expression, her eyes downcast.

Violet's docile nature left Tristan feeling nauseous and confused. Where was the spark he'd seen earlier when she granted him permission to explore as he willed beneath her skirts?

Violet shook her head in response to something William said, pulling free and wrapping her arms almost defensively around her waist. Seeing her unease stiffened Tristan's backbone. And when her gaze shot across the room to lock with his, he physically restrained himself from rushing to her side.

Aware that her attention had drifted to the viscount, Gadley gripped her arm again, his mouth flattening into an ugly line.

Pain flashed across Violet's delicate features.

"The bastard..." Tristan breathed.

"Tristan," Celia warned. "Don't. You've no rights when it comes to Violet."

"You go to her, then. Quickly. Before I rip the man's arms from his body."

Celia nodded, setting down her glass. Without another word, she hurried across the room.

Tristan had no idea what Celia said as she slid an arm around Violet's waist but William released her with a reluctant scowl.

In her usual charming way, his sister's mannerism remained bright and cheerful while engaging the gentleman in conversation. Finally giving a tight nod, William stepped back so the two women could dip their heads in a private discussion. A moment later, Violet searched out Tristan, their eyes locking.

A smile of gratitude curved her lips, softening them and reminding him how sweetly they molded to his. She was still smiling as Celia led her from the salon.

William watched them go, his face hard, cold, and oddly determined, and Tristan wondered why that sent a shiver of unease up his spine.

TRISTAN CLOSED the door and sat in a chair closer to the fireplace.

His father had not yet arrived, although, to be fair, it was a few minutes before the designated time. With a sigh, he considered making himself a drink but decided against it for the moment.

At five after four, his father entered the study. He appeared almost surprised at the sight of his son already seated by the fire. However, he quickly recovered and made his way to a small bar set up in the corner.

"Will you have a brandy, son?"

"Certainly." Tristan stood up, respectfully waiting for his father to approach with the drinks before he retook his seat.

Handing over a brandy snifter, Lord Darby sat in a chair opposite of Tristan with a heavy sigh.

Tristan studied the earl, noting the pallor of his skin and his heavy breath. Concern once again caused his own chest to tighten. "You don't seem well this afternoon, sir."

Father waved a hand in dismissal. "It's just the dampness of the spring mornings catching up to me." Taking a sip of brandy, he fixed Tristan with a steely eye. "Now, what's this business between you and Violet Everstone?"

Tristan shrugged. "Nothing other than the customary interest one would expect for a Darby Meadows guest."

The earl gave a sharp bark of laughter. "Customary? Your mother and I have witnessed your interest. Regardless of the potential alliance her father has arranged, Violet could be an excellent addition to the list we've assembled. We've not added her due to the arrangement we've had over the years with Everstone. It would require a bit of negotiation on my part, but if she is the one you want—"

"I've stated as forcibly as I dare, Father, that I've no interest in marriage to anyone. Besides, I regard Lady Violet as nothing more than a friend." *A friend I've discovered has the most delectable, ripest, peach-flavored lips. Lips I cannot get enough of. Would a rational person kiss a friend in such a manner? As if one's own life depended on tasting the sweetness of another's essence?*

"I can't understand your reluctance to pursue the possibility of finding a wife. After your experience with Grace, one would think you'd be willing to find someone you could call your own," Lord Darby scoffed. "And of the two, Violet is far more suitable in temperament and nature. You and Grace were too much alike, but not in the areas where it mattered most. It is why I did not encourage a match."

"While you are correct in your assessment of my lack of compatibility with Grace, the decision to remain a bachelor has nothing to do with the new duchess and everything to do with myself."

"Would you ever consider the Everstone girl?" his father pressed, leaning forward in his chair and fixing Tristan with an intent stare. "Even with the complete lack of gain she might bring to a marriage? It is my understanding that, at the moment, only her name is worth any value."

"My decision to marry, if and when it ever occurs, shall have nothing to do with a woman's monetary value. Nor her social standing, for that matter," Tristan said firmly. "I shall wed her because she wishes to marry me as much as I wish to marry her."

Darby regarded Tristan over the rim of the brandy snifter. "Admirable. Although that did not seem to be the sentiment during your pursuit of Grace."

Tristan stiffened. "I've changed much since then, sir."

And he had. Seeing the deep, unwavering love Grace and Nicholas shared certainly proved he was wrong in forcing his attentions on an uninterested party. It was a mistake he would never make again.

"It is not my intention to meddle in my friend's affairs, nor my son's, for that matter, but it has not escaped notice that the man Everstone selected for his daughter meets only the requirement of having a sufficient amount of funds." Darby sighed. "And Gadley is willing to exchange those funds for a blue-blooded name. Your mother, bless her gentle soul, is greatly disturbed by this. She carries a deep fondness for Violet. And Celia, well, your sister is beside herself. She's convinced, if a marriage takes place, it will destroy the girl."

"I don't see how you can do anything about it, sir." Tristan stood from the chair and rested an arm on the fireplace mantle. He felt claustrophobic all of a sudden. As if a trap were being set and he'd walked willingly into the teeth of it.

"I cannot," Darby said in a low voice behind him. "But you can."

"What the devil does that mean?"

"Perhaps, if you are thought to be a serious candidate for her hand, Gadley will withdraw his suit. A more appropriate gentleman may then be vetted for the poor girl. Lord Bowman, for example. He's a decent sort, and I've noticed his interest in her. I could endorse him to Everstone."

Tristan gritted his teeth at the thought of Bowman laying claim to Violet every night as her lawful husband.

"Really, Father," he snorted in disdain. "How did Mother and

Celia coerce you into endorsing such a hare-brained scheme? God's teeth. I've no interest in being a part of whatever fate Everstone has in store for his daughter, and very little faith our actions would make a difference to the good or the bad. That man is ruthless. He has been that way since you were both boys at Eaton. Had he not saved you from drowning that one day, you two would barely be acquaintances. If he stands to make a shilling off the sale of his daughter, who are we to stand in his way?"

Tristan's words proclaimed his disinterest, but a merciless stab of possessiveness gutted him. The thought of Violet bartered off was almost more than he could bear. Could his father see the lie on his face?

"That's all true, but Gadley is perhaps even more heartless. You've heard rumors of his dealings with the fairer sex, Tristan." Darby set a hand on Tristan's shoulder. "Think upon it, won't you, son? Our interference could mean a vastly different life for her."

CHAPTER 17

*C*elia managed it so that one of the numerous Buchanan cousins occupied the dinner seat beside Violet. Just out of the university and overflowing with tales of his escapades, Lawrence kept her entertained.

Violet did not mind the young man's steady stream of conversation. It spared her the task of appearing engaged. More importantly, it saved her from William's odious presence.

But while William glared his disapproval with the seating arrangements, Tristan was strangely remote. Seated just across the table with Fiona Blackerby beside him, he avoided eye contact with Violet. Like her, he escaped the evening activities planned after the meal. The knowledge he more than likely requested Fiona as a dinner partner made her heart hurt with such painful sharpness, she was left breathless.

Pleading a headache, Violet took the stairs as quickly as she dared following dinner, mindful of the curious stares her hasty exit garnered. A glance over her shoulder revealed William preparing to follow, a determined look on his features. Her pace quickened until she gained the safety of her room.

Legs trembling, she leaned against the bedchamber's solid oak door.

Bile rose in her throat at the thought of William laying a hand on her. His newfound possessiveness was a disturbing development. One she didn't know how to handle.

Strange how much easier she'd found it to stomach him before Tristan touched her. Before Tristan kissed her. Made her fall hopelessly, tragically, and even deeper in love with him.

Life before that, while hardly perfect, was certainly less complicated. The only expectation was that she should obey her parents. To do as they wished and marry whoever was chosen for her. She had resigned herself to a dull, loveless marriage, certain nothing of interest would mark her life. Before Tristan, Violet doubted she would ever experience the affectionate touch of a man.

It was almost comical, really, that she found herself in this position. *Her.* The most unremarkable, unmemorable wall-flower of the past two seasons was utterly devastated by one of London's most eligible bachelors.

She was essentially ruined. Oh, not in the classic sense. At least, not in a manner anyone would have any knowledge of. No one knew the liberties the viscount had taken with her, the places he touched her body, the ways he kissed her. If anyone discovered the truth of their stolen encounters, a wedding would probably be her father's first and foremost demand.

She clenched her fists tight against a swelling of indignant pride.

I'll never let that happen. I'll not have any man forced to wed me against his will. Least of all the brother of my dearest friend. What has happened between Tristan and me must remain a secret.

Any chance of happiness with another man had been destroyed by chocolate-colored eyes and a pair of artist's hands stained with faint traces of paint. And she could only blame herself for her current state of turmoil. If only she'd tried harder in keeping her distance from the charmer. Done more to resist. Hardened her heart. Hid her soul.

A sob broke free from the depths of her chest. "How will I ever forget Tristan when I am that awful man's wife?"

At the sound of Violet's voice, Carrot jumped down from the bed's counterpane and trotted soundlessly to her. Weaving around her legs, he meowed until Violet complied with his demands to be picked up.

Burying her face in the kitten's soft fur, Violet sniffled until her emotions were wrangled under control.

Carrot endured the moment stoically at first, then with a mischievous spurt of energy, he batted at a hunk of Violet's hair and bit the auburn curls as though they were a tangle of yarn to be played with.

Carrying the kitten, Violet stood at the window, gazing out over the moonlit grounds below. The sensible thing to do would be to follow her plan and stay far away from the viscount. What he made her feel was dangerous.

Recalling his actions in his studio sent a tide of warmth throughout her body. She'd teetered on the cusp of something magical when his fingers danced upon her flesh. It was all very wicked and dark, and when it abruptly stopped, she'd known a great frustration mixed with eagerness.

She was aware of her body's own physical reaction to his caresses; the dampness between her thighs that Tristan gathered on his fingertips being the most blatant of those physical signs. That he reminded her of this damning evidence with a teasing grin even while Lord Gadley stood in the foyer of his parents' home was a stark reminder she was just a pleasant distraction. A dalliance. Certainly not worth forgoing his treasured state of bachelorhood.

"I have agreed he shall paint your portraiture, Carrot, and I shall not go back on my word. But when that is done, I vow I will stay far away from him, for my own sanity, at least." She nuzzled the kitten's nose, listening to him purr with pleasure at the unexpected attention. "Nothing good can come from this madness I feel for him. Nothing but heartache."

VIOLET'S AVOIDANCE of William lasted until teatime the following day. Upon returning from a daily check of the mother cat and kittens, he caught her on the terrace overlooking the stables.

"There you are, my dear."

Impeccably attired in a dark green afternoon coat and trousers, William was dazzling in the bright sunshine. Hair the shade of the new champagne glinted with the sun's rays, and his pale blue eyes narrowed as Violet slowly ascended the steps.

"Lord Gadley. It's a pleasant afternoon for taking the air."

"Yes. I had hoped you would join me. However, your maid informed me you were off on some errand when I came to your room earlier." His eyes were sharp, taking note of her reaction. "Silly girl said you'd gone to the stables. I informed her she must be mistaken."

Taken aback by William's disapproving tone, Violet slowly answered. "Bridgette spoke the truth."

William's jaw clenched. "What was your business there? I know you don't ride. Your father made that very clear."

"I-I was merely looking in on a stray cat that recently had kittens. You see, I've been taking scraps..."

"What utter foolishness," William mocked. "You shall refrain from such activities from this point forward."

"Oh, but it is of no consequence to anyone else! Lord Darby's cook says the scraps are not missed, and I am careful that my visits do not interfere with the workings of the stable." Violet's heart pounded from speaking so boldly, but there was no other way to explain herself. Surely, William would understand. "The poor thing was a bit weak, as one might expect with eight new mouths to feed, but she's much better now and—"

"No wife of mine shall be gallivanting back and forth wherever and whenever she pleases. God only knows the disease and pestilence you might contract from those disgusting creatures." His eyebrow arched empirically.

"I'm not your wife yet."

The moment the words escaped her mouth, Violet realized she'd committed a grave error.

William drew himself up into a model of rigid indignation. "All in good time, my dear. As my wife, you will obey me or suffer the consequences." Cold blue eyes flickered over Violet with a renewed spark of interest. "Your father assured me you were easily handled, and over the past months, I've found that to be annoyingly true. This current exhibition of insolence is most surprising. Quite out of character for you. A lack of discipline due to your parents' absence is certainly the cause. We shall work extremely hard at overcoming this newly uncovered flaw. There are several ways one should deal with defiance, and I will take the greatest of pleasures in correcting your behavior."

William's statement confused Violet. How precisely did a husband 'deal' with an unruly wife? She certainly had no wish to find out. Nor did she have any desire that her parents discover she'd insulted the man. Should he withdraw the pursuit for her hand, the repercussions would not be pleasant.

"Please forgive my hasty words. I did not mean to offend but was only stating the obvious." Violet glanced down at her hands, then rubbed them lightly down the sides of her gown. "If you will excuse me, I must go change my gown for tea and freshen up a bit. Good afternoon, Lord Gadley."

Inclining her head in dismissal, she hurried past, but William snagged her arm, pulling her up short. His eyes bored into her own, lit now with a strange fire and something that resembled lust.

Violet stared at him in alarm. This man had never given her any regard other than that of bored acceptance. But there was an air about him now. It made her wonder; if there was no chance at being caught, what he might do to her. Skin clammy with fear, her heart rose in her throat as she prepared herself to scream for assistance if needed.

"Your father pressed me hard for a decision, Violet. And I obliged him before coming to Darby Meadows." William leaned forward. In a shocking gesture, he ran his nose alongside hers and breathed in her fear. It was apparent he exalted in its presence. "When your parents arrive, our engagement will be formally announced. After this little display of rebellion, I wouldn't dream of letting you go now."

VIOLET CRUMPLED the note into a ball and in a fit of temper flung it into the fireplace. Watching it burst into a tiny ball of flames was momentarily satisfying, but not enough to ease her emotions.

"The gall of that man," she muttered beneath her breath. "The absolute temerity."

Tristan had selected the time and place for Carrot's painting. Notification was sent to Violet via a hand-written message, delivered some hours ago by a servant rather than conveyed in person. Instead of the woodland setting she'd originally requested, he rather high-handedly deemed the fabulously ornate, overly large fountain in the center of his mother's garden as the location.

The very center of Buckingham Palace would be less populated than the popular Darby Rose Garden in the height of springtime.

Obviously, Tristan wished to avoid any time in her presence now that William had arrived. And while Violet agreed with the sentiment, it stung beyond all bearing he was making serious efforts to that end.

It should not bother her so deeply, but it did. It should not anger her, but goodness, her palms itched with a need to slap the man. And it should not make her heart ache, knowing he wished to end their association, but it hurt more than she wanted to admit.

She stewed upon that pain while preparing for bed, and Bridgette combed out her hair.

"I shouldn't care," she whispered defiantly. "I shouldn't care, and I don't. Because he never gave a moment's thought to anything other than his own pleasure. The selfish cad. Even when he was caressing me, it was for himself. Oh, how could I be so blind? So foolish? So eager to be used for his amusement?"

The longer she thought on the subject, the more upset Violet became until it was clear she must say something to Tristan or burst with the words seething inside her.

She waited until Bridgette left her for the evening, then waited another two hours for good measure. But even the passage of time did nothing to cool her temper. With a night rail pulled tight around her body and a self-righteous grimace stamped on her features, she shut the bedchamber door behind her with a decisive click.

"I shall simply inform the viscount I've no wish to be in his company any longer than necessary. In fact, it is I attempting to distance myself from him, rather than the other way around. He and Fiona Blackerby are welcome to each other..."

Violet mumbled this to herself as she made her way down the long hallway and turned down the corridor containing Tristan's suite. From previous stays, she knew the viscount's rooms were situated in a wing of the huge estate house affording both privacy and convenience to the rest of the residence. He was far enough away no guests would bother him, but close enough that he also wasn't regarded as an outcast.

It was after midnight. The servants had turned down the hall sconces some time before, leaving the long corridor dark with deep shadows. This wing contained only Tristan's rooms. There was no reason anyone else should be about at this time of the night, but as Violet drew close, the bedchamber door flew open.

A female form, her blonde hair barely covered by a pretty shawl, was suddenly thrust into the small pool of light cast by twin sconces bracketing Tristan's doorway. She wore only a flimsy nightgown and robe.

Violet grimaced. Much like herself.

"Go back to your room, Fiona," Tristan rumbled.

Violet ducked behind a tall armoire, holding her breath at the sound of the viscount's voice. It carried a lilt of annoyance and something else. Exasperation? Desire? She couldn't tell.

"But, Tristan, shouldn't we just— "

"No, we shouldn't. I warned you about this, that it can't happen again. Go back to your room. Quickly, before someone sees you."

Fiona's sultry laugh set Violet's teeth on edge. "Would that be such a terrible thing?"

"For you, yes. Before any real damage is done to your reputation, do as I say."

"You do lead a girl on a merry chase, Longleigh," Fiona simpered. "Everyone knows how terribly persistent I am."

Peeking around the piece of furniture, Violet's eyes widened at the sight of Tristan. Dear heavens, the man wore only loose drawers resembling a pair of trousers held up by a drawstring and a dark green robe which hung open. Golden in the light of the sconces, his bare chest rippled with muscles. A line of dark hair began at his navel and tracked to the waistline of the pants.

Fascinated by the expanse of flesh, Violet helplessly watched him take Fiona by the shoulders. He then spun her around so she faced away from him.

Leaning forward, he whispered something in her ear.

Fiona's eyes closed until Tristan gave her a little shove that placed a small distance between their bodies.

Her tone carried a husky promise of sex as she glanced back at him. "Don't offer unless you intend on delivering, darling."

"Go back to your room and remember what I said," Tristan replied, tersely.

"Oh, I'll remember," Fiona trilled, coming toward Violet who quickly ducked out of eyesight again. "I'll dream of it every night."

Tristan's response was to shut his door. Fiona simply shrugged, seemingly unfazed by the viscount's rudeness. Continuing down the corridor, a smug smile lit her features.

When the woman's light humming could no longer be heard, Violet ventured out from her hiding place.

Fury shook her. How dare he? How dare he carry on with that hussy? And all while acting like her champion against Fiona's cruelty at the same time.

The preening peacock. The insufferable cad.

Before she realized her feet were moving, Violet stood at his door. Her fists banged on the oak in a series of rapid knocks.

Tristan flung open the portal at the racket, and Violet barely had time to register his surprise before she was snatched from the hallway and into his rooms.

The door slammed shut behind her. The click of the lock struck with an ominous note.

"You'll have a devil of a time explaining why you are lurking outside my bedroom, kitten," Tristan purred. He easily held Violet against the wall with one hand lightly gripping the base of her throat. The other braced against the wood paneling beside her head, caging her in. "But oh, how I look forward to hearing why you are. Now, start talking."

CHAPTER 18

*V*iolet was magnificent. All flowing auburn hair and flashing amethyst-blue eyes. A flimsy concoction of ivory muslin wrapped around her body fired Tristan's blood to the point of boiling. Had she traversed the halls wearing *only* that?

Sweet Jesus. It was sinful. And arousing. And innocent. And infuriatingly distracting.

She glared up at him, a mixture of anguish and fury igniting the dark blue depths of her eyes. When Tristan thought she might speak, she did just the opposite.

The slap she delivered left a stinging red palm print on his cheek.

"How dare you," Violet choked out. "How *dare* you prattle on and on of your desire for me. Your *need*. What a blessed fool I've been. I'm mortified that just because a known scoundrel said I'm beautiful, I abandoned all good sense and believed his lies. I allowed myself to hope, to dream. All while you consorted with that—that horrid woman. How taxing you must find it, keeping us separate while chasing us both. Well, you no longer need to worry about maintaining pretenses, keeping those pretenses up,

Longleigh. In fact, you needn't have bothered with this charade at all. I never asked for your attention, nor demanded it. I'm hardly one of those frivolous women, salivating over you. Fawning over you. Craving a crumb of your regard. You and Lady Fiona are welcome to each other, you duplicitous blackguard."

Tristan felt a rising urge to clasp Violet against his chest, to quiet the outburst with kisses, but her fiery statement hit a sour note deep in his gut.

"The little kitten grows claws at last," he breathed. "While you practice sharpening those weapons on my admittedly tough hide, let me make one thing absolutely clear. I have not, and will not pursue Fiona Blackerby. The woman deludes herself into thinking she might trick me into marriage, but I'll have nothing to do with it, or her for that matter."

"Then why is she in your rooms after midnight?" Violet cried. "In her nightclothes… sneaking about the corridors."

"Why are you?" Tristan countered serenely.

His question shocked her. Violet gaped at him for a moment then fiercely blurted out, "I came to inform you I've no more desire to be alone with you than you do with me. Your intention to paint Carrot in such a public setting as your mother's rose garden, rather than the woods as I requested, is evidence of that. You'll recall I've been trying to avoid situations that might be considered improper—"

"You mean situations like appearing on my doorstep in your nightgown while the rest of the household are in their beds? Or perhaps the instances when you've sought me out in my studio, and instructed that I shut the door so we could be alone." Tristan's voice was silky-smooth. Dangerous. And on the edge of something even he didn't quite comprehend. He felt strung tight as a bowstring as they stared at each other, tension and heat crackling between them like a flashfire.

Violet struggled against his grip. "Let me go. Only a heartless monster would kiss me as you have done and then blame me for responding to it."

"I only point out that you seek my company. I am guilty of the same."

"You are keeping me here now. Against my will."

Tristan swore softly beneath his breath. "Be honest, Violet. Right here. Right now. Be honest with yourself and with me."

A part of him deeply regretted forcing Violet to acknowledge her own actions, but Tristan knew it must be done. He'd pushed an unfair advantage with his kisses and caresses; however, she could not play the victim forever.

Sucking in an outraged breath, Violet's eyes narrowed. For the longest time, she simply looked up at him as though attempting to unravel a mystery or a puzzle. Then her shoulders slumped. All the righteous anger bled from her body, leaving behind a dejected shell. Misery flashed across her heart-shaped face.

Her defeat happened quickly, the sight of it nearly breaking Tristan's embattled heart.

"You are right, Tristan. I-I have placed myself, and you, in positions which could irrevocably compromise us both. I did not even realize it until you pointed it out this very moment. How silly and sad you must think I am. I'm so sorry, and I swear, I've not attempted to trick you into something as serious as marriage. I would never do something so dishonorable." Surprisingly dark and thick eyelashes swept down, hiding her thoughts from scrutiny, that blood-red, bee-stung mouth of hers trembling as if she might cry at any moment. "But even if it's just been a lovely lie, even if I only serve as a temporary amusement, you should know I enjoy it. I shall live on those moments for the rest of my life, as pathetic as it sounds when said aloud."

Listening to her, Tristan realized something quite profound and unexpected. He had no idea how he got there, but there he was. Standing on the sharp edge of a jagged cliff with no sight of the bottom, and only two logical choices facing him.

He could agree with this shy, gorgeous, tenderhearted girl. Say he'd merely toyed with her for his own pleasure. Send her on her way with the understanding their lives would continue on separate paths. Their association would abruptly end, with the exception of exchanging pleasantries when they encountered one another in social settings, and that would be that.

Or he could leap off the cliff with his eyes closed. Take her hand. Take her with him. See where they landed.

His hand slid up the column of her throat, his thumb pressing the underside of her chin. Exerting pressure, he forced her head back, his fingers sliding so that they meshed in the silk curtain of her hair.

"I should send you away without a care for your feelings, Violet. But I cannot. And I won't. Because I am the devil himself. And the devil takes what he wants, damn the consequences. Do you think I don't want you? Because I do. God help me, but I do. Since that afternoon under the oak tree, I've tortured myself with thoughts of having you. I tried distancing myself so you wouldn't get hurt, but I can't let you believe I don't want you. I ache for you, Violet." Tristan's other hand snaked around her waist, pulling her tight against him. "I want you for myself. No other man has a right to see the beauty that is you."

Violet's body quivered, the tiny tremors rippling through her body as delicate and as finely wrought as the fluttering of a fairy's wings.

Tristan felt every single one like a shock to his own system. An overwhelming sense of protectiveness swept him. He needed to shield and comfort her. To make her smile and laugh. To stand between her and danger. It wasn't love. Of that he was positive. But he was deeply fond of her. And Hell's fire, he wanted her in his bed.

"You shouldn't tell such falsehoods. It isn't kind—" Violet said between clenched teeth. Little stars of tears illuminated her eyes.

"Do not doubt my words," Tristan growled back, exasperated that she could not comprehend her loveliness. "You are the most gorgeous creature I've ever laid eyes on. And the kindest. The most intelligent… most sensible…"

Violet's lips curved, causing the little dimple in her right cheek to peek out. "You have no fear of being accused of insincerity."

His head bowed toward hers. "I've no idea what will happen with you and me, but Violet, this attraction between us is real. What I feel for you is real."

"You'll forgive my ignorance, Tristan, but is this an offer of some sort?" Violet asked softly, a thread of sorrow lacing her words.

Tristan hesitated, remembering his father's plea. He could help her avoid a union with Gadley and other unscrupulous men like him.

The problem was, if he leaped off the cliff and took her with him, he would become the villain.

"In a way, it could be. Perhaps it's possible to change Gadley's mind when it comes to marrying you. And I can appease my father's insistent demands that I seek a wife without actually committing to the deed."

"You want me as your mistress."

Tristan chuckled. "What do you know of men and their mistresses, kitten?"

Violet's eyes flashed. "I know many gentlemen have them. The Earl of Ravenwood was known to consort with Lady Veronica before Lady Ivy entranced him. The same is true of Lord Bentley before Lady Sara agreed to become his wife. And you should know better than most that the Duke of Richeforte kept several mistresses, all at the same time, including that awful baroness. At least, until the duchess cast a spell over him." A pensive air came over her. "Apparently, those gentlemen no longer have need of a mistress. No one gossips of them anymore. Do you suppose marriage cures a man of the urge in certain instances?"

Tristan rubbed the underside of her chin with his thumb, marveling over its velvety softness. "I'd say those marriages are the exception, Violet, at least in the *ton*. As for the two of us, while I can give you pleasure the likes of which you've never known, I've no intention nor interest in having you as my mistress."

The insinuation he was not interested in marriage went unsaid.

Her disappointment was almost palatable. The thought she might want to actually become his mistress should not have excited Tristan, but it did.

"Why not? Would I be so terrible in the position?" Violet's mouth tightened with silent indignation. "Like anything else, I imagine it is a skill that can be learned. This business of being kept for a man's enjoyment and amusement cannot be all that difficult."

Swallowing past the lump of lust that rose in his throat at the thought of teaching her just how to go about becoming his mistress, Tristan brushed his lips over her forehead. "You are not mistress material, Violet. But rest assured, were I a weaker man, I'd lock you away from the rest of the world, and you would never leave my bed."

"So, this would simply be for appearances?"

"Yes. And for a bit of pleasure, if you agree," Tristan said.

"You will kiss me... and touch me, as you did before?" Violet asked hesitantly. "But you will not make me your mistress?"

"Yes and no." He deliberately kept his response cryptic.

"You won't entertain Lady Fiona while helping me," Violet

asserted with unexpected fierceness. "I will not compete with that woman, even if our arrangement is a false one."

Tristan had serious doubts of just how counterfeit things might be between them, but he nodded in agreement. "I've no interest in that woman. Shall I prove it right now?"

"How? Lady Fiona isn't here."

"Good thing, too," Tristan murmured. "This demonstration is strictly for your benefit. Besides, she would be terribly jealous if she saw me do this."

CHAPTER 19

ith soft tenderness, Tristan staked his claim.

First, he nibbled the outer edges of Violet's succulent lips, reveling in the little gasp of pleasure she emitted. Drawing the fullness of her bottom lip into the grip of his teeth, he gave it a series of lazy nips until she shuddered in response. Her hands came up, reflexively clutching his shoulders and the material of his robe.

Next came a full invasion of her mouth. No part was left undiscovered. His tongue swept along hers, encouraging her to mimic his actions. When she became bolder, meeting him halfway and feinting his tongue with her own, Tristan delved deeper, sweeping through and drinking her in.

She was so damned sweet, so responsive and warm, it was easy to get lost in her. To drown in her splendor. If it were possible to kiss her forever, he would happily do so.

But there were more accessible parts of her now. Areas he'd dreamed of seeing laid bare were pressing against him, her soft sighs ambrosia to his senses. With slow, careful movements, he let his hands coast down her sides, measuring the span of her waist through the thin robe before finally cupping the outside curves of her breasts.

Like an untried filly, Violet stiffened under the heavy weight of his hands. Tristan did not relent. With no words, he coaxed her into returning his kisses until she gradually relaxed. Sinking back against the wall, she did not voice a protest when he moved even closer. One of her hands curled around the back of his neck with such desperation it seemed she required his strength to hold herself up.

Then her fingers knotted in his hair, and Tristan found he was the one groaning with desire.

Tearing his mouth from hers, he set about exploring the elegant curve of her neck.

"I could feast on you all day, Violet. All night. And still find myself hungry for more," he murmured in between open-mouthed kisses and half-gentle, half ravenous bites of her flesh.

With every rake of his teeth, Violet shivered. "I—I think I would like that."

He nipped her ear with a chuckle. "I'll make damn sure that you do. Tell me, kitten. Did you enjoy what we did together in my studio?"

While he spoke, the ribbons to her nightgown were being undone. When he spread the edges of the robe apart, followed by the bodice of the gown, more of her body was exposed.

Violet swallowed hard.

"Yes. It was wonderful. But..." Her words trailed away as Tristan sucked in a breath at the sight of her.

Violet Everstone was absolute perfection. Creamy white breasts crowned with nipples of the palest rose hue could be considered works of art. Long auburn red hair curled in shimmery splendor around the full, lush curves.

Tristan wanted a taste of her so badly, his mouth was watering. With hands rough and gentle, he caressed the glowing bare flesh.

"I know, sweetheart. That damned interruption wasn't kind to either of us. There's more. So much more. Will you let me show you?"

Violet quickly nodded, meeting his gaze when he cupped her chin in the palm of his hand. "Yes, Tristan. I felt... empty when we left your studio that afternoon. As though I were supposed to be filled with... something... but it was snatched away instead. I cannot explain such an odd feeling. Frustrating and exciting at the same time. I liked it and hated it."

"I can remedy that," he soothed. "Can I take this off you? Yes? When you want this to end, or if I should move too quickly, you only have to tell me. I will stop immediately. Do you trust me to do that, Violet?"

"I trust you, Tristan." She bit her lip, eyes darkening to the shade of the flower she was named for.

She trusts me.

And Tristan wasn't sure if that was the exact moment of Violet's downfall or the beginning of his own.

"Lift your arms, kitten."

In one smooth movement, the robe and gown were pulled over her head. Left only with the dubious concealment her hair provided, Violet nervously pulled a chunk of it over her shoulder. Tumbling nearly to her waist in a thick mass of curling waves and tendrils, it carried the heady scent which was uniquely hers; a combination of lavender and vanilla.

Still on her feet were a pair of simply embroidered satin mules in the same blush pink hue as her nightclothes. She shifted from one heeled shoe to the other, but when she went to slip them off, Tristan's fingers traced the flare of her hip.

He breathed her in with a wicked smile.

"Leave them on. Ah, Violet. You are so damned beautiful. A secret treasure just waiting to be discovered by the right person. Now, be very still and I'll show you why I'm that man."

Violet did as instructed. She did not move, even when

Tristan experimentally ran a palm over the swell of one breast until the entire plump mound was within his grasp.

With delicate precision, he teased the pearled tip between forefinger and thumb, gradually applying more pressure until she made a sound of desperate hunger and shock.

Immediately, his mouth was there, soothing the sting he'd caused. He lapped at her, sucked her flesh deep, swirled his tongue around the aching, rosy tip. When she sighed, pushing against the subtle force, his teeth served as a reminder that he was master of the moment. The way he took her flesh, holding it between his teeth and lashing with his tongue soon had her crying for more.

"Remember, kitten," he whispered, moving in a leisurely fashion to her other breast. "You must remain still if this is to be done properly. When you thrash about, I will see it as an indication you would like me to stop."

"No, please, Tristan. Do not stop. I won't be able to bear it again if you do," she vowed in a voice low and shaky with desire. "Please. I'll be still. I promise."

"How prettily you beg me. It drives me insane with lust."

As a reward, Tristan lavished the same treatment on her other breast until she could not help herself from writhing against him. Her movements were countered by his hard grip on her hip, but it did not seem to matter. Violet shook from his ministrations, lost in the sensual world Tristan created with his hands and tongue.

It did not seem she noticed when he sank into a position which slowly placed him on his knees before her, pressing kisses in the shadowed valley between her breasts. He moved down the center of her ribcage, his hands smoothing over the round globes of her bottom before decisively gripping her hips.

Realizing that Tristan's face was on level with the junction of her thighs, Violet jerked away with a tiny cry of alarm.

His fingers flexed, tightened, caressed, the blunt digits

leaving little divots in the voluptuous flesh. Faint bruises would surely mark that pale skin by morning. "Sheath your claws, kitten." Hot and warm, his breath stirred the luxuriant patch of auburn curls. "Remember the emptiness you felt before? That hollow hunger inside you even now? I will make that go away. This is how I will accomplish it."

"It is indecent." The words got caught up in a little sob of frustration and hope that he would contradict her and do as he willed. Tristan had every intention of doing just that.

"Terribly indecent. And our secret, Violet. Ours."

With that, his tongue slyly eased past the shield of her sex's outer lips and the soft, pretty curls. Violet shuddered so violently Tristan wondered if he should stop. But a high, keening whimper of pleasure gave him his answer. Permission he should go on.

And now that he'd begun, there was no chance in hell he would stop. Because she tasted like peach brandy. Sweet and velvety with just a twinge of sharpness to counterbalance the honied undertones. It wasn't easy, but Tristan restrained himself from burying his face between her thighs and devouring her until she begged for mercy.

Even if she did plead for a respite at some point, he doubted he would grant clemency. Her taste was addictive. Enthralling. Consuming. He could lick and nibble and suck her for an eternity and it would never be long enough.

She helplessly rotated her hips in time with the direction of his mouth, her breathing whispery and soft. She sounded like a kitten being stroked. Tristan wanted more. He wanted her climax. Wanted her to come apart on his tongue. Wanted to hear her wail in response to the rasp of his teeth on her most delicate flesh. He could tease her like this, keep her on edge for as long as he wished, or he could get what he wanted most by more efficient means.

He was greedy, of course. Impatient as well, and waiting was impossible. So, he perfected the torment by tracing her body's opening with a long, blunt finger, testing the wetness there until his touch elicited a desperate moan from her lips.

"Tristan... Tristan," Violet chanted, her legs falling open further with invitation.

He slid the finger inside her, his mouth never letting up its assault. Licking her sweet flesh while shallowly pumping a digit into the tight recess of her body sent Violet over the edge of ecstasy.

Her hands, previously held flat against the wall as if she could not trust herself to touch him, now plunged into the thick waves of his hair. She held him to her, unashamedly demanding he continue this sensual assault while she rode the waves, climbed them to dizzying heights, crashing again and again.

When she flooded his mouth and his senses with the essence of her pleasure, when her flesh contracted around his finger, Tristan wondered how he would survive her.

Because without a doubt, Violet Everstone would be his ruin.

And in his current state of delirium, he might not even care when it happened.

iolet could not say with certainty how she made it back to her room.

The aftermath of those moments with Tristan was a bit hazy. Like a lovely dream with sharp edges and bright flashes of color. Certain moments and details etched into her mind. The rasp of his cheeks against the inside of her tender thighs. The quick flicker of his tongue against her sex and the bluntness of his finger filling her until she thought she might overflow.

There was the moment she plunged over a jagged cliff, calling his name, her hands clenched in his hair so he would not move away from her. A disturbingly primal thrill illuminated her soul when he gripped her hip tighter in response. His fingers bit almost cruelly into her flesh as though he wanted to leave marks of possession.

She wanted those marks. Wanted him. Desperately and without reason.

After that remarkable experience, she had drifted in a cloud of satisfaction. Tristan rose from the floor, murmured unintelligible words into her hair, then kissed her mouth softly. She could taste herself on his lips, salty and sweet, but it did not bother her like it should have. She let him soothe and pet her, and stood still while he rearranged her clothing.

There was no protest formed when he left her slumped against the wall and returned with a silky black robe from his wardrobe. Wrapping it around her, he muttered beneath his breath something about being damned if he'd allow her to go back through the corridors in the same half-dressed state in which she'd come to him.

Tristan did not speak at all as he returned her to her bedchamber. He seemed content in allowing the silence to hang between them.

Violet wasn't sure she could conduct an intelligent conversation anyway.

With a hand to her elbow, Tristan stopped her before they reached her doorway.

"I'll leave you here, Violet. It wouldn't do for anyone to see me outside your room at this time of night. Not when we are both so scandalously underdressed." He smiled, his teeth flashing white in the shadowy alcove he'd pulled her into. With gentle hands, he pulled his robe from her body. "And while my heart pounds seeing you in this, there would be no rational explanation for my robe being in your room."

Violet nodded. Of course, everything Tristan said made perfect sense. Only, there was a tiny portion of her soul yearning that he would not leave her. That he would follow her into her room. Lock the door. Kiss and caress her again until she could not form words and soared again.

Tristan's head cocked at her continued silence. "Are you well, Violet?" His voice dropped to a husky whisper that sent tingles chasing each other down Violet's spine. "I did not hurt you, did I? I wasn't too rough?"

His eyes, so darkly expressive and fathomless, watched her reaction.

Violet hugged herself, suddenly cold without the voluminous warmth of his robe. "No, Tristan. You did not hurt me. I'm fine, really."

There was a flash of relief in his gaze. "Good. Then I'll say goodnight." Very gently, he kissed her, then gave her a tiny nudge to encourage her feet to begin moving. "Meet me tomorrow in the rose garden for your beast's portrait, and we shall put my plan into action. Hurry to your room now."

She did as he ordered. Before the door closed completely, shutting out the light from the hallway sconces, Violet saw a slight movement.

It was down the corridor and in the opposite direction of the alcove where Tristan had already melted into the shadows. She peered into the darkness to determine if her eyes were playing tricks but could see nothing worthy of alarm.

Violet shut the door, wishing it were "tomorrow", already.

THE NEXT DAY, Violet made her way to Lady Darby's garden. She carried Carrot in her arms and laughed softly at the mewing sounds he made upon seeing a flock of brown sparrows foraging on the pathway.

Tristan was not waiting by the massive circular fountain, but an easel and blank canvas were already set up.

She did not expect him to be there. She'd come early for the purpose of allowing Carrot to become familiar with his surroundings.

Perching herself on the fountain's wide basin wall, Violet placed the cat on the ground.

Carrot immediately darted toward the birds, coming up short in his quest. The leash attached to the tiny collar restricted his stalking range. Giving a low yowl, he crouched by Violet's feet, tail twitching in frustration at being unable to reach the tiny birds.

Violet found it surprising that the garden was not populated. Afternoons usually meant a steady stream of visitors parading along the gravel paths. They admired the roses blooming in all shades and sizes, as well as the magnificent stone fountain in the garden's center. The musical sound of water splashing over the four tiers was soothing, the late afternoon light sparkling through the waterdrops enthralling. It was a beautiful spot to spend the afternoon.

"This is where you've run off to today. I've been looking for you, my dear."

William emerged from one of the five pathways designed like wheel spokes to end at the fountain. Coldly handsome as usual, his golden hair gleamed in the sun and his clothes were the epitome of fashion.

Adjusting the cuff of his jacket, he halted before her, an eyebrow shooting skyward. "What is that?"

Violet tightened her grip on Carrot's leash, noting the kitten moved closer until he was pressed against her skirts. William's appearance was suspicious. He would not have known she was in the gardens unless he'd been apprised of her whereabouts.

"It's the kitten I told you of. The one I rescued."

"Do you realize you and that creature share almost the exact shade of hair color? Remarkable." William glanced about the garden as if expecting someone might join them. "Do you often put it on a leash?"

"This is Carrot's first time outside since I took him from the stables. Perhaps it is a bit overwhelming for him. He seems a tad frightened."

"That he does," William agreed. "A weak constitution, I imagine. Certainly not fit for life as a pet."

Violet bristled at the insult. "Carrot is very brave, Lord Gadley. But this is a new setting for him."

Staring at the cat, who decided in that moment to both

scratch his ear and begin licking his coat in an impressive display of self-grooming, William grimaced in distaste.

"Filthy creature. I can only wonder at the number of fleas he likely harbors this very moment. Did you carry him here? Or does he walk while on that bit of ribbon you are holding?"

Fleas? Carrot had no fleas, of that Violet was certain. He was a fastidiously clean kitten. "I carried him, of course."

"Then no doubt, you are infested as well. This won't do at all, my dear. Not at all."

Before Violet could discern his meaning, William scooped Carrot by the nape of the neck. Held out over the water in the fountain's lowest basin, the cat issued a squealing roar of protest.

"Best we go ahead and eliminate him, my dear. You'll only find it more painful should you continue forming an attachment. Do not fear. I'll dispose of him properly."

Violet stared at William in open-mouthed horror. Did he intend on drowning her cat right before her very eyes?

"What are you doing? Put him down at *once*, Lord Gadley. How can you even think to be so cruel? If you hurt him, I shall never forgive you... never!" She cried in protest. Shaking off her shock, she jumped up from the fountain and attempted stealing the kitten back. William kept Carrot just out of her reach. All the while, Carrot twisted and turned in his captor's hold, scratching at whoever gripped the back of his neck.

"Give him back to me. Give him back!" Violet grabbed William's free arm, using it as leverage so she could get closer to Carrot. "Oh, please!"

"I forbid you to keep this animal, and I won't allow it in my home, no matter how prettily you beg. I've heard it said cats do not like water, so I suppose it will not be an easy go of it for the ugly beast. But we'll be rid of it, anyway."

Tears trickled down Violet's cheeks; however, they were not ones born of helplessness. On the contrary, they were the manifestation of some sort of madness overtaking her body. Stomping the crown of William's foot with the heel of her shoe, she succeeded in bringing his arm down enough that she could wrest the cat from his grip.

Violet glared at William, watching as he hopped in pain. Carrot meowed plaintively, his claws latching in her dress bodice as if he expected to be snatched from her arms at any moment.

"You horrid, horrid man. If you harm Carrot in any way, you shall pay dearly for it. I promise you that." She dashed tears away with the back of her hand.

Recovering enough that he could bear weight on his injured foot, William grabbed Violet. Eyes glittering with fury, his face darkened to an unflattering shade of mottled red. Holding her arm in a punishing grip, he pulled her so close their noses nearly touched. To an outside observer, it would appear they shared an intimate kiss.

"Why, you little bitch," William hissed. "Don't think I won't make you regret your impudence. Once you are my wife, I'll do as I please with you and that damned cat. If I choose to drown him or quarter him, you'll have no say in the matter. Indeed, you won't have much of a say on anything of note."

William was the only second man she'd ever dare strike. The imprint of her hand on his skin bloomed redder than the roses surrounding the fountain.

He responded by jerking her closer, squeezing her upper arms until Violet was sure bruises were forming. A fresh surge of tears welled in her eyes, and the cold rage on William's face was enough that she was frightened into silence.

"Perhaps I should teach you that lesson now—" he snarled.

"Release her, Gadley."

Tristan's voice echoed sharp as a gunshot in the serene peacefulness of the garden. Violet gulped in a breath of pure relief, a sob threatening to escape despite her best efforts to remain calm. The viscount looked incredibly tall as he stalked toward them. More than that. He was invincible.

William's hands tightened cruelly around Violet's arms, but his features rearranged themselves into a pleasant mask.

"Your concern is unnecessary. Lady Violet and I were simply having a discussion. You see, we cannot agree on the issue of this animal becoming part of the wedding contract negotiations." His smile, while sharp, remained congenial.

"And I'm telling you to let her go," Tristan said in the iciest tone Violet had ever heard him use. "Or must I convince you?"

William's grip loosened as he regarded Tristan with growing suspicion. He finally noticed the easel and the fact the three of them were alone in the garden.

"What's this about, Longleigh?" Brushing a hand over his elegant coat so any stray cat hairs were removed, William sounded thoroughly disinterested in whatever the answer might be. "A garden tryst of some sort?"

"I have promised Lady Violet a portrait of her pet."

William's laugh was derisive. "You waste precious time on that venture. Not to mention squandering materials best used on worthier subjects than that flea-ridden creature. Have you gone mad, sir?"

Violet sidled away with the cat cradled protectively against her chest. William's icy-blue eyes narrowed when he realized she was out of reach now.

"Far from it. The clarity I have at this very moment is astounding," Tristan drawled.

Daring a peek in Tristan's direction, Violet was stunned by the almost visible waves of cold rage emanating from his person. Would he rip William Gadley to shreds using nothing but his bare hands?

Tristan's eyes flickered to Violet. His gaze softened, warming the tiniest bit.

"Come here, Violet."

Violet did not care he murmured her given name in a conspicuous breach of social etiquette. She did not even care that William heard it. The connotations of Tristan's informality in a public setting should have set off alarm bells, but Violet felt only relief.

She ran to Tristan, fighting the urge to launch herself into his arms. Instead, she made herself stand calmly beside him, avoiding William's intense scrutiny by crooning to the oddly silent Carrot.

Tristan moved so Violet's body was shielded by his own. Without a single touch, he conveyed possessiveness.

A small, mean smile of understanding curved William's lips. "You appear very comfortable with one another, Longleigh. Ordinarily, I might find it alarming." His laugh was taunting. "But I've little concern you'll steal our sweet Violet away from me, considering your dedicated aversion to matrimony. I do find it interesting, however, that you've already forgotten how the Duchess broke your heart when she married another. One cannot blame you for following a set pattern of pursuing a woman who will never be yours."

CHAPTER 21

*I*f it were possible to punch William Gadley in the mouth and not ruin the festivities planned for May Day, Tristan's fist would have already found its mark.

He curbed the impulse to beat the man senseless; a hard-fought battle if there ever was one.

"It is impossible to forget the Duchess of Richeforte. The duke certainly agrees with that," Tristan replied tightly. He did not comment on the assertion he had no interest in stealing Violet away.

If Gadley only knew the things he'd done already, the man wouldn't be so quick to dismiss him as a threat.

That Violet might believe he was still in love with Grace twisted Tristan's stomach. If it wasn't for Gadley watching them so closely, he would disprove that misconception in the most decadent way possible.

"My opinion regarding marriage is none of your concern." Tristan forced the words between clenched teeth.

"Here now, Longleigh," William scoffed with a wave of an elegant hand. "No need creating a row. This is a private matter between Lady Violet and myself. Soon, our engagement will be announced, so she is as good as my wife already. We only require a ceremony to make it official, although it would create quite a stir if done in haste. Gossips do love to spread their rumors, regardless of facts."

Tristan wondered if tales of Gadley's true nature had reached Violet's ears. For the thousandth time, he questioned her father's motives. Were the gains so significant that he would sell his daughter to this polished braggart?

"You are not the only man interested in Lady Violet. I find her company so delightful I've been unable to keep myself from seeking her out." Tristan set a canvas roll down on the table beside the easel. It contained vials of ink powders as well as an array of his favorite brushes. "Now, I'll ask that you vacate my mother's gardens. You see, this is a place of exceeding beauty. Your actions have tainted that."

William shrugged off Tristan's pointed warning. "I had no intention of staying. The cloying scent wreaks havoc with my constitution. I cannot abide it for any length of time." Executing a precise bow, he gave Violet a chilling smile. "Do not fret, my dear. Very soon, you will be mine, and we shall finish this conversation privately."

Tristan watched the man take his leave, practically sauntering down the garden path he'd originally entered from.

Turning back, Tristan took Violet's elbow and felt the fine tremors shaking her body.

"I apologize for arriving late. I was... detained." It was Fiona's fault he wasn't there while William Gadley was busy proving how despicable he could be.

The need to sweep her into his arms, to comfort her was overwhelming. He'd never experienced this level of intense protectiveness before—not even with Grace. Why he felt it so strongly for Violet was a mystery he might never solve.

He was quite sure he despised being so attuned to her. It left him feeling a bit out of control. Turned him dark and moody and so unlike his usual jovial self, he wondered if others could see the transformation.

Keeping his voice purposefully even, he asked, "Are you all right?"

Her laugh was wobbly. "Of course, I am. What a silly question."

"You've been crying." Tristan drew her to the fountain, sitting her down on the basin wall. "Did he hurt you?"

Violet shook her head in response, but he knew she wasn't being completely truthful.

"I should break his hands," he muttered beneath his breath as he sank beside her. "And I will if he ever touches you like that again."

Violet said nothing as he gently removed Carrot from her arms and placed him on the ground. Surprisingly, the kitten neither hissed nor attempted to scratch Tristan during this. Progress was surely being made on that front.

She rubbed her upper arms, the dress sleeves concealing bruising Tristan suspected was already forming. "Poor Carrot. He was so frightened. As was I."

"I welcome the opportunity to teach the man a lesson."

"I can't allow you to intervene again on my behalf," Violet replied softly. "Gadley is oddly determined to marry me, for reasons I don't fully understand. He and my father have already decided the course of my life."

"The hell they have," Tristan growled. "What of *our* arrangement? Have you forgotten it already? I *will* make Gadley rethink his pursuit. He desires a compliant and meek wife, yet I watched you land a blow to rival that of any boxer at Gentleman Jackson's. You are capable of defiance, Violet. Courageous enough to defy a man who does not deserve your kindness and doesn't give a farthing for your loyalty."

"You nor I have little say in the matter," she replied with a harsh laugh and a wave of her hand. Sobering, she tucked a stray curl back into her coiffure. "I wasn't myself when I agreed to follow your scheme. And I certainly wasn't thinking clearly when I struck Lord Gadley. Oh, Tristan. I'm neither defiant nor brave. I'm simply a foolish girl who forgot the reality of my own circumstances. This marriage is inevitable, and I must resign myself to it."

Tristan considered her words in silence, offering neither denial nor sympathy for her plight.

Sighing heavily, Violet gazed up at the clouds scuttling in to darken the skies. "You should begin with Carrot's portraiture. The day will fade quickly while we discuss matters neither one of us have control over. Besides, when my parents arrive at Darby Meadows, the freedom I enjoy now will be restricted."

Tristan fought the urge to yank Violet to him and prove just how brave she was. She should know her quiet, rebellious nature ignited his blood. He should tell her he derived great pleasure in seeing her confidence grow. Most of all, he wanted to tell her that he loved the sparkle in her eyes when she challenged *him.*

He said none of those things, however. It was impossible when the words lodged in his throat with all the sharp edges of an unexpected fish bone swallowed at dinner.

With a frown, he scooped Carrot up, placing him in Violet's lap. The kitten swatted his hand for taking the trouble, but the tiny scratch did not bother him as much as Violet's sad smile of resignation.

"Very well, Violet." He would abandon the argument of her impending engagement for the time being. "I shall only be a moment setting things up."

In little more than an hour, Tristan completed the rough outline of the painting. Carrot would be immortalized on canvas with the garden fountain as the main backdrop and banks of roses providing a subtle softness along the edges. Facing forward in a sitting position, with the glow of the afternoon sun creating a halo effect, the kitten would appear both regal and playful.

Tristan easily captured the mischievous lift of Carrot's mouth, his whiskers gilded in golden sunshine, and the funny little crook at the end of his tail.

If it were not just a portrait of a cat, he might have thought it rivaled his best work.

No one intruded while Tristan painted. He'd made sure of that earlier, posting a footman at the beginning of each pathway. When he began laying brushes aside at the end of the hour, Violet stood, intent on seeing the progress. Carrot followed, stopping occasionally so he could roll upon the smooth gravel stones in obvious delight.

"Wait," Tristan held up his hand, halting Violet's progress. "I'd rather you not see it until it is completely done."

She smiled. "I told you before I won't criticize."

"Even so." He turned the easel so it wasn't possible to catch a glimpse and met her halfway. "By May Day, I promise you shall have your painting."

Using his index finger, Tristan traced the line of her jaw then the shell-like perfection of her ear exposed by the upsweep of her hair. The late afternoon sun lit the shiny, auburn strands until they gleamed like autumn fire.

He wished her hair was unbound. He would pay a fortune to see it loose, flowing down her back like a silk banner. He imagined how glorious she would look naked with the soft light of dusk illuminating her creamy white skin, those violet eyes glowing with desire for him. For some reason, a vison of her in the Darby Meadows conservatory taunted the edges of his brain as well. He would paint her draped in amethyst-hued silk, surrounded by all the exotic flora he could gather.

Tristan's hand slid further until his fingers buried in the wealth of her hair, and he teetered on the verge of claiming her mouth. A giant vise imprisoned his heart, leaving him short of breath at the thought of drinking her in.

Violet's eyes fluttered shut. Leaning into his touch, her lips parted in anticipation of his kiss before abruptly catching herself.

Stumbling back, her white teeth worried the plump, soft flesh of her bottom lip. "I-I must go select my dress for the dance tomorrow night. Of course, it's not the grand ball which comes at the end of everyone's stay here at Darby Meadows, but it shall be amusing just the same."

Her fragile resistance both pleased and frustrated Tristan. The excuse she gave was flimsy at best but he allowed her to retreat with a smile, silently promising he'd have that kiss sooner or later.

"I shall claim every waltz. If for no other reason than to prove my interest in you is genuine."

Violet's head tilted. "But it's not, is it? Everything is for appearance. For Gadley. My parents. Even your own father." Bending down, she picked the kitten up and began walking up the pathway, leaving him behind. "Thank you for painting Carrot. I know I will love whatever you create."

"Every waltz, Violet," he called after her, the statement sounding more like a threat than a promise even to his own ears.

But any opportunity to touch and hold Violet, even if under the guise of an innocent dance, could not be missed.

And the barriers she hopelessly erected between them?

He would damn well ignore those. What else could he do when the taste of her coating his mouth, the feel of her body clenching around his fingers, was all now etched upon his soul?

He wanted more, and that meant a ruthless pursuit of Violet Everstone.

∿

A BURST of activity in the grand hall and the barking of dogs announced the arrival of new guests.

"They are here!"

Tristan straightened the cuffs of his coat, frowning as he glanced over his shoulder at Celia standing at the top of the staircase. His sister was known for her disregard for propriety, but usually, it was not displayed so exuberantly when his parents stood in full view.

"What the devil—" Tristan murmured, coming to a halt in the middle of the stairs.

Celia squealed again, clapping her hands in obvious delight. She flew past him, holding aloft double handfuls of her skirts to achieve greater speed. If she wasn't careful, she would likely take a tumble down the steps and land in a heap.

"Richeforte and Grace! They've arrived!" Celia tossed over her shoulder, now that she'd moved past him. "Hurry, Tristan!"

"Celia!" Their mother admonished with an exasperated smile from where she and the earl stood in the grand foyer. "Remember yourself, if you please. The Duke and Duchess are not addressed so informally."

"But, Mother," Celia laughed. "Before she became 'Her Grace', she was simply Grace to us. Oh! I can hardly believe she's here. I've missed her so terribly."

Tristan remained immobile on the staircase. He'd not seen Grace or Nicholas in months, and while the awkward situation between them was settled long ago, a strange nervousness confounded him.

How would Violet react to the news?

The footmen and Herman, their dreadfully dour butler, bustled about as Tristan descended the stairs. The arrival of a duke and duchess would throw any proper household into a frenzied hub of activity, and Darby Meadows was no exception.

"Hurry down, Violet!" Celia said. "Her Grace will be so happy to see you."

Tristan glanced over his shoulder. At the top of the steps, her face pale and white, Violet hesitated in her own descent. For a second, he saw a flash of something in her gaze when their eyes met.

Dread. And a bit of sadness as well. Tristan's stomach twisted.

With enviable control, Violet masked her emotions, a smile curving her lips. Catching up to Tristan, she took his arm when it was silently offered.

They entered the foyer together as if they were a true couple. But Violet refused to look at him. The smile she wore was reserved for Celia and his parents.

"Her Grace adores you, you know," Mother said, holding out a hand to Violet. "Come closer, dear. Stand with us as part of the family. Tristan, darling, you may stand here."

The spot indicated was beside Violet, and Tristan knew immediately what his mother was about. She wanted it known Violet was accepted as a candidate for marriage into the family. The two of them standing shoulder to shoulder sent a powerful message.

Violet released her grip on Tristan's forearm. Celia grabbed her hand, squeezing it with a gentle smile. "Yes, you are a part of our family for a certainty, Violet. Regardless of circumstances, and anything else that may happen."

Tristan stood where his mother instructed. He wanted very badly to reach out and wrap an arm around Violet. The way her feet shifted told him she was incredibly nervous. Most concerning was his abrupt willingness to soothe her, even if it meant attracting undue attention.

"His Grace and Her Grace, The Duke and Duchess of Richeforte," Herman intoned as the double doors were ceremoniously opened.

Being so closely attuned to Violet, Tristan noticed immediately that her entire body stiffened. And God help him, her chin even trembled the tiniest bit before she regained control, exhibiting an even wider smile for the benefit of those gathered around.

Celia leaned over, whispering something in her ear, and Violet gave an imperceptible nod.

What is Celia saying to her? And why do I care so much?

CHAPTER 22

"*H*e cares for her as a sister. Remember that, Violet," Celia murmured in her ear, and Violet could only nod.

That rushing feeling of dread she experienced at the sight of Grace breezing through the ornate doors could not be quashed.

Notorious for her lack of social airs, the duchess radiated all the strength and energy of a summer storm. Exquisitely dressed, her hair arranged perfectly, save for a few loose strands which slipped from her coiffure with a will of their own, she fairly gleamed with happiness.

"Oh, do hurry, Richeforte. Hurry!" Grace exclaimed, several steps ahead of her husband. Spying Herman, she laughed and closed the distance between them. "Herman, how wonderful it is seeing you again. I must say, your proclamation skills have not changed one bit, not that I thought they should. You announce everyone so perfectly. Don't you think so, Richeforte?"

"Of course, darling," came Nicholas's droll response. The duke strolled in Grace's wake, seeming unconcerned with his wife's brash nature and her unusual behavior when addressing servants as if they were old friends. He smiled indulgently as Grace returned to his side, her hand slipping into his. Even to the casual observer, it was obvious the two could not tolerate being separated for even a short period of time.

"Our gracious hosts await us. Shall we?" Nicholas nodded toward Lord and Lady Darby.

Were they not already accustomed to their former ward and her impulsive nature, the earl and countess may have been shocked. But, having had guardianship over Grace for a lengthy period of time before her marriage to the duke, they were thankfully immune.

Grace blushed, and Violet felt a tremor of jealousy pierce the armor surrounding her heart.

How very beautiful Her Grace is. And how ardently she and the duke gaze at each other. As if they cannot bear to look elsewhere.

Glancing at Tristan, Violet expected to find his attention focused solely on Grace. Instead, his intense gaze centered on Violet herself. His eyes, usually lively and full of humor, were darkly penetrating as he watched her with a barely disguised hunger.

Only Richeforte's low laugh succeeded in drawing Tristan's eyes away, and even that was done in a reluctant manner.

"Welcome, Your Grace," Lord Darby bowed first to Nicholas and then Grace. "Your Grace, you are even lovelier than the last time we saw you on the joyous occasion of your wedding day."

Grace did not hesitate embracing her former guardian, followed by a fierce hug for Lady Darby. "How good it is to see you all. I've missed your dear faces." Breaking free, she turned toward Celia with a delighted laugh. "And you, Celia. How I have missed you and your enchanting smile."

Celia allowed herself to be swept into Grace's arms.

"How wonderful you look, Your Grace." Celia giggled. "It appears marriage agrees with you and the duke. Never have I seen two people with such an air of contentment around them."

"The rigid rules of society shall not dictate our visit," Grace said, leaning back to shake a finger at the family she lived with for so many months following her mother's death. "I am simply 'Grace' to all of you. Or 'Lady Grace' if you are compelled to be so formal." She grinned at Tristan with unabashed affection. "Hello, Longleigh. You look fit and well, as always. Perhaps more handsome, too, which surely isn't fair to the other gentlemen visiting Darby Meadows."

Tristan's smile was warm and charming. "And I'll respond with the observation your beauty is a welcomed bright spot." With a genuine laugh of camaraderie, Tristan addressed the duke. "Richeforte, your presence always enlivens a gathering. It has been customary since the day we met."

"In that retrospect, that was not always a pleasant thing to witness." Nicholas shook Tristan's hand, his brow arching. "But it is fortunate that the hospitality of Darby Meadows is always assured, as are the affections I have for you and your family." When Grace nudged him with her shoulder, her gaze finding Violet and softening, the duke's emerald green eyes widened the tiniest bit.

Giving Tristan a curious glance, Nicholas reached for Violet's hand, gently pulling her to him. Several guests had gathered, and from the corner of her eye, Violet saw William standing in the entrance to the hall, an expression bordering on panic stamped over his features. Fiona Blackerby stood close by as well, her mouth set in a thin line of jealousy.

"Ah, the lovely Lady Violet," Nicholas said. "Now, it must be said this May Day Affair is truly blessed with all the beauties of England in attendance."

"How kind you are, Your Grace." Violet thanked the stars above when her voice held steady and clear, despite her surprise that the powerful duke remembered her name. She couldn't remember a time when Richeforte actually recognized her existence. Giving the duchess a shy smile, she murmured in acknowledgment, "Your Grace."

She couldn't bear to look at Tristan, not knowing if he stared at the duchess in rapt adoration, or perhaps now regarded Violet with vague disappointment.

Grace laughed, wrapping an arm around Violet's waist. "None of that, now. We've been friends long enough that I will not tolerate such stuffiness. I'm so pleased to see you, Lady Violet. Your quiet, sweet nature is always a balm to one's soul."

Violet blushed until she was sure her cheeks were an unflattering shade of red. Her pulse thundered violently when Tristan commented, "Sometimes, a quiet nature is simply a mask hiding a fierceness of spirit."

"A brilliant observation," Lady Darby said, giving her son a nod of approval. "Come, let us get you settled into your rooms. Lady Grace, I'm sure you would appreciate a chance to freshen up after your journey."

"Your Grace, would you care for a brandy?" Lord Darby inquired, turning to Nicholas.

"I held hope you would ask, Darby."

Celia clapped her hands. "Oh, Grace! You arrived at just the right time. We are to have dancing tomorrow evening in the west parlor. The doors will be open to the terrace and the gardens. It will not compare to the May Day Affair Ball, but still, it is dancing all the same. Oh, do say you and His Grace will attend."

"I most certainly will. Nothing could keep me from it," Grace replied. Moving so until she stood between Celia and Violet, she linked her arms through those of the two girls. "Come with me to my rooms and help me decide what I should wear. Richeforte spent an ungodly amount adding to my wardrobe while we were away in France." She sent her husband a dazzling smile. "Even though he knows I'd be just as content wearing last season's gowns, provided I also have breeches and boots."

"It is money well spent when the finished products enhance your beauty." Nicholas grinned at his wife. "And you still have your breeches and boots. It appears I can deny you nothing, honeybee."

Ducking her head, Grace whispered in a conspiratorial manner, "He spoils me without a smidgen of embarrassment. It is quite remarkable." Raising her voice, she called out to Nicholas as Lady Darby led the way from the foyer. "Don't be long, darling."

Nicholas tilted his head toward Tristan while addressing his wife. "I wouldn't dare, Your Grace. Longleigh, will you join us for that brandy?"

Violet caught Tristan's eye. With a self-aware shiver, she realized he still watched her closely, as if attempting to learn a secret about her. While friendly and cordial in his interactions with Grace, he certainly did not exhibit any signs of previous or current infatuation.

Tristan's attention returned to Nicholas and his father. "A brandy would be most appreciated."

Violet watched Tristan as long as she could, pulled along as she was with Celia holding her arm.

Grace kept up a steady stream of chatter as they descended the stairs.

"You must tell me everything I've missed during our time in France. It seems a great deal has taken place. Good things, I'm sure. Violet, I find myself most curious about you. Have you and Longleigh developed affections toward one another? You do make such a lovely couple. You've always harbored a tender spot for him, and he has finally discovered one for you. Oh, Lady Darby, how excited you must be. To gain Violet as a daughter is certainly a blessing."

Violet came to a halt, forcing the other two girls to fall backward. Even Lady Darby paused, glancing over her shoulder.

"Your Grace, I'm afraid your observations are far from

correct. You see, you misunderstand..." Violet was not comfortable correcting the duchess, but it wasn't right to foster the misconception that she and Tristan were embroiled in a relationship. "Longleigh and I are not..."

"But you could be, Violet," Celia insisted fiercely, taking Violet's arm while urging her to continue walking. "You must admit Longleigh has been very attentive since he arrived. He has never shown so much interest in you as he has these past two weeks."

"Celia, dear, do not meddle in your brother's life," Lady Darby said in a stern manner as she opened the doors to one of the suites. "Nor Violet's, for that matter."

"I noticed his eyes never left you, Violet," Grace observed as they entered the rooms set aside for their visit. "The viscount looks at you as one might expect when two people are in love. Even when he believed himself head over heels for me, awkward as it was, he never seemed so... absorbed."

The subject of Tristan's former infatuation with Grace was casually stated even as Violet cringed.

Oh, God. How will I survive the constant reminder Tristan was in love with her?

"I'm sure you are mistaken. Longleigh carries no affection for me other than that as a family friend," Violet managed with a slight wince. "Please, may we speak of other things?"

Her face felt as if it were on fire as she turned to the windows, gazing out at the rolling meadows. Perhaps the glitter of tears in her eyes would go unnoticed.

"I am sorry, Violet. I did not mean to upset you, truly," Grace said quietly. "It seems I've become one of those women who believes everyone should be married when not so long ago I was firmly set against it. The viscount is very dear to me and to Richeforte. We only wish him happiness. I thought perhaps you could be the one who might help him find it."

"Longleigh has no interest in marriage. Not anymore."

Violet's words hung in the air, an uncomfortable reminder of why Tristan decided marriage was not for him.

"He cares only for pleasure and merriment," Violet continued, spinning around to face the other women. "His lack of interest in finding a suitable wife is well known, but Lord Longleigh's views on matrimony are none of my concern. When my father and mother arrive, my engagement to Lord William Gadley will be announced. I am to be his wife."

Celia looked as though she might swallow her tongue in an effort to keep her opinion quiet. Angry disappointment leaked from her, but she remained silent. Lady Darby nervously bustled around the room as the servants began carrying in the baggage and the duchess's clothing trunks. She wiped a tear from her cheek when she believed Violet was not watching.

Grace regarded Violet for a long moment, then slowly replied, "Forgive my impulsive words, Violet. Richeforte always says I chatter too much. Perhaps he is right, although I do hate admitting it." Her honey brown eyes were sharp though, leaving Violet to wonder if Grace could see through her affected indifference.

"Thank you, Your Grace." Violet nodded. "Longleigh himself would agree we have no connection other than through our families."

She refused to remember how connected she'd been to Tristan just a few days before. The overwhelming, terrifying pleasure she experienced when his mouth pressed against her skin. Remembering that blissful interlude was dangerous.

And it was dangerous to wish Tristan would repeat it.

VIOLET EMERGED from the strand of trees and stood at the edge of the small clearing.

The oak was still there, despite the fact it seemed centuries ago that she had fallen and landed on Tristan in an awkward heap of legs and velvet skirts. With a heavy sigh, she advanced until she was directly beneath the outstretched limbs.

Craning her neck, she peered through the thick canopy of leaves in an attempt at locating the nest. Chirping noises could be heard, but until a pair of robins fluttered overhead and landed on a swaying branch, Violet was unsure the nest still existed.

She exhaled in relief. If both parents of the fledglings were present, then it was a good indication the nest still held occupants. Moving closer to the base of the tree, she listened very carefully until she finally heard multiple chirps. Following the sounds, she located the spot where she'd climbed up before and saw a fluttering of tiny wings on the sturdy branch.

"Oh, you dear things. So, you are leaving the nest at last," Violet exclaimed with a pleased smile.

Gratified by visual proof that the robins had survived in her absence, Violet leaned back against tree's rough bark. The stem of a vibrant, yellow wildflower was absently twirled between her fingers. She had plucked it along the way through the meadow after slowing her frantic escape from the house.

A grimace twisted her features as she thought of her actions. It was cowardly, but there was no choice other than to flee at the first available opportunity.

Standing in the sunshine that was Grace Willsdown March, proved entirely too painful. Violet's heart and cheeks had begun aching with the effort of smiling as if nothing were wrong. She withstood the torture for as long as possible, all the while wondering how long she must pretend. How long must she keep up the façade that she was not madly in love with the man who perhaps *still* loved the duchess?

"Are the robins still alive?"

Violet clutched the wildflower with such force it ended up crushed between her fingers. So immersed was she in despair, she failed to notice Tristan's approach. His footsteps had fallen with quick softness on the grassy soil, and now, he stood only feet away.

Quickly dashing a tear from her cheek, she turned toward him, smiling brightly as if his presence did not affect her in the slightest.

"They are."

Tristan cocked his head when he heard the cheerfulness of her tone. Hands clasped behind his back, he stalked toward her.

"I thought perhaps there was a dire outcome, based on your tears."

Violet's teeth clenched. Could she conceal nothing from this man? "I don't know what you mean, Longleigh."

Frowning, Tristan reached the oak, leaning a forearm against its surface. The look he gave was intensely scrutinizing. "You cannot hide such things from me, Violet."

"How did you know where to find me?"

He gave her a crooked smile. "No one else may have noticed you running past the library windows, but I certainly did. Naturally, I followed what I believed to be your path. I wanted to assure myself of your safety. So, here we are."

Tristan stood so close that his trousers brushed against her skirts, and his fingers, if he were to flex them the slightest bit in her direction, would actually slide over her hair. Violet swallowed hard, praying he would not do that. She would crumble like a house made of straw if he dared touch her right now. Her feelings skated too close to the surface, barely held in check with the tightest of reins.

"Yes, here we are." She dared glance up at him and was immediately sorry. Dark with concern, his eyes bore into hers until she squirmed under their intensity.

"Why did you leave?" Tristan questioned softly.

"I felt like taking a walk." Violet averted her gaze, remembering she held a crumpled blossom in her hand. "I needed some fresh air." Tossing the flower aside, she told herself she would not look at him again. "Well, I should go back now."

Before she could push off from the tree, Tristan shifted so that his body blocked hers. "Violet, wait. At the very least, tell me what has upset you."

Violet was certain she would not survive it when his fingers drifted down until they rested lightly in the hollow of her throat. He stroked the indention there with a feather-soft caress.

"It is nothing, Tristan. Nothing you should concern yourself over, anyway."

"I don't believe you." He leaned forward, his nose touching hers almost playfully. "Shall I kiss the truth out of you? Make a game of it? For every truthful answer you give me, I shall kiss you until your toes curl."

Violet bit her lip against the thrill elicited by the mere mention of kissing. *How I wish it was as simple as that. I wish I could treat whatever is between us as a bit of sport. But I've not the heart for it. And I'm too weak to deny him.*

When she did not reject his suggestion outright, a wry smile lifted Tristan's lips.

"Kitten, you remember, don't you, that I've promised nothing in this game of ours? A game you agreed to. Mutual pleasure is the extent of things, and if you are unwilling to continue in such a manner, you need only say the word. I will not force anything upon you that you do not wish to experience. But decide now if I should keep you or let you go. I find my patience grows treacherously thin."

Violet's mouth tightened. "I do not require a reminder that you merely toy with me. I realize this is a farce and the outcome matters very little to you."

"Oh, kitten. If only that were the truth. You mean more to me than you can possibly understand." Tristan's mouth hovered above hers, his hand never leaving her throat. Those long, strong fingers curled around the column of her neck as if he intended to contradict his own promise of releasing her.

"Now, I am the one who cannot believe you, Tristan. And I've no intention of kissing you to discover if what you say is truth or fabrication." Violet quickly ducked beneath his arm. With deceptive calm, she strolled away without a single care he might haul her back against him.

Glancing over her shoulder, she found him watching her retreat with a puzzled expression twisting his features.

"Violet, this discussion is not over. And this kiss, this kiss will happen, eventually. You know that."

"I know nothing of the sort." Violet was proud that not even a sliver of shyness was evident in her voice. "Oh, and Tristan? You have no need to worry for my safety here at Darby Meadows. I've explored every inch of this estate over the years and know it as though it were my own. Your show of concern is touching, however. Insincere, but touching. I'll see you back at the house."

CHAPTER 23

*H*enry Bowman twirled Violet around in a lively Scottish reel, passing her off occasionally to one of the Buchanan cousins.

Tristan leaned a shoulder against the parlor's doorjamb. A scowl darkened his face as he watched young Lawrence swing her around until her laughter rang out above that of the other girls. When Lawrence let her go, Henry caught her back up again, her hands clasped tight in his.

It was damned hard not to stalk into the middle of the swirling couples and snatch Violet from their grasps. And while he stood sulking, contemplating this unreasonable fit of possessiveness for a woman he had no claim over, the duke took up a stance beside him.

The way Violet left him in the forest the day before still rankled a bit, although he wasn't sure why. The confidence in her words, in her very essence, should have thrilled him. And while it did on some level, on another he could not dismiss how easily she walked away from him.

"Longleigh, the fierceness of your gaze is enough to strike fear in a man, even those unaware of the danger," Richeforte said with a smile coloring his voice. "Why not just toss the lady over your shoulder, carry her out of here, and be done with it?"

"What the devil are you talking about, Richeforte?" Tristan spared the man an aggravated glance as he leaned against the wall beside him.

"The Everstone girl, of course. I simply wonder why you do not take matters into your own hands."

Tristan said nothing, even when Nicholas chuckled.

"Ah! I am correct then, despite what my dear wife told me. You and Lady Violet have formed an attachment. I wanted to make mention of it earlier, but was unsure if your father is aware of matters. How long has this been going on?"

Tristan's scowl grew even more savage. "Nothing is going on."

Nicholas's arms crossed over his chest. "Those heated glares of yours indicate otherwise. And do you see the unintended consequences? The gossips believe they are witnessing some type of quarrel between you and me." The duke laughed beneath his breath. He then executed a slight bow for the benefit of two ladies whispering behind their fans while staring at them. "If you would only claim the lady, you can avoid all those unnecessary rumors."

"Damn you, Richeforte. I've no intention of claiming any woman." He'd already been forced to make that clear to Fiona Blackerby. The lady was more persistent than he'd given her credit. Earlier, he abruptly, but politely, left her in an alcove while she detailed how they might meet for a private rendezvous in the conservatory.

"Neither did I before Grace Willsdown decided differently. It's no use denying it, for I recognize your expression. I wore the same not too long ago." Nicholas's emerald gaze swept the large parlor, softening when he spied his wife near the terrace doors. "Damnation, if I don't wear it still. My sweet duchess bedevils me every moment. And how I adore her because of it."

A reluctant smile eased Tristan's frown. "That is understandable. Her Grace is an exceptional woman of great beauty and kindness. You are lucky to have won her. I say to devil with the gossips if they cannot comprehend my genuine happiness for you."

"I know, my friend." Nicholas rested a hand on Tristan's shoulder. "I'm grateful we put that disagreement to rest." His expression was somber. "Grace says Lady Violet has captured your heart, and I find myself in complete accord. I anticipate you will offer for her hand soon?"

"You are as bad as my own father," Tristan grumbled. "Indeed, my entire family has conspired together in this effort to push me into marriage. I think it is an obsessive sickness with them, to be honest."

"Happens to all of us, eventually. And in your case, Lady Violet is an excellent choice to spend the rest of your life with. Lady Celia adores her. She meets your parents' approval, which is always a massive advantage. She's gentle and sweet. It appears she's as infatuated with you as you are with her. And her very nature screams for someone to take care of her. To take her in hand and offer protection. Which compliments your own desire to become a lady's veritable knight in shining armor. Symbolically, of course. No one expects that you will begin jousting simply to win the lady's hand."

"And you've discovered all this in the short time you've been here at Darby Meadows?" Tristan could not help the mocking tone in his voice. It was troubling that Nicholas could see through him so clearly. Was he so transparent in his dealings with women? No doubt he enjoyed a good romp as well as any other man, but deep inside his soul, Tristan found Nicholas's words frighteningly accurate.

Nicholas's eyebrow arched. "It's quite noticeable, really. Even now, while disparaging of the very idea you and Violet have formed a connection, you can scarcely take your eyes off her.

"Pardon my bluntness, but you are wrong, Richeforte," Tristan retorted with a slight grimace. He forced himself to look away each time Violet spun past in another man's arms. "Lady Violet is not the meek young lady she appears, and I've no interest in having her as a wife. Any perceived affection between us is simply for the purpose of dissuading Lord Gadley from taking her as a wife. You see, she and I have an agreement of sort. I am assisting her in avoiding marriage to the man."

The stare Nicholas leveled on him was unflinching. "And what do you gain from such an unusual arrangement?" In a tone suddenly cold as ice, the duke murmured, "Answer carefully, Longleigh. Very carefully."

"Do you think I would debauch an innocent?" Tristan demanded, then quickly added, "Do not respond to that. It is simply a ploy, Richeforte. That's all. One devised for her sake only."

"Then you are doing a poor job of it. Not once have you claimed Lady Violet for a dance. Or even procured a glass of lemonade for her. All you've done is stand and glare at the gentlemen pursuing her favor. How precisely will this work to dissuade Gadley from wanting to wed the girl?"

"You are a meddlesome bastard, Richeforte," Tristan growled.

No one needed to know just how far he'd gone in debauching Violet, the liberties he'd taken. Scanning the crowd to hide his unease, Tristan caught his mother's eye where she stood beside the earl.

Tristan forced himself to return her happy smile. The countess did adore Violet, to the point she regarded her as another daughter. That attention was the reason behind Violet's many visits to Darby Meadows, her closeness with his family. Lord and Lady Everstone believed their only child safe from scandal while in Lady Darby's care. She stood as chaperone in their absence. Indeed, much of the credit for Violet's unsullied reputation was because of his mother's influence.

A reputation he seemed destined to destroy simply because of his irrational desire for the girl.

Unexpected nausea roiled inside Tristan's stomach, lurching high in his throat. The memory of everything he'd done choked him with guilt. Acrid bitterness washed through his mouth in a fleeting instant.

What he had done was monstrous. What he would do if given another chance was far worse.

When the musicians shifted from the liveliness of the reel to the haunting lilt of a waltz, Tristan shoved off from his stance against the doorjamb, intent on exiting the parlor. He must make his escape before Violet's eyes found his. Before she questioned his failure to pull her into his arms for the dance. He had, after all, promised her he would.

Instead of fleeing, however, he found himself inexplicably looking for her amongst the swirl of pretty velvet and silk gowns.

His sharp gaze located her near the entrance to the terrace, Lawrence Buchanan bent over her hand. The young man pled his case for the honor of sweeping her into the dance. Violet only laughed, shaking her head in denial while attempting to separate herself from the other couples selecting their partners for the waltz.

A crushing weight suffocated Tristan. An overwhelming need to prove Richeforte wrong drove his next actions. Averting his eyes, he ignored the possessiveness stabbing his insides. A possessiveness that demanded he snatch Violet away from the crowd so he would not have to share her.

Nicholas's low chuckle reeked of understanding pity. "It appears your fall shall be harder and far beyond my own, Longleigh. You should prepare yourself for the consequences of the aftermath."

"Your advice is unnecessary. There will be no consequences to face. Why should I shackle myself to one woman when there are so many who desire my company? I can think of no reason to throw myself into that prison. Bachelor life is surprisingly carefree."

The duke shook his head at the display of stubbornness, but Tristan vowed it would not dissuade him. Abruptly sketching a bow to the duke, he turned his back on the gaiety.

"If you will excuse me, I've developed a sudden thirst, and it seems only whiskey will suffice."

As he made his way down the hall, his lips twisted at the idea Violet would make an excellent wife.

My wild Violet possesses the capability of driving a man quite mad. How is it possible to defend one's heart against all that hidden fierceness coated in sugar candy sweetness?

And as for his own inner craving to rescue the damsel in distress?

It was a defect in his character that must be cured. Quickly, before something inevitable happened to them both.

VIOLET STRAINED her neck looking over Lawrence's shoulder.

Where is Tristan? Just a moment ago, he stood in the doorway with the Duke of Richeforte, and now he's vanished.

"I say, Lady Violet, are my skills lacking so completely?"

"What?" Violet murmured, preoccupied by the sight of Richeforte uncrossing his arms and sauntering in the direction of his wife.

"You seem distracted," Lawrence explained. "To the point I fear my waltzing abilities must be deficient."

Violet dragged her gaze back to the young man. "Of course, they are not."

"But you *are* distracted." The young man's chiseled features were enhanced by a breaking smile. "I swear I will not be crushed to learn you are searching for Longleigh."

"Don't be silly, Mister Buchanan. Why ever would you think I have the slightest interest in your cousin's whereabouts?"

"Don't you?" Lawrence tilted his head. "Have an interest, that is?"

"No, I don't," Violet stammered as the waltz slowed, drawing to an end.

Her cheeks flushed pink with the lie. She had *too* much interest in Longleigh. Damn her curiosity, but she wondered if his disappearance was tied with what she'd witnessed earlier in the evening.

Violet had spied Tristan cozied up with Lady Fiona Blackerby in an alcove earlier. He had been smiling, those full, sensual lips twisted in the attractively sardonic manner he was infamous for. The one that playfully teased with darkness and hints of wickedness until a girl wasn't sure if she straddled the edge of being kissed into oblivion or carefully strangled and caressed by the viscount's large, capable hands.

Either option was intriguing

"Blast it all. Here comes Lord Gadley," Lawrence huffed in exasperation as the waltz ended on a final flourish. Sketching a bow, he then straightened, intentionally towering over Violet. "If I miss my guess, I suspect you've no wish to have the man claim your next dance."

She shivered. "You would be correct, Mister Buchanan."

"Then there is only one thing for it. Follow me, staying as close as you can. I believe I can at least get you to the terrace unseen. You may then do whatever mysterious thing it is that ladies do when they disappear during balls. It's the perfect solution for avoiding Gadley."

Lawrence was already moving while he spoke, weaving through the crowd with Violet's hand clasped in his. She fell into step behind him, grateful for his assistance, although he marched at a speed much faster than her legs could match.

But the ploy worked. In the bustling cluster of guests, Lawrence successfully led her to the outer terrace without Gadley witnessing their escape.

"There. That was a bit of sport, wasn't it?" Lawrence crowed, his chest puffing out slightly with his success.

"Most certainly. How clever you are, Mister Buchanan," Violet replied, catching her breath. "I may make use of your skills for the rest of the evening."

"At your service, my lady." Lawrence swept a deep bow, giving her a grin before pressing a kiss to the top of her gloved hand. "Now, to avoid talk of impropriety, I shall return to the parlor. You recall how to reenter the house, correct? Go down these steps toward the rose garden path, and the main hall entrance is just beyond the conservatory. You may slip back into the house and return to the dance with no one the wiser. And if you don't return, I'll simply relay to my aunt that you were not feeling well after our waltz and retired for the evening."

"You are exceedingly kind," Violet said in earnest.

Lawrence laughed and gave her a wink. "Longleigh would have my head if I treated you in any other fashion."

Once Lawrence left her on the terrace, Violet stood for several moments, debating what to do next. The sounds of the gala were still discernible, courtesy of the terrace doors being flung open. That no other guests ventured out to enjoy the pleasant night air was somewhat surprising. The far-reaching glow of the moon was bright, so bright one could easily make out the tall hedges of the rose garden in the distance, the gravel stone pathways bathed in ghostly white.

Would it be so terrible not to return to the gaiety of the dance? She could stroll through the garden. See the fountain sparkle in the moonlight. Listen to the crickets and attempt to solve their mysterious message. Stare at the stars while tracing their pattern with a forefinger. All could be done before retiring to her room.

And accomplished in the most solitary fashion. Which made Violet unaccountably sad.

What enjoyment could be found looking at stars, or strolling garden paths if one did so alone?

Feminine voices interrupted her thoughts. On another portion of the terrace where the open doors created a rather private alcove, two young women stood with their backs to the gardens. Side-by-side, they watched the dancing while sipping lemonade.

Violet immediately recognized one as Lady Fiona by her profile and the upsweep of gleaming blonde hair. The other, a Miss Patricia Clipperson, had arrived just that afternoon with her widowed mother. Violet was only marginally acquainted with the young lady.

"Well, he certainly seems to be over the duchess. He's hardly given her a moment's notice tonight, other than accepting that little peck on the cheek she gave him. Did you see how fiercely Richeforte glared? However, when he shook Longleigh's hand afterward, I think he almost looked apologetic."

"Of course, he's over her. Longleigh was never in love with her," Fiona huffed, snapping her fan shut with a flick of her wrist. "That was simply a momentary infatuation, its ending hastened when Richeforte stole Her Grace for himself. Longleigh was over her in less time than it takes to snap one's fingers. Now, his attention is centered elsewhere."

"Obviously," Patricia laughed. "It has been placed square on Lady Violet."

"Don't be absurd. The viscount is completely enamored with me. Although we must keep our love secret," Fiona countered, her tone tight with annoyance.

"Truly?" Patricia's skepticism was obvious. "Longleigh appears fascinated by the Everstone girl. Which is quite odd, considering she always appears as if she might faint dead away if anyone so much as winks in her direction."

"Don't be fooled by our little façade, dear." Fiona's laugh was shrill. "That wallflower is simply a convenient ruse to keep attention off us."

When Fiona gripped the other girl's forearm, Violet's own hands clenched into fists. Her fingernails dug through the gloves until half-moon imprints were left on her palms.

"Longleigh pleaded that I go along with this little deception. At least until our parents finalize the details of our engagement. It's all so very complicated, you see. I only agreed because his sister despises me, despite my efforts to befriend her. Celia will do anything to keep us apart, so secrecy is a must. She's held such high hopes that Lady Violet would become Viscountess Longleigh, and eventually, the Countess of Darby. But rest assured, any attention he shows that insipid girl is to satisfy his sister. Nothing more."

Violet bit back a moan. *Whatever Fiona says can't possibly be true. It can't be.*

"Your subterfuge is working, then. But, Fiona, I've only witnessed Richeforte, and perhaps the Earl of Ravenswood, regard a woman with the same intensity as Longleigh exhibits while watching Lady Violet. He stares at her as if he might devour her at any moment. Or drag her off to his bed. I've never really noticed before because, I mean, she's such a shy thing, but she really is very lovely." Patricia took a contemplative sip of lemonade. "Several of the gentlemen seem rather taken with her."

A sound of complete aggravation escaped Fiona.

"Well, that shows how much you know, Patricia. Longleigh can barely stand that quiet, plump mouse, but he does what is necessary for our future together. I can depend on you to keep our secret, can I not?"

As the music changed to a fast-paced polka, the women began moving away.

"I won't tell a soul. But still, I can hardly believe it…" Patricia shrugged, her words trailing off.

Could Tristan and Fiona really be in love?

A feeling of numbness settled over Violet. It wasn't true. Not after everything Tristan had said to her. Had done with her willing participation. Not when he kissed her with such desperate sweetness.

He could not be that duplicitous.

She refused to believe it.

It can't be true…

Wrapping her arms around her waist, Violet let out a little hiccup of despair and began walking in the direction Lawrence indicated.

She knew every entry into the manor house. Knew every path and corridor as intimately as if they belonged to her. She'd practically grown up at Darby Meadows, and for Violet, that was both a curse and a blessing. The close proximity afforded the opportunity to adore Tristan while at the same time she suffered the acute agony of longing for him.

Yes, she knew this house. Knew its secrets and its charms. And out of all the nooks and crannies, the open corridors, the elegant parlors and stately public areas, the massive Darby conservatory held a distinct place in her heart.

She adored it even more than the secluded third-floor studio where a dark-eyed, deceptively complex, outwardly light-hearted artist created beauty on swaths of canvas.

The conservatory was a special place, infused with magic and the heady scent of foreign flowers and earthy soil. Here, beneath a sky made of glass and darkened by rainclouds, Violet fell in love.

Violet remembered that day well. Remembered Tristan rising with a scowl, irritated by the interruption. She would never forget how her heart nearly stopped at the fierce beauty of his features, his chocolate brown hair tumbling over his brow before it was pushed into unruly obedience with a quick thrust of his fingers. His scowl melted into a smile at the sight of his sister.

When the young viscount bowed over Violet's hand as Celia made the introductions, she had cursed the blasted shyness striking her mute. The rain drumming against the glass walls and ceiling echoed the pounding of her young heart until Violet wondered if she would faint for the first time ever.

And Tristan, dark eyes full of mischief, well accustomed to female adoration in all forms, had merely winked in acknowledgment of her speechlessness.

Yes, the conservatory was a special place indeed.

Melancholy for silly, childish dreams and memories of visits over the years called Violet there now. As if pulled along on a silken thread, she glided forward. The night whispered in approval, enveloping her in velvety darkness until the magnificent iron and glass structure loomed ahead.

The outer doors hung slightly ajar, emitting a sliver of light. The head gardener was meticulously fussy regarding such matters; few braved his wrath when it came to the care lavished on the fragile specimens within. These doors were never left open.

Slightly fogged glass windows glowed with lamplight. There was the faint outline of numerous plants and exotic trees, but it was impossible to determine if anyone had actually slipped inside or if a servant left the doors cracked open by mistake.

Violet pushed past the large, double doors, breathing deeply of the richly scented air. Mindful of the need to retain the warmth and humidity, she tugged at the heavy portals until they shut behind her with a low clang.

I should continue on my way to the main house.

And she would, too. In a moment.

There was a quiet hush inside the cavernous space. Leaves rustled slightly as an unseen breeze from an unknown source swirled the air with a feather's touch. An occasional chirp came from tiny sparrows that found their way inside the glass sanctuary and built nests within the branches of lemon and orange trees. The musical tinkling sound of the water fountain, dripping and splashing over the basin's confines, was broken occasionally by the appreciative croaking of a frog.

It seemed she was alone inside the conservatory.

Violet sighed, her tension easing away. She dearly loved this place. More than the Everstone manor house tucked away in Derbyshire or her parents' spacious townhome in London. She suspected both residences were likely levied to the hilt, and their continued ownership rested on her future marriage.

But those problems were easily forgotten here. This would be one of the last times she could enjoy the quiet solitude of the conservatory. Here, she could nurse her heart.

Crushed stone pathways meandered through vine-covered arbors and past secret niches inhabited by Greek statuaries. The jungle-like greenery and lush blooms were crafted so the pathways ended at a central water feature and the benches surrounding it. Decorative lanterns composed of glass and set on stakes at shoulder height illuminated Violet's way.

She would gather her thoughts here and summon her strength. Reflect on what she'd overheard on the terrace. More importantly, she could determine how to survive marriage to any man who had the misfortune to be someone other than the viscount.

The sound of ice clinking against glass alerted Violet that she was not alone. She froze, mindful she could be intruding upon someone's stolen moments.

But curiosity strained against the boundaries of decency.

Who is there? Do I want to know? Do I dare find out? Please don't let it be Tristan and Lady Fiona. I will simply die. From embarrass-

ment. From heartache...

She could turn around this very moment. *Should* turn around. Should leave before she ever laid eyes on whoever was by the fountain; leave before that person or persons *saw* her.

Her hesitation was futile. Her chest tightened, her throat closing up and preventing speech.

Tristan sauntered into the middle of the pathway ahead of her. A tumbler containing some sort of liquor dangled loosely from his hand.

Their eyes locked. Darkest blue held hostage by deep, wicked sable.

A shiver of unadulterated excitement wracked Violet. It was useless to even attempt hiding it when it possessed the strength to buckle her knees.

How glad she was that he was here.

How it frightened her that he was.

Tristan smiled, recognizing the effect he had on her. Just as he had all those years ago. Long before the devastation of his smile ever reached its full potency, he surely understood its capacity to destroy a woman's willpower.

It had been honed, sharpened over time into a perfect weapon of destruction. Perhaps in preparation for this very moment. This moment when all of Violet's defenses were slashed to ribbons. There was no hope for her, after all.

She would surrender everything to this man.

Even if meant her ruin.

His hand stretched toward her.

"I've been waiting for you, kitten."

CHAPTER 24

*V*iolet took a deep, steadying breath.

"Have you?" Peering at Tristan in the flickering light, she inched closer. "How could you possibly know I would be here, of all places?"

Swirling the contents of the glass, Tristan watched her from beneath lowered lashes. His hand waited for hers to slip into it. "I overheard Lawrence's instructions. And somehow, I knew I would find you in this exact spot, although I don't even know why I thought it."

Worrying her bottom lip between her teeth, Violet steeled herself before slipping her hand into the warmth of his. "I suppose you came through the west breakfast room. It's the only entrance other than the one used by the servants."

Tristan's gaze fixated on her mouth. "You drive me to distraction when you do that." He uttered a low curse. "And damn your uncanny knowledge of my home's footprint. You seem to know every inch as if it were your own."

"Had I continued past the conservatory, gone to my room, what would you have done?"

His head tilted as he pulled her closer against him. "I

honestly don't know. Maybe broke down your bedchamber door. Maybe finished off the bottle of whiskey I started earlier." Setting the glass on the ground, he rested his forehead against hers and breathed deep. "Why do you always smell so damned delicious, Violet? It's a scent I cannot erase from my consciousness. It haunts me at all hours of the day and night."

Violet trembled when Tristan's lips brushed her forehead. His arms tightened around her waist until she caught the faint, sweet aroma of liquor.

"What are you doing, Tristan?"

"Damned if I know."

Violet debated what she should do. Part of her wanted to tear away. Run from the embarrassment of future rejection.

But a rebellious side reared its head, demanding answers to the questions. Demanded she stand her ground and take what she wanted for once. To live for herself instead of duty and obligation and expectations. Dangerous thoughts but unstoppable once acknowledged.

Violet pulled back so she could stare into Tristan's dark eyes and see the truth for herself.

"Are you in love with Fiona Blackerby?"

Confusion warred with amusement for a split second. Then wariness crept into the dark depths of his gaze. "What the devil are you talking about?"

"Is there a secret engagement? Are you... using me to hide your relationship with Lady Fiona from your sister?" Violet nearly choked over that last part.

Tristan's jaw clenched. "Using you... Have you taken leave of your senses? Have you not heard me when I repeatedly deny any interest in that woman? A secret engagement. That's surprising, when it's well known I've no interest in marrying at all. Where have you managed to hear such drivel?"

Violet's chin lifted. "From Fiona herself. I overheard her conversation with Patricia Clipperson. She was adamant that you must hide your relationship from Celia so your plans remain intact. She said I am a pawn that keeps others from learning the truth."

Releasing his grip on her, Tristan threw his arms in the air in frustration. "She said those things to hurt you, kitten. There's not a shred of truth to any of it."

"She had no idea I overheard her, Tristan." Violet's voice trembled, but her words were laced with steel, her amethyst eyes sparkling with fire. Holding herself rigid, she fixed him with a steady glare. "If you are truly involved, tell me now. I prefer saving myself the embarrassment and heartache and to just be done with whatever is between us."

Tristan whirled back. "I've nothing to do with that woman! Why do you persist with such lunacy?"

"I will persist. I will until I understand you!" Violet cried out, her pain leaching out. "She is a poor substitute for Grace, but Tristan, Fiona is the closest you may ever get. I see that. I accept it. I can't even hate you for the attraction you must feel for her. You'll never have Grace, but you can have someone like her by your side."

"Do you think I am so shallow as to want a woman simply because of her appearance? There is a great deal more to it than that. More than you can possibly understand."

"You are right, Tristan. I don't understand," she replied quietly. "And I don't think you even know what you want. Or who you want, for that matter."

"Well, I most certainly do not want Fiona Blackerby! And I don't want Grace, either. Goddamn it." Tristan swore fiercely, raking a hand through thick, dark hair. "The only one I want is you, Violet. *You.* But what I want and what I deserve are two separate beasts. You really have no comprehension of just how different we are. You would forsake everything all in the name of true love, while I loathe the very thought that sacrifice should be for anything other than the pursuit of pleasure. Perhaps it is better you do not discover my true nature. It is darker and more cynical than you can imagine."

They stared at one another, the atmosphere charged and crackling.

Tristan's hands fisted at his sides, a muscle ticking in his stern jaw. His eyes gleamed with shadowy desires and unsaid things. It was as though he stood on the edge of a perilous cliff. Teetering on the verge of snatching her up.

Ravishing her.

Destroying her.

Breaking her.

And she would let him.

"Then take me, Tristan."

Her words were quiet but forged of iron. She'd made up her mind.

She would have this moment for herself. This flash of madness she would always remember. An ember of warmth she would hold close when suffering the coldness of being William Gadley's wife.

She would have this for herself. Not for Tristan's benefit, but her own.

Her chin rose higher. She stood straighter. The tears on her cheeks dried until the only indication she'd even wept was a spiky fringe of wet eyelashes.

"I won't marry you, Violet," he snarled.

She met his gaze without flinching. "I won't marry you, either, Tristan. Not even if you beg."

Tristan's hands clenched harder, surprise flashing in his eyes. He looked as though he were on the verge of exploding with... something. Violet just wasn't sure what.

"If you are angry with me," she murmured, "for daring to want you, I am sorry for that. What would you have me do instead?"

"Go away before I completely ruin you."

She nearly smiled at the fierceness of his words. "I've no wish to go anywhere other than where I am at this very moment, Tristan."

"Fine. I'll go."

His words were little more than a growl, but Violet recognized them as a peculiar sort of mechanism for keeping her at arm's length, even when he obviously wanted everything from her.

"If you do, take me with you," was her earnest reply.

Violet stepped closer, a temptation she suspected he could not resist, her eyes sparkling with challenge.

A curse escaped him, then he was sweeping her against his body again, peering down at her as if she were a mythical creature who'd suddenly appeared in his world. When he spoke, it was with a sad reverence.

"By God, there she is. My sweet, wild Violet. I've untamed you at last, haven't I? To my own detriment, and my shame, I've untamed you."

His lips claimed hers before she could acknowledge that yes, he'd done just that. Transformed her from a wallflower into something wild and free. A creature who would do whatever she desired.

Whatever *he* desired.

She kissed him back.

Violently. Tenderly. Desperately.

Her gloved fingers tangled in his hair, the strands sliding over the silk material. Suddenly, she wanted to rip the proper accompaniments away. She wanted the feel of his flesh, warm, bare, strong, flexing beneath her palms. But she could not bring herself to stop kissing him, not even for a heartbeat, to strip the gloves from her hands.

A tiny groan escaped her throat when forced to acknowledge a simple fact. The abundance of his clothes almost matched her own. Formal evening coat, tightly fitted waistcoat, cravat, linen shirt, high starched collar, flat-front trousers, braces. All the items were singularly insignificant but, taken as a whole, greatly impeded her ability to discover as much of him as possible.

The kiss grew increasingly wild. Tristan ravaged her mouth, their tongues tangling in an erotic duel while his arms locked around her waist, holding her tight. Not that she wished to escape. When he moved back the slightest bit, Violet eagerly followed so their lips remained sealed. The restraint he showed thrilled her while at the same time, filled her with an odd feeling of frustration.

She wanted him to lose control. With her. With himself. With everything unsaid and undone between them.

Tristan finally placed a bit of space between their bodies. But unable to give her up completely, he bit and nibbled at her lips, his own gloved hands sliding into the intricate updo of her hair. His fingers threatened to pull it all apart, to dislodge the pins and send the entire mass of dark auburn curls tumbling around her shoulders in wild disarray.

"Fuck, Violet. We can't do this here." His words came out rough.

The unexpected curse sent a sharp pang of excitement dancing along every nerve ending Violet possessed. Whimpering, she pressed even closer.

"I want you, Tristan. I don't care what happens tomorrow. I don't care what happens after that. When I am someone's wife," Violet said, staring up into his chocolate-brown eyes. "I want this for myself. I-I shall make no claims on you, no demands except this. Show me what fire feels like. Show me what it means to burn under your touch. Show me so I will have it as a memory forever when I shiver from the iciness of another man's hand. Do this for me. I beg you."

Tristan's eyes glowed hotter. A muscle ticked in his jaw, and his hands gripped her head tighter, fingers flexing until several pins finally succumbed to pressure. They fell to the ground, lost in the crushed stone like tiny glittery treasures.

A strange mixture of rage and desire emanated from Tristan in rolling waves. It seemed he both hated and loved her words.

Violet shuddered. She'd never felt such undiluted *need* before. The obsession to experience another's emotions, to understand them and force it all to the surface. She'd always been one who felt things intensely, whether it be sorrow for someone less fortunate, joy for another's happiness, or pity for those who were intentionally cruel. But this went far beyond that.

If Tristan suddenly stripped her gown from her and made love to her there on the conservatory floor in a blazing flurry of frustration and regret, she would not stop him. She would revel in it because it would match her own roiling emotions. And if he kissed her tenderly, stroked and cajoled before pressing his body inside hers with sweetness and careful attention, she would accept that, too.

She had become something of a mystery, even to herself in this moment. She wanted this man with no reservations. No shame. No strings. No expectations.

Tristan still watched her, his internal struggle evident in the clench of his jaw and rigid posture. But even more telling was the bulge which ruined the perfect flatness of his trousers.

Violet's eyes drifted over that part of him pressing against her. Arousal, primal and sharp, jolted her.

He wanted her just as much as she wanted him. Maybe more.

Realizing where her gaze had fallen, Tristan let out a strangled groan.

"If you only understood what you are asking me to do, Violet..."

"I do. Well, I don't understand the particulars of the act, having never done it. But I know I want you. And you want me.

And rather than Lord Gadley take what is mine, I choose to give it to you instead." Her amethyst-colored gaze shimmered with unshed tears. Her hand curled around the back of his neck, pulling him into her. "Help me do this, Tristan. Help me before it is ripped away by a man I do not love."

With those words, her fierce plea, Violet won the battle.

Tristan bore down on her, engulfing her in his embrace, his mouth crushing hers almost painfully. He kissed her until she was breathless and dizzy, until his arms were all that kept her from falling in a boneless heap of desire at his feet.

"Then you are mine, Violet. For a few hours, at least, and what happens between us tonight will remain our secret."

CHAPTER 25

Tristan did not speak as he led Violet through servants' entrances and along corridors most visitors to Darby Meadows were not even aware existed. To be fair, she uttered not a word either, her hand gripping his as though he were a lifeline found in stormy seas.

They avoided detection with the exclusion of two scullery maids. The girls, having just finished their duties, bobbed matching curtsies and turned away. Any curiosity regarding the viscount and the lady accompanying him paled when compared to having their supper and falling into a warm bed.

Higher and higher they climbed until the door to Tristan's studio was reached.

Tristan turned to Violet, holding both her hands in his. Her eyes met his with solemn determination.

"I would be damned for all eternity if I did not give you one final opportunity to change your mind, Violet." He wondered at the hoarseness of his own voice. Something deep inside him hoped she would not decide this was a terrible idea after all.

Her head tilted. "This is what I want, Tristan. You may not

love me, but I'll wager you hold far more affection for me than my future husband. I want this with you and only you."

Standing on tiptoe, she pressed her lips to his in graceful supplication. A gentle kiss that first trembled with shyness then blossomed with boldness. He allowed her to decide if the kiss should continue. Let her decide if her mouth would press harder to his and if her tongue would slip inside to stroke alongside his own.

When she did, Tristan could not contain the groan that shuddered through him.

Reaching behind him, he turned the doorknob, drawing Violet into his sanctuary of paints and canvases and illusions. The thought occurred he might never let her leave now that he had her in there once more.

She followed willingly, the pale green hue of her gown glowing in the dimness of the room. Falling back against the closed door, her arms wound around his neck, keeping their mouths linked.

Tristan knew a moment of such yearning for her that he felt shaky with it. It was useless ignoring its existence. He only hoped that gorging himself this one time would bring a lifetime of satisfaction and kill any future cravings.

Tearing his mouth away, he kissed the arc of Violet's neck, savoring the flavor of her skin. The sweetness of her flesh was addictive. It was fortunate the room was dimly lit by a full moon shining just outside the huge windows. He did not want to stop devouring her long enough to even bother with lighting a lamp or candle.

But he could begin divesting them both of their clothes.

In quick fashion, Tristan stripped his gloves away. He followed that with a slow, methodical removal of Violet's silk gloves, one digit at a time, pressing gentle kisses to each fingertip before delivering a quick nip from his teeth. And each time, she gasped with delight, her breathing growing faster.

Her eyes dilated with pleasure as the passionate assault continued, his lips landing where they willed on bare patches of her skin.

"I love your hair, kitten." Shrugging out of his formal coat, he tossed it over a nearby chair holding three blank canvases. His fingers were suddenly clumsy on the heavy gold buttons of his waistcoat, but within moments, he was free of that, too. "It's quite lovely. May I?"

At Violet's nod, he slipped a few additional hairpins from the intricate hairdo, and it tumbled in an ember-sparked waterfall of deep red.

"So damned beautiful." Tristan inhaled a shaky breath, meeting Violet's stare with a chagrined smile. Lifting one of the auburn locks, he watched it curl around his hand and wrist. "I confess a weakness for the very sight of it. I wish to see it draped over your body. Feel its softness drifting over me." His gaze grew darker, hungrier. "Most of all, I want it wrapped around my fist when I pull you to me for a kiss, so you cannot escape."

"I've no wish to escape." Violet shivered; her bottom lip caught between her teeth while fumbling at untying his cravat with little success. "I want all those things and more, Tristan."

Brushing her hands aside, he quickly unknotted the length of silk around his neck.

When he paused, considering what might be done with that bit of cloth, Violet's head tilted in curiosity.

"What is the matter?"

A wicked grin spread across Tristan's face. "Something you are too innocent to understand and too untried to experience this first time, my darling." He tossed the cravat to the floor. "Perhaps someday I will show you."

There will never be a 'someday' for us.

He was reminded of his own vow that this could *never*

happen again. He knew his sudden frown made her nervous. She clasped her hands together but wouldn't look away.

"Light a lamp, Tristan," Violet requested in a soft voice. "Whatever happens here does not need to be hidden in the shadows. I'm neither afraid nor ashamed, and I... I wish very much to see you. All of you."

Tristan responded with a fierce claiming of her mouth before he took her by the hand, leading her to an oversized settee situated in one corner of the room. It'd been placed there years ago for the purpose of grabbing a few moments of sleep while he furiously painted. Nowadays, it was mostly used as a holding spot for various canvases.

Pushing those to the floor, Tristan set Violet on the settee's cushion then went about doing as she asked. As a golden glow flooded the room, he watched as she kicked off her heeled shoes. With a stocking-clad toe, she traced a swirling vine pattern woven into the rug.

With deliberate intent, he removed his own boots. Next came his shirt, the buttons surprisingly difficult to navigate with her eyes trained so intensely upon him. Pulling the tails from the waistband of his breeches, the shirt fluttered open, revealing the wide planes of his chest and a crisp scattering of dark hair.

Violet never looked away, her gaze locked on his lean, muscular form as he moved toward her. She rose gracefully when he reached for her hand.

"Spin around, darling," he murmured. In the lamplight, it was easy to see the flush warming her ivory-hued skin. Dark eyelashes fluttered downward like silk fans, concealing the violet depths of her eyes, but she did as he asked, pirouetting without hesitation. He released her hand but not before noticing how it trembled the tiniest bit.

Her head bent forward, unconsciously making his task easier. Sweeping the fragrant locks of her hair aside, he slipped the gown's buttons through their moorings. Inch by inch, the silky skin of her back was revealed, the tender nape of her neck begging to be kissed and explored.

Tristan could not withstand the invitation. As her dress pooled around her waist, exposing the intricate cage of an ivory brocade corset and silk ribbons, he pressed a kiss to the back of Violet's neck.

Violet jolted forward, surprised by the heat of his mouth. A moan rose in her throat when Tristan simply wrapped an arm around her waist and hauled her back into place against his body.

The dress was pushed down until it formed a colorful puddle on the floor. The corset ribbons were quickly loosened to the point the contraption simply slid away by force of gravity. All that remained now was Violet's plain, white chemise and a set of bow-topped stockings.

Tracing the line between her ear and the top of her shoulder with a fiery trail of kisses, Tristan muttered his appreciation.

"How very beautiful you are, Violet. A painting come to life with your sunset hair, jewel-colored eyes, and velvet skin. You fit my hands as if crafted for me, all silky curves and heat. I cannot wait to taste you again. To feel you come on my tongue, your hands clenched in my hair, holding me tight as I make you explode. I intend to make love to you with such thoroughness, you will never forget this night. I'm going to bury myself so deep inside you, your body will remember mine for an eternity."

He spun her around so they stood face to face, their breaths mingling. Tristan slipped a finger beneath the strap of her chemise, lifting it slightly.

The swell of her plump breasts threatened to breach the low neckline. It tempted his willpower. Made him want to rip the flimsy garment from her body. Somehow, he restrained himself, but his hands still shook as he stared down at her.

"May I remove this, Violet?" His voice lowered to a raspy plea. "Will you allow me to have you as I wish?"

Violet swallowed hard, her eyes closing briefly before opening to regard him with a fierceness he had never witnessed in her before.

"Yes, Tristan. Dear God, yes." The words came out in a near hiss, a mixture of arousal and curiosity and a tiny bit of trepidation. She still wanted him. Wanted him as desperately as he wanted her, and there was no going back now.

With a swiftness that robbed her of breath, he yanked the chemise over her head. When the garment was tossed aside, his beautiful Violet stood before him in nothing but her white silk stockings.

With blazing, fire-bright eyes, Tristan admired her perfect form. His hands smoothed over her flared hips, and his fingertips trailed over the curving planes of her belly. He should strip those stockings from her legs. Kiss his way down to her dainty feet, but there was always later.

For now, he wanted to look his fill of her.

Keeping their gazes locked, he cupped her full, pert breasts in the palm of each hand.

Violet blushed, automatically raising her arms to shield her nakedness, but Tristan wouldn't allow that. With gentle persuasion, he eased her arms down, showing her wordlessly how he wished to touch her without restraint. Her hands eventually landed on his shoulders, and Tristan wondered if she was using him to remain upright.

His gaze roamed her figure, noting every lovely curve and swell. Particularly entrancing was a tiny constellation of freckles scattered on the angle of her left hipbone.

The dark, rose-colored marks formed a half-circle which trailed toward the curls between her thighs. Those innocent marks, the only blemishes he could see marking her body, called for his lips to trace and learn. They were a roadmap to pleasure, and he promised himself he would discover each one and memorize their shape with his tongue.

Using his thumbs, he wickedly strummed pale, pink nipples until they tightened into diamond-hard nubs. Her heart beat so wildly he felt its drumming, could see the leaping of her pulse in the hollow of her throat

Violet bit back a gasp as he explored her, her teeth tugging her bottom lip. When one of his hands drifted to the space between her thighs, she recoiled a half-step, but as before, Tristan stopped her.

Tugging her back to him with a soothing sound deep in his throat, he leisurely caressed the patch of soft, auburn curls.

"Be still, love." Spreading her heated flesh and repeatedly dipping his finger inside, he gathered the moisture and bathed her with it.

"But it is impossible." Violet gripped his forearms, fingernails digging into the fabric of his shirt as he slowly began driving her mad. "Oh, God," she moaned. "Tristan, don't stop. No... don't stop..."

"Yes, my little wild Violet. Yes. Yes. Yes," Tristan whispered, his fingers moving in tight circles on the pearl hidden by the folds of her vagina. He bit at her sweet, plump lips and sucked her tongue into his mouth, lashing it with his own while his other hand kept her off-center by pinching and flicking her nipples. Within moments he had worked her into a fever pitch, her arousal flooding his hand as he urged her to a shuddering climax.

"There, my sweet darling. There..." he shushed as she panted with satisfaction and hid her face in the crook of his neck. "That was only the beginning. We've so much more to discover."

"Tell me what to do, Tristan. I want so badly to please you..."

Tristan kissed the top of her head, brushing his lips over the silky tresses. Her breathless words sent a strange, possessive thrill shooting through him, making it difficult to breathe. Why she affected him so deeply, he could not understand.

Very slowly, he drew off his shirt, loving the way her eyes widened at the sight of his naked chest. She devoured every detail, every dip and line, every ridge, every muscle. And the way her eyes gleamed told him she was hungry for more, especially when her gaze dropped to the painful bulge in his trousers. She assessed his body almost ravenously before reaching out a forefinger.

Tracing the dark trail of hair running from his navel to below the band of his trousers, dazed pleasure softened her features.

"What should I do?" she breathed in wonder, her fingertips roaming the slabs of his abdomen.

Tristan chuckled, cupping her chin and tilting it upward. "You don't have to do a damned thing, kitten, but if you must, you may begin by unbuttoning my trousers."

CHAPTER 26

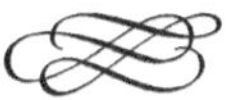

Still trembling from the orgasm Tristan coaxed from her, Violet hesitated, unsure just how one went about removing a man's garments.

Licking her lips, she stared into the dark brown eyes watching her so closely. This business of removing his clothes should be no different than removing her own. But the logistics of it eluded her.

"It is of no matter, kitten," Tristan said soothingly, his hands covering hers. "I should not ask something so wicked of you."

Violet did not understand what came over her when she abruptly sank to her knees. Her hands, still captured within Tristan's larger ones, rested at his waist. Tilting her head back, she met his startled gaze. The air between them swirled thick and heady, like a garden bursting with fragrant blooms in the warmth of a late spring afternoon.

"Don't you know, Tristan? I want to be wicked. I want to be wicked with you. For you."

Untangling their hands, Violet's fingers rested on the buttons of his trousers. The impressive bulge of his shaft jumped in response.

"Violet," he growled.

She ignored the desperate warning in his tone. Shifting on her knees only moved her closer. Carefully, she unfastened the trousers' buttons. As the fabric gaped open, more of his lower abdomen was revealed. There were slabs of muscled flesh there, too, and chiseled, matching grooves defined his hips.

Violet swallowed hard, smoothing her palms over those V-shaped divots.

Where her own body was soft and pleasingly rounded in certain areas, Tristan's seemed crafted of iron. There was nothing forgiving or tender in the planes and lines of his physique. Realizing that this male perfection was hers to fully explore made her hands shake the slightest bit.

Tugging further on the garment revealed the upper swell of Tristan's cock.

Her exhaled breath of surprise swept over his flesh. Deep inside her belly, arousal launched another quivering arrow.

Tristan muttered a fierce curse.

"Kitten, if you do not stop, I shall lose control. And for this, I shall need a great deal of control."

"But I want to see you," she whispered, gazing up at him through lowered lashes. Her fingers slipped inside the opening of the trousers, encountering crisp hair before gingerly closing around the bulge she found so curious.

Touching Tristan was like nothing she expected. He was so wonderfully warm. And smooth. Velvet-wrapped granite.

In the flickering lamplight, she was shocked when he grew even larger, the length of flesh hardening until it practically throbbed within the circle of her hands.

How extraordinary that I can feel his heartbeat...

A quick peek revealed Tristan's jaw locked in an unforgiving clench, his eyes closed as if in prayer. One hand hung frozen in the air just above her head, fingers twitching just enough that Violet wondered what his intent might be.

It seemed he wished to slide his fingers through her hair. Maybe caress her cheek, or something similar. Violet wasn't quite sure *what*, but whatever he decided, she would let him.

Distracted by the pulsating shaft within her grasp, her hands began moving in exploration. Up and down. Cupping. Circling. Tracing.

"You are so incredibly... hard, and yet, soft at the same time. I never expected..." Her words trailed off when Tristan let out a guttural groan. Both of his hands abruptly closed into tight fists.

"For fuck's sake, Violet. Do not do this to me. And do not breathe. Do not move. Do not—"

Violet did not wish to stop, but perhaps she was hurting him. He certainly appeared to be in pain. And if it would help him to touch her while she discovered the mysterious differences between a man and woman's body, she didn't mind at all. In fact, everything inside her was screaming that he should place his hands on her once more.

With a small frown, her hands squeezed the hard flesh. "You may touch me, Tristan. I want you to."

"You will be the death of me," he muttered, his hand delving into the ruined remains of her once elegant updo. "I swear you are killing me now with your hands around my cock."

The weight of her hair cascading down her back felt incredibly erotic. While the word he used in describing his member was unfamiliar, Violet immediately recognized its significance. Tristan's current state was the direct result of her own bold actions.

Is it my inexperience that causes him pain?

As the thought crashed through her brain, Violet instinctively sought to make things better. She would ease Tristan's discomfort. Offer a small portion of herself in supplication.

In a sweet kiss of apology, her lips delicately brushed the head of his shaft.

Tristan's hand abruptly tangled in her hair, tightening with such intensity Violet let out a small cry. Pleasure, deep and almost painfully sharp, seized her. The primal thrill shocked her senses.

Then she found herself pulled tighter against his body, held firmly in place between his thighs. Fear swamped her desire. Would he push himself inside her in this manner? Breach the barrier of her teeth with force as lust overtook him?

But Tristan did nothing more. Although his hand trembled, he did not move, perhaps aware he danced far too close to crossing an imaginary line.

A strange calm washed over Violet.

He will not harm me.

Nor would he demand more than she was willing to give. It was somehow liberating to realize she *needed* his hands on her like this. Gripping her with restrained fierceness. She liked how he seemed on the verge of going a little insane at the thought of possessing her. It matched her own internal madness to have him at any cost.

Before another heartbeat passed between them, Violet surged forward. Her mouth closed over the cushiony soft head of his cock in curious, inexperienced exploration.

That brief moment, with his body pressed so intimately between her lips, ignited a firestorm.

Tristan clutched Violet's shoulders, hauling her up from the floor with such speed she was momentarily dizzy.

She was then crushed against him, his voice a fierce growl in her ear.

"Enough."

He devoured her mouth, kissing her hard and deep. Kissing her until she was so caught up in the wild splendor of it, she did not realize he had kicked out of his trousers and was lowering her to the velvet settee. Her body was shifted until Tristan had her positioned as he desired, with her head resting on the upholstered softness of the low, decoratively carved arm while he sprawled between her opened thighs.

"Are you ready to become mine?" The whisper was murmured against her lips, his mouth searching and ravenous.

I've always been yours. Forever, Violet wanted to say, but she held her breath, swallowed the words instead. Drowning in his dark brown, gold-flecked eyes, she slowly nodded her head.

"It shall pain you for a moment, but after that, I promise nothing but pleasure, Violet." He rocked against her, making her shockingly aware of his shaft. "And there will be no chance of a child, I swear it."

Could something that large, something so hot it could be a lit flame against the tender flesh between her legs actually fit inside her?

It would. And she grew weary of waiting for him to claim her. This, *this* was fate in all of its glory.

"I trust you, Tristan. I know you will not harm me if you can avoid it." Her arms wound around his neck. "Please, I want you so desperately, I ache with it. Do not stop, even if I cry out."

Tristan's forehead touched hers while, at the same time, his cock pushed against the damp folds of her cleft. "My wild girl. Forgive me for this. Forgive me for needing you to the point I cannot think clearly enough to determine right from wrong."

"Nothing about this is wrong," Violet declared with a stubborn lift of her chin.

His smile was a bit wistful, but he nodded in agreement. "Hold tight to me now, love."

One second, Violet was empty; the next, Tristan was filling her, steadily inching forward, stretching and burning her until she felt the need to squirm away. When she did move, Tristan grasped her hip, his fingers biting into the soft flesh.

"Do not move, my sweet darling. Be still just a moment longer," he said in a harsh mutter. His hips flexed, and Violet gasped as the pressure increased until it felt she was overflowing. "I'm barely inside you, and there is still more to come." Pressing fevered kisses to her mouth, her neck, her jawline, Tristan's other hand came up and braced on the settee arm above her head.

Capturing her gaze, he held it with such force Violet felt almost frightened. He looked like a Viking plundering a new treasure trove.

"Do not look away from me, Violet. I want this moment seared on your brain for an eternity."

She nodded, unsure what he meant by such a fierce declaration.

Surging forward, Tristan quickly broke the barrier of her virginity and sealed their fate.

Her heartbeat pounded in her ears. A wordless cry of pain rose up from her throat and was swallowed with a tiny whimper.

Tristan's eyes smoldered with possessiveness. With lust. With something so elusive Violet could not place a name to it.

"I'm sorry." He dropped another kiss to her lips. "Remember, the pain is fleeting."

He was right. The sharp ache was already receding as the seconds passed. But steady and patient, Tristan waited, waited for something inside her to shift and accept this intimate invasion. Their breaths collided and mingled while the bombardment of her senses was processed and analyzed.

There was the dull throbbing, of course, but also fullness and heat. Flickering flames grew and spread, sparks firing like Chinese firecrackers.

Tristan's body buried so deep inside her ignited every nerve ending, prickling her skin until goosebumps rushed over her in waves. His broad chest brushed the tender peaks of her breasts, his stomach pressed intimately against her lower belly. Violet was so sensitive, every touch or caress, no matter how feather-like, sent unfamiliar tingles cascading through her veins.

Suddenly, it did not hurt as badly as it had moments before. Suddenly, something raw and all-consuming was swamping her senses. An urge to move, to undulate, to kiss and be kissed rose inside her, and with a moan, she surrendered.

Would he kiss her as he had before? Would his hands roam her flesh, finding new points of pleasure and driving her insane with need?

Tristan's smile was both wicked and warm. "Has the pain lessened, kitten? Are you ready now?"

Violet offered a softly murmured, "Please", in response.

He never looked away and neither did she as he began moving inside her.

Shallow, exploratory movements soon morphed into full, demanding thrusts where his pelvis collided with her sensitive pearl, his cock hitting so deep it touched another magical spot inside her. Her legs came up, instinctively wrapping around his narrow hips as she hesitantly matched the rocking lunges.

Was this the right response? She didn't know. She only knew that everything he was doing felt heavenly. She felt both owned and dominated as Tristan's hand gripped her hip, holding her in place for the taking.

Her own body's response startled her. Her movements become increasingly focused while, at the same time, strangely erratic.

Because even if Tristan's deep plunges sent tiny frissons of pain trickling over the pleasure, she could not remain still.

Her hands tunneled through his dark hair, clutching fiercely each time he kissed her or took the peak of her breast into the inferno of his mouth. Her hips rose and fell in tandem with Tristan's, accompanied by his murmured encouragement. Something wonderful and terrifying commanded her now. There was no stopping or hiding from it.

And she could no more stop herself from loving him than she could keep the sun from rising every morning.

The pleasure grew. More. More. More. Until her eyes fluttered shut against an overwhelming tide of emotion.

She was drifting. Flying.

Drowning.

"Look at me, Violet." Whiplash sharp, Tristan's voice dragged her back to him.

She obeyed and the glittering, possessive want in his eyes split her universe apart, rushing her into a dazzling world of sensation. A low, choked sob broke free from her throat as she arched against him. It echoed in the quiet of the room, and Tristan growled with satisfaction as her climax rolled over them both.

"Yes, that's it, my beautiful girl. My sweet kitten. You've given me your first kiss. Your first climax. Everything. And now this. No one else shall have these things from you. *They. Are. Mine."*

With a half-intelligible, strangled curse, he began thrusting harder and harder until Violet wondered if the world would explode with the exquisite tension.

Then abruptly, without warning, Tristan tore himself away, pulling out from her body.

Violet cried out against the loss, but he was already moving back from her, erecting space between them.

"I can't hold back... I can't." Rising on his haunches, Tristan gripped his cock in one hand, stroking and squeezing while Violet watched in startled, but dreamy fascination. Despite their bodies now being separated, his dark eyes burned into hers until everything felt a hundred times more intimate.

At that moment, she could see into his soul. And she wanted nothing more than to drown there in the velvety depths of his desire.

"Violet..." The words spilled out as he exploded with a guttural cry. Hot seed pumped from his shaft in a visceral display of lust, splashing onto her bare stomach. Throwing his

head back at the culmination of climax, hair disheveled from Violet's fingers, he could have easily been mistaken for a wild creature celebrating a fresh kill.

And Violet was utterly, completely entranced.

Shuddering from release, Tristan partially collapsed on top of her. His arms slid beneath her shoulders, keeping the bulk of his weight suspended so she wouldn't be crushed.

Violet's fingers threaded through the thick waves of Tristan's hair as he nestled into the crook of her neck. She stroked the dark locks while his breathing eased back to normal and their hearts lessened their brutal pounding.

Pressing a gentle kiss to her lips, he held her even tighter, his breath warm against her ear.

How Violet wished they could remain like this forever, although the settee was becoming uncomfortable, and the fluid on her stomach, smeared by the contact of their bodies, was turning damp and sticky.

She would pay a king's ransom if it meant they would never have to leave this room.

The words he'd uttered while possessing her were stamped into Violet's brain, turning everything crystal clear and clearing away the fog of incredible pleasure.

Tristan Buchanan might be determined to fight whatever had grown between them, but perhaps the unthinkable had occurred.

Perhaps, she had wormed her way into his heart after all.

CHAPTER 27

Violet did not move when Tristan finally pulled away from her.

Leaving her on the sofa, he retrieved his trousers and slid them up over slim hips. His eyes lingered on her figure with such latent heat, Violet felt the need to conceal her nakedness. But her gown and corset lay on the floor, out of arm's reach. Draped over one of the blank canvases near the window was her chemise, its haphazard placement the result of Tristan flinging it aside.

That left her with a pair of silk stockings which were certainly no help. They only provided cover from toe to just above her knees.

Biting her lip in consternation, Violet watched Tristan deliberately turn away.

He disappeared into what she assumed was a small water closet. There came the sound of drawers opening, then splashing water. Just as quickly as he left, he returned to her, the lamplight casting him in shadow.

"Here," Tristan murmured, sinking into a sitting position by her side. In his hand was a small cloth and a glass containing clear liquid. "Drink this."

Propping herself half upright, Violet was acutely aware of her nudity. Accepting the glass, she took a cautious sip. "It's water."

A smile tugged at Tristan's firm lips. "Of course, it is. I'm sorry it's a bit cold."

Violet cocked her head. "I don't understand."

"Warmer would be better, but we must make do."

Using his free hand, Tristan encouraged her knees to fall apart, exposing her in such a way she wasn't sure if it was erotic or shameful. Before she could draw a breath, the cloth pressed between her legs.

"Oh!" Violet hissed, instinctively grabbing Tristan's huge hand. Her fingernails dug into his wrist.

Her attempts at shoving him away proved unsuccessful. It was like trying to move a boulder with a twig. The private flesh he believed needed ministrations was tender. Sensitive. She tried wiggling free of his control, even while realizing the shock of the cold, damp cloth was rather soothing.

Tristan pinned her with an unreadable stare, dark brown eyes stilling her movements.

"Let me, Violet."

There was no room for negotiation in his low tone. Trembling, and so embarrassed that her cheeks felt on fire, Violet slowly released her grip.

With calm, gentle strokes, Tristan cleaned her. The cloth, now tinged a faint pink with the blood of her virginity, was folded in half. The fresh side of the square was then used to wipe away the evidence of lovemaking from her belly.

Tristan watched Violet closely, his own expression solemn. There wasn't even a glimmer of lust as he took care of her. When he was finished with the task, he stoked a fire in the fireplace grate, tossing the cloth into the flames.

Finally, he located her chemise and pulled it over her head, then settled onto the settee beside her.

With his back against the furniture's cushion, he tugged Violet until she reclined against him. Tucked between his spread thighs, with her back to his front, she let him position her as he wished.

"Stay here with me for a while, Violet," he said, his lips brushing the top of her head while he spoke. Muscular arms wrapped around her waist.

If she wanted to escape, he was not making it easy.

"You do not want me to go?" The question came out tremulous despite her best effort. She was tense, her spine so rigid it kept a small space between their bodies despite the close proximity.

"God, no." Gathering the bulk of her hair in his fist, Tristan arranged it so the lustrous waves tumbled over her opposite shoulder. Now, he could kiss the side of her neck unimpeded. Running his large fingers through her hair, he patiently untangled a few snarls. "Quite the opposite, kitten. I want you to stay. Surely, no harm can come from simply enjoying each other's company in the little time we have together. Do you not find this pleasant?"

Violet relaxed with his words, sinking into the hard planes of his bare chest. The heat of his skin burned her through the linen of her chemise. Molded against him like this, held with such exacting care, she felt secure. Safe. Cherished.

For so many years, she'd longed for something like this to happen between her and Tristan. Would it be so damaging if she took this for herself? Kept it as a secret treasure? It would be a moment to remember Tristan by long after they parted ways.

"Yes," she shyly answered. "It is lovely. I wish—"

With a little shake of her head, Violet clamped her lips together.

Tristan lifted a curl from her shoulder. It wound about his

finger like a silk ribbon. "What do you wish, Violet?" Curiosity tinged his words.

Clinging would only make matters worse, Violet decided. She was determined not to be like so many of his conquests; determined to walk away when it was truly over. "It doesn't matter, Tristan. Really, it doesn't."

With a heavy sigh, Tristan pulled her tighter against him, his arm becoming a welcome vise over her midsection. Violet rested her fingers lightly on the muscled forearm, absently tracing veins which stood out in relief when he flexed the tiniest bit.

Her touch drifted aimlessly until she reached his hand where it curved along the line of her belly. The fascination she had with his hands still existed, even more so now that she'd experienced their effect on her body.

A smile tugged at her lips when he entwined their fingers together. Lifting her hand to his mouth, he gave it a soft kiss.

"You are an odd, little creature, Violet."

"You are not the first to say so, and being odd has a few surprising advantages. My shortcomings are easily overlooked. Even where my own parents are concerned, I'm quite forgettable." Violet's tone turned pensive. "There's never been any cause to worry for my virtue. Or fret I would receive improper attention from a gentleman. And until you, I've never considered doing anything remotely scandalous. My shyness has concealed me from the world. No one sees me, which is both a curse and a blessing, I suppose."

Pushing her upright, Tristan gripped Violet's shoulders and turned her upper body so they faced one another. There was a faintly distressed glitter in his dark eyes, his voice carrying a subtle undercurrent of puzzled torment.

"My words did not come out as I intended. Odd is not an insult, at least not when it relates to how I regard you. I simply meant... hell, I'm not sure how I meant it. But, in my opinion, being odd is precisely what makes you unique. Special, and so different from everyone else. Everything about you dazzles the eye, and I'm always left breathless. I do *see* you, Violet. And now I find it impossible to look away."

Tristan crushed her mouth then, delving deep with thorough, intense sweeps of his tongue. He kissed her as though he'd just invented the act and needed her for the purpose of perfecting the motions.

Violet surrendered at once, her hands bracketing Tristan's cheeks. She delighted in the passionate embrace, the unyielding pressure of his arms, and mostly, the scorching heat of his body stoking the flames of her own. With a whimper, she scooted closer to him, snuggling against the wide planes of his chest and breathing deeply of his masculine cologne.

Tristan always smelled so heavenly. Wintergreen and spice. That teasing touch of leather. How she would miss him…

With effort, he finally released her lips, giving one lingering nibble along the corner of her mouth. The smile he gave her was crooked and slightly apologetic.

"I'm sorry for that. It seems I can hardly be near you and not begin kissing you in some manner."

"I don't mind," Violet whispered, determined to take each and every kiss and store them away in her memories. "Keep kissing me, Tristan."

"Will you solve a puzzle for me first?" His finger traced the expanse of skin left exposed by the gaping neckline of her chemise.

She regarded him curiously as his touch trailed up and circled the shell of her ear. When she shivered in response, he chuckled while his hand half-curled around her neck, his thumb finally resting in the hollow of her throat. He held her there in that manner for a long moment, a slight frown marring his brow as he watched her. Violet had the impression he was attempting to resolve his own question without her assistance.

"In a few days, all guests will be invited to ride in the Darby Fox Chase. For as long as the Buchanan family has held the Darby title, this chase has been held three days prior to the May Day Affair. It's tradition, as you well know."

Violet nodded, her stomach tightening. She was intimately acquainted with the Darby Fox Chase.

"And in all the years you've been a guest in my father's home, I don't recall ever seeing you take part. Of course, when you were younger, I admittedly would not have paid much attention. But I'm sure I would have taken notice of you more recently. Especially as you would likely ride alongside Celia. Then, there is something you said to me when you and I rescued the beast in the stables. Do you remember what you said?"

Violet shrank a little but bravely lifted her chin. "I recall saying quite a bit during the course of that particular morning."

At her subtle, yet flippant reply, Tristan's hand closed fractionally firmer, fingers curling over the nape of her neck while his thumb stroked the careening pulse in her throat. Did he have any idea how this small gesture both excited and frightened her?

As if well aware of it, Tristan's lips quirked upward. "You said you did not ride," he reminded her softly. "That horses frighten you. You mentioned an incident, and for some reason, I wondered if I had something to do with that fear. I would like very much if you would ride beside me during the chase. And if you are frightened, I would like to remedy that situation. Tell me, Violet. I can help you."

Her laugh was a humorless sound.

"The incident was of little matter then, and even less now."

"Tell me regardless," he urged.

Violet tried moving away, flustered by Tristan's persistence and the apparent sincerity of his request, but he would not allow it. When his hand tightened again, it seemed directly connected to the odd flutter of lust in her stomach.

"Violet, I want to help you."

"Why would you? Besides, do you think Lord Gadley cares whether or not I can ride?" she shot back, cringing on the inside at the abomination of uttering the man's name in this room. "His only interest is correcting my behavior. In fact, he says he will take great pleasure in doing just that." Her voice wobbled despite efforts to steady it. "I doubt I'll be allowed out of his sight once we are wed, much less given leave to venture to the stables whenever it strikes my fancy."

"Correct you?" Tristan's jaw tightened. "The hell he will."

Violet nibbled at her bottom lip. "Let's not tangle ourselves in that argument again, Tristan."

"Kitten." Increasing the pressure on her neck, Tristan tilted her head back until their gazes locked. "Biting your lip like that distracts me. Now, I concede the discussion on your possible marriage; however, you will tell me what I want to know."

When she stubbornly remained silent, Tristan sighed and tugged her closer.

"Tell me because I'm asking you." His lips brushed her forehead. "Not because I demand it."

CHAPTER 28

"You will not remember the event the same way that I do," Violet said in a small voice. "If you remember it at all."

"Go on." Tristan noted Violet's cheeks were now stained pink. "What happened?"

"I've never told anyone about that day."

She bit her lip again, then thought better of it when his intense stare drifted to her mouth.

"I'd just turned fourteen that year, and you were home with friends you'd known at school. At first, I thought they were much like yourself. Young, handsome, so very charming. While I worshipped you from afar, the three of you made merry that week."

"I recall that particular spring. We'd all graduated the university and were feeling rather pompous." Tristan grinned widely. "Lord Trentham and the Earl of Granger were always up to some sort of mischief."

"Yes, mischief." Violet's full pink lips tightened. "They thrived on it. Sought it out, in fact. The morning of the fox chase, you were all in high spirits as everyone readied to ride, including Lord Trentham's sister, Miss Ellen. I'd been given one of the slowest hunters in your father's stables. He was a steady animal and gentle, which was fortunate as I am a novice when it comes to horsemanship. Mother does not believe it is a skill I must excel at. Why ride when one can always travel by coach or carriage?"

"But you have obtained a rudimentary grasp of what is involved, correct?"

"Yes, thanks to Celia. She insisted I learn the basics. And so, I did. Not for her sake but for yours. I swallowed my fear and learned to stay atop a horse simply so that when I visited Darby Woods every spring, I could ride in the Darby Fox Chase, too."

Tristan's heart squeezed painfully at the thought of this lovely girl adoring him from a distance. She did not care he was unworthy of that devotion. Then or now.

His pulse quickened, however, wondering how those two friends, admittedly rather wild and impulsive in those days, fit into the events as she relayed them.

"I hung back from the rest of the group. You were all so eager to begin, and your horses were just as excited. I remember how they pawed and snorted. And I was so fixated on you—" Her smile was sad as she said this. "So worried that you enjoyed Lady Ellen's company, that I hardly noticed Lord Trentham and Lord Granger circling back. When the fox was set free and everyone else burst into action, your friends did not follow. Instead, they moved in, their horses rearing and prancing so close they jostled mine. Lord Granger's mount was particularly vicious. It swung its rear toward my horse and began furiously kicking."

"I remember that mare of his," Tristan mused. "Granger always said she was slightly mad, but none could beat her on open ground. She ran like a fiend, to the point of collapse if he allowed it."

"When they circled me, my gelding reared, desperate to get away. I could hardly retain my seat."

Tristan sat up straight, tense with the realization she might have been harmed.

"They laughed at me. And when I saw Ellen riding beside you, and she smiled as though pleased, I became so angry. I wanted to snatch her down from her horse by her hair, but of course, I could not do that. Lord Trentham told me you did not want me following you as I had that entire week. That you wished to be alone with his sister, and as your friend, he was helping you to that end."

"His sister was a little flirt who would have done anything to land a husband," Tristan stated grimly.

He recalled the lengths Ellen had gone in her attempts at wrangling him into a romantic situation. When he proved resistant to her advances, she moved on, trapping Granger in marriage instead the following year. Now a countess, the gossip mill reported Lady Granger was just as miserable as her carousing husband.

Violet frowned as if Tristan's statement troubled her. "Lord Granger's horse was so wild, and I was so afraid, but my poor gelding was terrified. He finally bolted when the other horse bumped him one too many times."

"Oh, kitten," Tristan murmured, his arms tightening around her. "Were you injured?"

"I tried hanging on. It knocked the very breath from me when I landed, and the thought of being trampled was terrifying. One never truly realizes how very large a horse's hoof actually is until it is stomping the ground next to your ear. Before riding off, Lord Trentham said that unless I wished the incident repeated, I was not to follow you. By then, with my horse already galloping back to the stables, I had no choice. Besides, I was so bruised from the fall, I could hardly lift my arm. My lip was bloody, and there was a nasty scrape on my knee. Later,

Celia asked what happened, but I told her and my parents the same story. That I was thrown because of my own inexperience. I was ashamed your friends were tasked with keeping me away as though I were a bothersome pest."

Tristan sighed and pulled Violet closer. She resisted for a second before allowing him to press her head over the spot where his heart beat. Neither moved nor spoke until Tristan broke the silence.

"That was very cruel of them, Violet, to lie with such audacity and fail to offer assistance when you were injured. Had I been aware of their actions, I would have beaten the hell out of the pair of them. Even if I was a rakehell myself, I would not have condoned such behavior. And I never had any interest in Lady Ellen. I tolerated her because of my friendship with her brother. I have a feeling it was she who orchestrated the event. She pulled a similar stunt later that year which resulted in her marriage to George. Oh, darling, I'm sorry you were subjected to their malice."

"I believed you directed the actions of your friends. I should have known you would not be so heartless," Violet said in a muffled voice. Then, a tiny laugh escaped her. "There's a distressing abundance of women willing to go to great lengths just to be part of your life."

"Two is not an abundance, kitten."

"Do you forget the actress who just last season claimed you were to wed once production shut down? The gossips reported you vowed to end the play's run if she did not say yes to your proposal of marriage. Of course, very few believed her since you were also in pursuit of Grace around that time." Violet's head lifted so she could gaze deep into his eyes. "Do not fear I will do the same, Tristan. I may be no more than a shy wallflower, but I possess some pride. And I'll not scheme and lie to gain a husband."

Tristan ground his teeth in silent frustration. It did appear there were several plots to shackle him with a wife.

None of the women Violet mentioned interested him in the least. Then or now. However, if he ever decided he wanted a wife, the woman in his arms at that very moment would be his choice.

And how his father would rejoice at that bit of news.

"No, you would not lower yourself to such deceptive measures, Violet. Perhaps that is why I am obsessed with having you while I can. While it's possible. You are the unattainable. I may have my pleasure, and give you yours, with no worry that tomorrow will see me standing at the altar. It is a defect in my character that allows me to take your innocence with little qualm."

Violet's soft hands brushed over his abdomen before her arms slipped around his waist. Her grip tightened almost convulsively as she embraced him.

"If there is a flaw, it is mine to claim, Tristan. I gave myself to you. Few men would reject what I offered. I am a woman who has become willingly wicked, even if there is no gain to be had and no promises for a future." Her voice turned fierce. "But I'm not sorry. I'll never be sorry for this."

Tristan could think of nothing to say to that resolute statement. He simply held her, contemplating how anyone could ever overlook a girl of her caliber.

Violet Everstone was a hidden treasure. He was a fool for having been blind to her for so long. And he would become a bigger fool when it was time to let her go and he allowed it.

"Will you allow me to help you overcome your fear of horses? You may find comfort in such a simple pleasure as riding one day." He smoothed her hair back away from her temple, pressing a soft kiss to the top of her head. "There is something to be said for a quiet morning ride through the forest, or across a green meadow. If you were properly introduced to it, you would enjoy it more than you think possible."

She shivered just a little in his arms, no doubt remembering the day his friends terrorized her.

The irrational urge to find those men, to bloody their faces with his fists so they could experience the consequences of their cruelty surprised him. He'd always shown consideration and respect for the fairer sex, but this was different. This was a visceral need to punish anyone who might hurt this sweet girl.

It was a need to protect what was his.

"If you really believe it will help." Violet's voice was small, her breath warm against his chest. Her perfume tickled his nostrils.

His body was already responding again, ready to claim her a second time. When she shifted, the blood thumped quicker in his veins.

He couldn't let her go just yet. The night was not over, and the thought of not tasting her one more time before this door closed on their relationship was stomach-wrenching.

Tilting her chin with his forefinger, he stared down into her dark violet eyes, memorizing all the myriad shades of blue swimming in their depths. The lighter flecks of color reminded him of diamond dust.

"There are many things that become easier after the initial undertaking. And definitely things you will find more pleasurable the second time around." He brushed a kiss over her full lips, playfully tugging the bottom one between his teeth before releasing it.

She smiled shyly. "You are not talking about riding, are you?"

"Of course, I am. But what we are doing now is just another way you can gain some confidence." His lips twisted upward. "Shall I show you, little kitten? Or should I allow you to slip away from me to the safety of your room?"

Violet's breath quickened. She scooted forward until she

faced him, her body nestled in the space of his legs, her chest to his, her hips caged by his thighs, her belly pressed against his rapidly growing shaft.

"We can do... *that*... again?"

Tristan chuckled at the hopeful tone of her question. "We can. We can do anything we wish. Anything *you* wish. And this time, you will take the lead. Whatever you want, even if you don't know what it is just yet, I will do for you. I will help you discover what your body wants, and I'll show you how you may please yourself. You have all of the control, Violet."

Her head tilted. "I think I like that idea."

"Then let us begin with a kiss," Tristan replied, his voice husky at the thought of being at her mercy. "Kiss me how you like. Anywhere you like. And any question you have, I will answer as we go down this path together."

The diamond dust in Violet's eyes sparkled with curiosity. Trailing a finger along the firm line of his jaw, she murmured, "The stubble of your whiskers tickles when you kiss my neck and shoulders. It makes me shiver but in a good way. As if warning me something better is coming. Does it tickle when I kiss you?"

"Violet." Tristan took a deep breath, steadying his desire while she peeked up at him beneath the thick sweep of her lashes. "Your kiss lights a fire deep in my soul."

A glimmer of pleased satisfaction lit her features as her finger moved along to his earlobe. "And if I bit you here, as you have done to me, would it feel like something sharp twisted its way into your heart, leaving you unable to breathe?"

Leaning forward, her breath whispered over his jaw before warming his ear.

"I imagine it would." His voice was already shaky with longing before her teeth gently nipped his earlobe.

A groan escaped his lungs. His cock hardened almost painfully, thrilled by the hint of savagery she was showing him.

Encouraged by the sound he made, Violet repeated the action, this time taking more flesh between her teeth and slightly tugging it. Then, in a flash, she let go and leisurely licked the spot.

Before he could fully react to that intriguing maneuver, her tongue was swirling around the contours of his ear, her fingers sifting through the thick waves of his hair and curling around the back of his head so he was held immobile for exploration.

Lust cascaded through Tristan. Rarely had a woman taken the time to tease him, to discover the erogenous zones of his body with the exception of his cock. Violet Everstone and her inexperienced caresses were driving him insane with need.

His fists tightened. If this went on much longer, he would not be able to stop himself from rolling her over and driving into her sweet, curvy body over and over until the world either exploded or froze in its orbit.

"When I'm with you, Tristan, when you touch me, kiss me, it feels like a thousand fireflies lighting me up from the inside. Every time, the pleasure is so overwhelming I feel like I am coming apart at the seams. As if the entire world is inside me and bursting out. Does it feel that way for you, too?"

Her mouth slowly tracked down the slope of his neck to the area where it met his shoulder. She smoothed a hand over the muscles of his chest, measuring the bulges and tracing the defined lines of his pectorals. Her lips drifted lower, brushing kisses over his flesh until she reached the flat disk of his nipple.

"I feel everything you feel, Violet," he grunted. "Magnified until I spend my days going crazy wanting you."

"Is it like that no matter who you make love to, or is this something special we only feel with each other?" Her inquiry was followed by the tip of her wicked, little tongue swiping at his nipple just before the bit of flesh was sucked into the heat of her mouth.

Muscles tightening, Tristan very nearly shot off the settee.

Against his better judgment, one hand found its way into the wealth of her hair.

Clenching a chunk of auburn curls in his fist, he struggled against the urge to snatch her up and kiss her to within an inch of her life.

"It's not like this with anyone else." Tugging her head back, he forced her to meet his gaze. "It's *never* been like this before. No one, *no one,* makes me feel like you do. And with every jealous thread of my selfish soul, I am determined that you never forget my hands on your skin. My mouth on yours. Our bodies joined together."

With the quickness of a jungle cat, Tristan moved to a sitting position and settled Violet so she straddled his lap.

This placed her chest at eye-level. The temptation was greater than any mortal man could resist. Nuzzling the soft, fragrant skin bared by the gaping chemise, Tristan ran his tongue over the shadowy valley between her breasts, searching for her nipples through the flimsy cloth. Finding one, he drew it into his mouth and tasted her until the chemise's fabric grew damp and transparent.

His hands skimmed the span of Violet's waist, slowly dropping even further until the curves of her buttocks rested in his palms. Gripping her tighter brought her flush against his aching shaft, and with an excited moan, Violet's fingers plowed through the thick waves of his hair. She pressed him to her breasts, her breathing intensifying with each passing moment as he feasted.

"Open my trousers and free me," he muttered around a mouthful of her creamy flesh.

Violet barely fumbled while following the command. Shifting her body, she quickly navigated the buttons and helped him shed the garment with just a touch of awkwardness.

She giggled against his lips when he finally kicked them aside.

"You should consider more easily accessible clothing, Viscount."

"If it were up to me, neither of us would wear a stitch when we are together." He kissed the underside of her chin, his hands returning to grip the bare globes of her bottom.

"How scandalous of you. Imagine the reactions at afternoon tea if you had your way. We would certainly turn heads."

"If I had my way, we would spend all day and night making love," he replied with a husky laugh. "To hell with tea and anything or anyone outside this room. I have a feast of violets in my arms and no need for anything else."

Violet bracketed his face in her hands, staring down at him for a long moment, her fingers stilling until they no longer twisted in his hair. She appeared dazed by his ardor.

"You say the sweetest, most wicked things, Tristan. Sometimes, I wonder if I should believe…"

Tristan swore beneath his breath. "Every word is the truth, Violet, even if I cannot offer more than what I give you in this moment. Now, if you are not too ill-used by my selfish addiction to you, would you like to learn how to ride?"

She kissed him softly. "We're still not talking about horses, are we?"

"I want you too badly to jest about such matters at the moment." Squeezing her plump buttocks until she sighed in dreamy surrender, he positioned her body until it would take only a surge of his hips to breach her. "Spread your legs wider, Violet. Lower yourself onto me. Take me deep inside you. Move as you will and don't stop until you've found your pleasure by using me. I want your heartbeat branding my flesh with your name."

CHAPTER 29

*T*ristan felt so damned good, so sinfully hot and forbidden there against the junction of her thighs, Violet knew she could not deny him. Although her flesh was tender and her internal muscles were already clenching with anticipation that it would most likely hurt, she did as he said.

He's so beautiful like this. Demanding. Impatient, although a veneer of cool wariness shields his heart. He wants me. Me. Despite my flaws and ignorance of the ways between a man and a woman. How is it possible I've become a woman willing to give him anything he desires when he truly offers nothing in return?

When she was completely impaled upon his body, when her buttocks rested atop the muscles of his upper thighs, when she was so full of him it was hard to breathe, her bottom lip tugged between her teeth. He was huge, and her flesh protested the invasion.

It hurt more in this position. She felt stretched. Tiny. Powerless, especially when his large hands gripped her hips so tight that her skin would be surely marked by bruises. A tear formed, the salty drop clinging to her eyelashes.

But even though it burned like fire, there was a wicked

ecstasy in the way his shaft throbbed inside her. A pleasure found in the fullness that prickled her skin with awareness each time he shifted or breathed too deep a breath. This frenzy of sensations robbed her of all common sense.

She began to move and was startled when he stopped her.

"I know I am hurting you, kitten. You are so goddamn tiny; it can't help but hurt. I need you to be still for just a moment. I need you to take your time, wait until you are sure of your movements before you even make them. Let your body adjust to mine, and when you are ready, I want you to do whatever is necessary to make yourself feel good. Until the pain I'm causing right now is gone and forgotten."

"Yes, Tristan," she whispered. How would she know when to move? Or when she was ready? That first time, he'd made those decisions for her. Now, insecurity reared its head. "But I—"

With the pad of his thumb, he swiped away a tear from her cheek. "I want to feel you come around me. And I will wait until you decide when that happens. Understood?"

Violet nodded. Of course, the pain would ease. Just like it did before. And unimaginable pleasure would follow. As it had before.

The only agony she would experience after that was the heartache caused by his exit from her life.

For an eternity, or maybe only minutes, Violet was still. Absorbing him. Remembering him. Tucking away bits of Tristan she could savor for years. Every breath he took was an echo of her own. Every kiss he pressed to her skin, a mirror of those she wanted to give him. Every squeeze, every caress, every whisper, tied with ribbons and stored in her heart.

When her heart was full, she began moving. Slowly at first, learning how the undulation of her hips and the clench of her inner muscles made him groan with desire. She discovered that with his hands helping her rise and fall, she could also lean back and watch his cock plunge into her body. And when she needed something else, something *more,* something harder, Tristan took her hand, teaching her how to touch herself where they were joined. Showing that her own fingers could glide over the silky folds of her flesh. It felt her heart would pound from her chest as the pleasure spiked higher.

"Come for me, my wild Violet," he crooned darkly. "Come for me."

She watched him watching her, entranced by the intense, possessive light in the depths of his coffee-colored eyes. Her fingers moved as if commanded by him, his cock striking so deep it felt otherworldly, until something within her exploded without warning.

The climax washed over her in glorious waves. Violet shook from the sheer force of it. She tried hanging on, she truly did, but Tristan's hoarse shout of conquest dragged her even further along a glittering precipice. The waves battered her, draining her and then somehow filling her back up.

She let the rolling tide have her. Let Tristan take her until she was no longer sure if she was still on earth or had somehow plummeted into a world full of fire and brimstone.

Words that should never be spoken aloud flowed from her soul. Words she'd kept secret from this man.

"I love you, Tristan. I love you..."

With a sob, Violet fell forward against his neck, but he jerked her head back up. His mouth claimed hers with a ferocity that was both thrilling and confusing. A split second later, he yanked her up and off his shaft before crushing her against him, trapping his pulsating flesh and his seed between their bodies.

His groan, muffled by their kiss, reverberated through Violet. For a moment, she wondered what he might have said at the moment of his climax had their mouths not been sealed together.

Would he have whispered how much he cared for her?

Would he have declared her as his own?

Would you have confessed your love for me, Tristan?

The words meant nothing to him but everything to Violet.

Now, he had them and the last remaining piece of her heart.

~

AN AWKWARD SILENCE fell between them as Tristan once again cleaned away all evidence of their union. After lighting another lamp, he pulled on his trousers before gathering her belongings and placing them on the settee.

He tugged her hand until she stood, then began helping her dress, pulling her corset strings tight while she stood in docile surrender.

Violet's gaze, however, frantically bounced around the studio, committing every detail to memory.

This would be the last time she ever saw it, and her breath caught in a painful gasp at the thought.

"I'm sorry. Did I pull too hard?" Tristan's lips hovered over the curve of her neck. With the corset strings loose in his fingers, he waited for an answer, his breath warm and still carrying a tinge of whiskey.

The anguish devouring Violet made speech difficult; she shook her head.

Tristan's movements gentled just the same, his knuckles grazing her skin with such reverence she thought she might scream with the unfairness of it all. Her dress was settled over her head, twitched into place by his capable hands, and buttoned with lingering fingers.

My heart and virginity... all lost within the confines of this room. But I'll take this memory to keep me warm during a lifetime of frost in another man's bed. This was my choice. My choice, one I'll never regret—

Violet stilled. Her gaze widened, her pulse thumping with

alarming force as she tried making sense of what she saw across the room.

"Kitten? Are you all right?" Tristan inquired in a soothing manner, taking her by the shoulders and turning her toward him. He frowned at her distant stare, clucking his tongue. "Perhaps you require a brandy. Maybe something stronger. I have whiskey here some—"

Perplexed by the continued silence, he followed her gaze then stiffened. His fingers curled around her shoulders, then realizing he might be hurting her, he let go.

"What is that, Tristan?" Violet brushed past him, moving so slowly and deliberately it felt she was part of a strange dream.

"It's nothing," he replied with deceptive calm. No attempt was made at stopping her, but a quick glance over her shoulder revealed the tightness of Tristan's jaw. His eyes glittered with an emotion Violet could not identify.

She halted in front of the canvas propped on the biggest of the three easels. This painting was the largest, with the details just beginning to sharpen under the artist's brush.

But Violet recognized herself.

It was *her*, as Tristan had pointedly described his fantasy only weeks before. It was her, splayed on the table and naked. A sketched outline of a wine goblet and the almost transparent rendition of a crystal bowl concealed the small swell of a stomach and the junction of her thighs. An arm crossed over her breasts, and her head was propped in the opposite hand. Auburn red hair tumbled over ivory-hued shoulders, and her face —

Oh, God. Her face... A tiny smile redolent with lust illuminated that portion of the canvas. Mysterious and maddening, full lips tilted at the corner though reluctant to share a scandalous secret. And for her eyes, he'd given her dark amethyst jewels so deep and rich a man could drown in them.

A dizzying blend of love and lust shaped the delicate brushstrokes he'd lain. Possession tinged the colors. Denial honed the lines.

It was a masterpiece no one would ever lay eyes on.

In the real world, she was a timid, insecure wallflower.

But on Tristan's canvas, she was transformed.

She was a goddess of wildflowers, blooming where she pleased.

Violet touched her lips with trembling fingers. Were they truly that full and stained with blood? "Is this how you see me?"

For a long moment, she wasn't sure he would answer, but then Tristan sighed heavily.

"I told you once before, Violet. I see *you*."

He sounded almost weary, maintaining the distance between them as Violet's attention turned to the second painting.

This one was breezily innocent and closer to completion. It depicted her stretched on the green grass with her back against the trunk of a huge oak. Scattered about was a stack of books, an open basket with grapes spilling from it, and sleeping in her lap was a tiny orange kitten. A bird's nest was barely visible, almost hidden in the foliage of one high, sweeping oak branch. And beside it, a lovely, little red-breasted robin gazing down at the girl below.

The third painting was the forfeit from their wager.

It was Carrot by the Rose Garden fountain, the sunlight setting his fur aglow, a mischievous glint in his wide, green eyes. The fountain sparkled behind him, red roses tumbling everywhere. Her dear, little kitten sat posed with a sort of regal grandeur that reminded Violet of a lion surveying his kingdom. It was magnificent and whimsical, and it shattered her heart into a million pieces.

"Why?" Her voice cracked with the question. "Why have you painted me? I don't understand..."

Her heart thumped faster, waiting for his answer.

Waiting...

"I'm a painter," he replied at last in a voice cool and detached. "It's what I do for amusement. I paint all manner of subjects. Hell, whatever catches my attention at the moment might end up on a bit of canvas."

Violet whirled on him, choking back a sob at the subtle note of cruelty in his tone.

"And I... I caught your attention for the moment." *I will not cry in front of this man. I will not. I cannot.*

A strange, almost pained expression crossed Tristan's features before his shoulders lifted in a shrug. He had yet to don his shirt, and the movement made his bare chest ripple with muscles. "Of course. You are a beautiful woman. Why wouldn't I immortalize you on canvas?"

Violet's chin lifted. "Is that all you can say to me? Is that all there is to it? I interested you for a brief time because you thought I was beautiful. Temporary, but beautiful."

He scowled. "Should there be more to it than that? For God's sake. This—" He waved a hand toward the easels. "This is nothing. Do not look for hidden meanings behind a few brushstrokes, Violet. I painted a meadow full of lovely, but rather ordinary sheep once. Doesn't mean I formed a lasting affection for sheep."

Had he stabbed her with a hunting knife, slipped it right between her ribs while twisting the blade, he could not have hurt her more.

Head held high, Violet stalked past him to the settee and scooped up her shoes and gloves. She debated taking the time to don them, not relishing the idea of traversing the manor's halls in her stockinged feet. A sobering realization struck her; she could not spend a minute longer in this man's presence. There was the very real threat of bursting into sobs if she so much as glanced his way.

Making it to the door without a single teardrop sliding onto her cheeks was an accomplishment of massive proportions.

Pride that she could restrain her emotions fought against the despair welling within her. If she could maintain her composure for a few seconds more, that pride would triumph and she could escape. Tristan would never know how badly he had sliced her with his derisive comments.

The doorknob rotated in her hand. She needed solitude to cry every bit of the pain out of her soul. She needed to hide from the world until she gathered the tattered pieces of herself back together.

But… Violet hesitated.

She turned, expecting Tristan watched her departure with an air of relief. Instead, resignation stamped his features into harsh lines. A hint of sorrow, possibly imagined by her broken heart, darkened his eyes as he stared at her.

"I wish I didn't love you, Tristan. I wish I hadn't told you that I do," she choked out. "It is an emotion wasted on you. I only realize now that it has been that way for a long time. Of course, that is my fault, not yours. You did nothing to encourage my feelings for you in the beginning."

Her head tilted as she regarded him. Her voice, so tortured at first, became stronger. Invincible. Brave. "You should know that I feel sorry for you, Tristan. Because you believe you see people. That you see me, but that's not true. You cannot see what blinds you. And you waste precious time ignoring what is right before your eyes. I have the awful feeling you will spend the rest of your life in the dark. Surrounded by light and love and happiness but too afraid to share your own with someone."

Glancing about the room one last time, Violet gave Tristan a wobbly smile. Tears stung her eyes, despite her best efforts at keeping them contained.

"Goodbye, Tristan. I do hope you remember me fondly, when you remember me at all."

Slipping through the door, she closed it with a finality that crushed her heart.

Desperate to escape the terrible weight of her crumbling dreams, Violet broke into a run once she was in the corridor. Tears held back so bravely, now streamed in tiny rivers down her cheeks, forcing her to dash them away with the back of her hand.

She did not turn back, not even when a faint crashing sound echoed from behind Tristan's studio door.

She *couldn't* turn back. Not now.

After all, there was no longer anything or anyone in that room worth turning back for.

CHAPTER 30

*I*nside Tristan's head, tiny devils bashed and clanged with gleeful amusement. They showed no signs of stopping.

Persistent.

Explosive

Merciless.

Perhaps if I open my eyes, they will cease.

Or if he rolled over, shoved his head under the pillow, and ignored the excruciating pain, they might magically go away.

The banging noises increased.

Fuck.

Perhaps he deserved it. Yes, he deserved it. Every last bit of the agony ripping him apart from the moment Violet left was truly earned.

With a groan, Tristan flopped onto his back, flinging an arm over his eyes to block out the sliver of sunlight piercing the crack in the drapes. That sunbeam was as sharp as a fisherman's spear, and it stabbed him where he lay on his bed.

"Tristan?" The doorknob rattled, the key holding in the lock despite the fierce shaking it received. "Tristan?"

The devils had a voice. Verging on the hysterical, but a voice nonetheless. How interesting for the devils.

"Oh, God, please. Please open the door." A slight hesitation, then increased battering followed. "Are you there?"

The devils in his head sounded just like his sister. But that couldn't be right.

Celia pounded the door again. "Tristan!"

There was a desperate shrillness in her tone. Why? And why did his heart seize up with the immediate thought something was wrong with Violet?

Rolling from the bed onto the floor, Tristan landed in a half-drunken heap on his rear-end.

"Shit," he mumbled, giving an angry swipe at an empty decanter beside him. It once held a full measure of whiskey. Now, he watched it spin in a lazy half-circle on the hardwood floor before it stopped, the mouth facing him in an accusing manner.

With a growl, Tristan kicked it away so it joined the other one. The clatter of glass hitting glass was unnaturally loud in the quiet of the room.

Well, not so quiet. Celia still banged her fists on the door in a most impolite fashion.

Didn't she know he was nursing a heartache? And a headache to boot? Wasn't it obvious he should be left alone in his cave? Permitted to lick his wounds with no interference?

Getting up from the floor, he automatically reached for a robe before realizing the clothing from the night before was still draped over his body. The trousers were unbuttoned, his shirt hanging open haphazardly. He was without his shoes; however, they were nowhere to be seen. A vague remembrance of picking them up and throwing them in a rage at some insignificant painting inside his studio flitted across his consciousness.

"Tristan. I know you are there; I can hear you. For the love of God, please open the door. You must hurry before it's too late."

Too late? Too late for what? Whatever it is, it doesn't matter. Nothing matters anymore. Not now...

He buttoned his pants while stepping over the bottles, giving the ruined interior of his room a cursory glance. He was obviously in quite a state the previous night if the wreckage surrounding him now was any indication. Destroying his own personal belongings was incredibly immature, certainly, but it must have satiated some deep need within him.

Flinging open the door, he glared at Celia with a scowl so dark, so fierce, she actually stumbled back a step.

"What do you want?"

His voice sounded as though it had been keelhauled across the bow of an ancient pirate ship several times over. It was rough, raspy. Shredded from emotions he never thought he would experience. Raw with regret from the injury he had inflicted on a person so dear to his heart. He was exhausted following his attempts at drowning the pain that crushed him after she left.

It hadn't worked.

Celia stared, her eyes big and round and so similar to his own, it was like gazing into a mirror.

"Will you save her?" Tears streaked her cheeks; her eyes were red and puffy. She was garbed in an afternoon riding habit, a jaunty hat still fixed to her windblown curls. Mud splattered her boots. Celia would never traipse through the house with boots in that condition. "*Can* you save her?"

"What the devil are you talking about?"

"Violet ..." Her voice trembled.

Tristan grasped his sister by the shoulders, nearly lifting her off her feet. "What about her?"

Celia had never seemed so small, so defeated before. Her heart was breaking for some unknown reason.

Tristan's own heart began pounding with uneasy fear.

What the hell is going on?

"They will force her to wed," Celia sobbed. Damn if she wasn't making any sense.

Tristan's frown darkened his eyes to a shade nearly ebony in color. "Who is forcing her? Wed to whom?"

"Her parents… they arrived this morning. Someone accused Violet of spending her nights in Lord Gadley's rooms. This person claims they caught Violet and Gadley in a romantic liaison in the conservatory. And that you, you saw them together, too."

She rubbed her arms when Tristan set her down, eyes panicked with concern and puzzled that her brother was in such a state of dishabille.

The entire day had passed while he rolled about in a drunken stupor. Who knew what hell Violet had faced during that time?

Rubbing a hand over his throbbing forehead, Tristan barked, "Christ! What time is it now?"

"Just after four o'clock. They've been in Father's study for over an hour. Setting terms for her marriage to Gadley. It was thought you were with us during our afternoon ride, but when Father discovered you had not gone, he sent me to find you right away. It can't be too late to save her. I refuse to believe it's too late. Until they take her away from Darby Meadows, there is still a chance, Tristan."

Tristan buttoned his shirt, raking a hand through his tumble of hair to bring it to some order. Turning his back on his sister, he quickly tucked the shirt into his trousers.

Realizing what those actions meant, Celia jumped to help.

Pouring water in the washbasin, she wet a cloth so he could wipe his face down, and put toothpowder on the brush. She then ran to the armoire and dragged out a pair of boots.

"These are lies, Tristan. Violet despises William Gadley. There is only one person she loves, and I do not need to say aloud who that man is..." Celia's voice trailed off, unsure what else to say on the subject. Then she shook herself. "Hurry, Tristan. *Hurry!*"

In less than two minutes, Tristan was ready. For what, he wasn't precisely sure, but quite possibly his task would be saving the fair maiden from the clutches of a villain. Violet should be free to choose her own husband. Not forced into marriage as a result of falsehoods and the greed of her parents.

He didn't know how he could save her without risking his own neck, but he would try his damnedest.

TRISTAN WAS SHOCKED to find Nicholas sprawled in a chair outside his father's study.

The duke watched his approach with hooded, green eyes, his manner languid and deceptively relaxed. But that was all for show. Tristan knew his friend possessed the instinct and quick reactions of a feral wolf.

When Tristan reached him, Nicholas unfurled himself. He used his body as a means of blocking the door while gripping Tristan's shoulder with one hand. He squeezed it tight with warning.

"Nothing inside that room is your concern, Longleigh."

"What do you mean? Of course, it is—" Tristan replied, tersely.

Nicholas's advice was genuine. "As a man avoiding the state of matrimony, you should tread lightly before placing yourself in the midst of these particular negotiations."

Raised voices came from inside the room. A woman began crying, the sobs seeping through the oak door.

Both men tensed. Then Tristan shoved the duke's hand aside. "Get out of my way, Richeforte."

Nicholas regarded Tristan for a moment, his thoughts unreadable. Together, the two men had cut quite a swath through London, enjoying actresses and dancers and mistresses aplenty until Nicholas fell for his duchess. The duke had always been an expert at concealing his inner emotions with icy control while Tristan perfected the art of the carefree bachelor, hiding behind the lighthearted façade.

Tristan wondered if he could keep that same lifestyle now. He didn't think he could. It would be so much harder to hide now.

Concern for Violet's wellbeing etched his features.

"She needs me, Richeforte."

Nicholas's lip twitched with a ghost of a smile.

"I've no doubt about that." The duke stepped aside with a slight bow. "Fair warning, however. Should you go in, do not expect to come out without a wife."

"Don't be ridiculous," Tristan snapped, his hand on the doorknob of his father's study. "This is likely a misunderstanding easily explained."

Pushing through the door on that statement, he shoved it shut behind him with more force than was necessary. His gaze immediately sought out Violet as the occupants of the room collectively turned his way.

Violet was seated near the large windows on a settee upholstered in dark blue brocade. She was a ray of sunshine despite eyes swollen from crying and a face so pale she appeared ill. Her curvy form was immaculately clothed in a gown of periwinkle blue, all that glorious flame-sparked hair he'd run his fingers through just the night before now scraped into a bun so severe not a single tendril escaped.

She was not crying at the moment. At the sight of him, her gaze lit up with an undisguised joy before it hardened and grew distant. Tilting her chin higher, blood red lips in a tight line, she simply glared as though he were the reason behind this madness.

It was Violet's mother who wept. Lady Everstone wrung her hands in distress, occasionally blotting her cheeks with a silk handkerchief. Lord Everstone, standing beside the chair his wife currently occupied, wore a thunderous expression directed at his daughter and no one else.

William Gadley stood with an arm propped nonchalantly on the fireplace mantle. A sharpness glinted in his eyes for a moment, but then a sigh of bored elegance masked any irritation at Tristan's intrusion.

Tristan's mother, Lady Darby, was perched on the settee beside Violet, close enough that their skirts touched. She held the girl's hand as though offering some manner of support, while his father, seated at the massive desk from which he ran his earldom, rubbed his forehead.

Tristan recognized the gesture as one of frustration.

"How fortuitous that you've finally arrived, Longleigh," William said with a cold smile. "You are the additional witness required to put this matter to rest."

"Witness?" Tristan's eyebrow arched high. Glancing again at Violet, he was disturbed by the fact her stare did not soften even the slightest.

"Yes, witness," Lord Everstone boomed. Directing his ire toward Violet, he swore, "Damnation, girl. Must we bring forth every person on this estate with evidence of your inappropriate behavior? There are surely more than the two we know of."

His enraged blustering had no effect on his daughter. She simply refused to look at him, her gaze remaining locked on Tristan. Tristan's mother, bottom lip caught between her teeth to stop its trembling, glared at Lord Everstone in disgust, then patted Violet's hand as though it would soothe away the older man's harshness.

"What a piece of baggage you are! My own daughter! I've

raised you up a proper young lady, and just see the gratitude you show. That you are capable of such outrageous behavior with this man is a scandal we shall never live down." Violet's mother sobbed into her handkerchief.

Tristan froze in place. *Have we been found out? Is that why they rush to marry her off to Gadley, so scandal may be avoided?*

"You will marry Lord Gadley, or by God, I'll disown you," her father threatened.

Violet's eyes shifted away from Tristan at that. She stared at her father as though she were sizing him up for battle, before shrugging her shoulders.

"What coin shall I bring to your empty pocket then, Father? Not a farthing, I'm afraid."

William laughed. "You're not without some value, my dear. There is the ungodly amount of funds already paid to Lord Everstone which grants me the pleasure of claiming you as my bride. Come now, Violet. Admit what we've done. There is no sense in fighting the inevitable."

Violet's stormy gaze settled on William. "I'll not begin a marriage on a lie, my lord. We both know we've not shared intimacies in any form."

"And how do you explain my possession of these very distinct hairpins, sweetling? You watched me pick them up in the conservatory." With a grin, he reached into his coat pocket.

Two glittery hairpins decorated with paste-jeweled violets lay in his extended palm.

Tristan could not believe what he was hearing. Did they honestly believe Violet had slept with this man?

"Son? I hesitate asking this of you, knowing what the answer will likely be." Lord Darby waved a hand at Tristan. "Can you collaborate Lady Fiona Blackerby's account? Tell us what you saw in the conservatory last night."

"Lady Fiona..." Tristan could not conceal his confusion. "What the devil does she have to do with any of this?"

Lady Darby's frown was compiled of great disappointment and sadness. "She has personally witnessed Violet leaving Lord Gadley's room late at night on several occasions since his arrival. He does have Violet's hairpins, which her mother confirms as hers. And last night, Lady Fiona revealed you and she entered the conservatory together where you encountered Violet and Lord Gadley in a… compromising situation."

Tristan glanced at the man, fists clenching tight to see his smirk of victory.

It was true Violet lost some of her hairpins inside the conservatory. Tristan scooped two of them up himself; they were in his studio along with the others.

Was it possible Fiona went searching for him last night? If she visited the conservatory, she would have seen Tristan and Violet in their impassioned embrace. Perhaps she found the hairpins after they departed and then involved Gadley in this scheme. It was a plan ensuring they would both get what they wanted.

Violet shot daggers at him with her eyes, and Tristan immediately knew her thoughts.

Finding Violet there instead of Fiona, he had simply used the most convenient female.

"Not a word of that drivel is the truth," Tristan said slowly, watching Violet's reaction. "Violet was not in the conservatory with Gadley. And I assure you she *never* visited his room for any purpose, at any time of the day or night."

"I've a witness who says otherwise, and Violet's personal items that prove it," Gadley scoffed. "I'm surprised at you, Longleigh. Lady Fiona looks so much like the Duchess of Richeforte and you seem well-suited. Why would you contradict the woman you really want? After all, there is your secret engagement, although it's certainly not a secret now. I do hope you'll do the honorable thing and marry the lady as quickly as I intend to marry Violet."

Tristan's blood boiled. Clearly, Gadley and Fiona cooked up this plot together. It was perfect, really. Marriage to Gadley meant a quick disposal of Violet while a path into Tristan's bed was efficiently cleared for Fiona.

And he would be tricked into standing at the altar.

The scheming little bitch...

In three strides, Tristan crossed the room, seizing Violet's hand from his mother's. She did not resist when he hauled her up onto her feet.

Cupping her chin in his palm Tristan stared deep into her eyes.

"Who was with you in the conservatory, Violet?" He snarled the words, growing more furious when her mouth remained a line of stubbornness. "Tell them."

"I was not in the conservatory last night, Lord Longleigh." Her voice was cool, the denial as smooth as her brow. She hung limp in his grasp.

Tristan almost shook her in his frustration. "Damn you, Violet. Do you want to marry him? Do you?"

Fear of marriage to William sparked like distant lightning in her eyes before it was shuttered. "Of course not."

"You will do as you're told, Violet. Your failure will result in consequences you can't possibly imagine," Lord Everstone growled.

Lady Darby interjected softly, "Oh, my dear girl. You always have a home with us." With a fierce glare for Violet's mother, she added, "How can you allow your daughter to be bartered in such a manner, Eloise?"

Violet hung in Tristan's grasp, giving no response to either her father's threatening words or his mother's sympathy.

Tristan understood at last. She would sacrifice herself, her reputation, and her honor rather than force Tristan into claiming her for his own. She'd made a promise she would never scheme nor lie to become part of his life. And that promise was kept by withholding the truth. If he only agreed with her statement, he would be free of her.

There was no doubt in Tristan's mind that Violet's parents would forcibly marry her to any man who paid their price.

"I say, Longleigh, I must object to you holding my fiancée in such a manner." William pocketed the hairpins and withdrew a snuff box from the same pocket inside his coat.

After pinching a generous amount and inhaling it, he pointed an index finger at Violet. "Violet, once we are wed, this outrageous behavior will cease. I won't have my wife whoring herself out to any man willing to fuck her beneath my very nose."

With the roar of a furious lion, Tristan released Violet and lunged toward William, intent on destroying the man. Two quick jabs to the man's face and one to his stomach occurred in a matter of seconds.

Somewhere in the room came the sound of his mother's shocked cry, and Lord Darby's chair scraping as he quickly stood. Lady Everstone let out an alarmed scream.

Violet's moan of despair was the first sign of emotion she'd shown other than disgust.

"No, Tristan. Don't. Please…"

But Tristan could not stop.

Holding the usually elegant man by the throat, his hands crushing the precise folds of his cravat, Tristan bit out, "I was the one kissing her, holding her, Gadley. I've caressed every inch of her soft skin. My lips discovered all her secrets and destroyed any resistance. And my hands sent those goddamn hairpins scattering everywhere by the conservatory fountain. I've taken everything, each little piece of her. Because she gave herself to me. *Me*. Not you. Anyone but you."

CHAPTER 31

"That was a foolish thing to do."

Tristan whirled on Violet, brow furrowing with her quiet declaration.

"And what would you have me do, kitten?" he bit out between clenched teeth.

"Let me go."

Violet watched his eyes darken into stormy pools of frustration.

"Impossible." Raking a hand through his hair, Tristan grimaced in sudden pain. Shaking his fingers out, he flexed them in an attempt at easing the ache. Violet wondered if he might have broken his hand on Gadley's jaw.

He restlessly paced the empty room, muttering beneath his breath before lifting a decanter from the side cabinet in the corner. Liquid splashed into a tumbler, and he downed the alcohol in one quick swallow.

Only the two of them occupied Lord Darby's study at the moment, and Violet nervously regarded Tristan as complete awareness of what just transpired began seeping in.

The ramifications of disobeying her father would not be pleasant.

Earlier, when Nicholas burst in, it had taken him some effort in prying Tristan off William where they grappled and rolled on the floor. Once they were separated, Violet's father escorted the man away from the room, hurrying past Celia and Grace and a crowd of curious onlookers who had gathered in the hall.

Appearing perilously close to fainting, Lady Everstone retreated to her rooms, still sobbing into her handkerchief and aided by an unsympathetic Lady Darby.

Lord Darby had turned to Tristan before leaving the room as well, saying rather sternly that he expected his son would do the honorable thing.

Whatever that statement implied, Violet had no wish to find out. But surely, Lord Darby did not think Tristan would actually marry *her*.

"You will be free of me. And I will be free of you," Violet said, hoping the sorrow deep inside her did not leach out through the words.

"Fiona wants you badly," she continued. "So desperately that she will lie to have you. And had I not intruded in the conservatory; you would not be having this conversation with me now. If you would admit our relationship has reached the end of its tether, Tristan, we could move on. We knew when this began it could not last."

"I am expected to let you go without a second thought," A scowl marred his features, "so you may sacrifice yourself? For what purpose? For whose benefit? That animal who insulted you by calling you a whore? You know as well as I do that your father will not stop until you are someone's wife and the debts his irresponsibility created have been paid."

"They cannot force me into anything." Holding onto that stubborn belief was probably naïve, but Violet did not care.

Tristan laughed., "They can and they will, Violet. Let me handle this in the manner I see fit."

"Fiona was waiting in my room last night when I left you. She said before she could meet you in the conservatory to discuss your secret engagement, I intercepted you. And after throwing myself at you, you took what was freely offered. As any man would." Violet's smile was derisive. "She called me a whore, which is no worse than being a wallflower, I suppose."

Tristan advanced on Violet so quickly she retreated from simple reflex. But the attempted evasion was of no use. Both her shoulders were within his grasp before she could gasp in surprise.

"Violet, utter one more word regarding Fiona Blackerby and her vicious lies, and I shall turn you across my knee," he growled. "If kisses and caresses do not convince you of my interest in you, I'm positive a spanking will do the trick."

"You would beat me?" Violet cried out.

"A spanking is not a beating." Tristan pulled her in closer, tighter. "It will clarify matters for you."

The heat of his body was scorching, and Violet realized suddenly just how exhausted he appeared; how bloodshot his eyes were. Notwithstanding his tussle with William, Tristan was disheveled, his cologne a faint memory beneath the remnants of new and old whiskey.

"I don't deserve to be treated as property." Violet's chin rose higher. "Gadley swore he would punish me for any defiance. I see you are no different."

"The difference, Violet, is your value to me. It is without price, and I will pay your father's debt if it means saving you from William Gadley," he muttered, cupping her chin in the palm of his hand. "And property or not, you would be safer with me. Do you understand what I am saying?"

"I do." Unsuccessful in jerking away from his grasp, she glared at him. "Since I am now ruined for polite society, you shall pay to have me occupy your bed. And I must endure physical punishment as proof you prefer me as a mistress rather than Fiona as a wife. In the end, you would own me as you would a herd of sheep."

The taunt was a reminder of his cruel words the night before, and he winced to hear them.

"St. Simon's Cross, but you are the most stubborn woman I've ever come across," Tristan swore roughly. "Have you not heard a word I've said?" He gave her a little shake.

"Of course, I heard you. You don't love me." Violet's manner was one of stone. "And we've already established how foolish I am to have fallen in love with you."

"Neither do you love Gadley, but that was no obstacle when you were to become his wife," he shot back. "So, here it is, Violet. The only solution I can offer is to marry you. The question remains, however, if you will marry *me*."

VIOLET DRESSED for dinner that evening with grim determination.

She would not hide in her room. She'd done nothing wrong, other than following what her heart demanded. The only remorse she could muster was a result of falling in love with Tristan. Their intimate moments shared no part of her regret.

A soft knock interrupted Bridgett's buttoning of Violet's gown.

"Shall I answer, milady?" the maid inquired with a concerned glance toward the door.

Violet nodded. "If it is Mother again, you may let her in."

Earlier, she'd been too raw and emotional to engage in an argument. She merely listened as Mother cried and wailed and, in the process, the jaw-dropping extent of their family's debt was laid bare.

Violet could hardly believe the amounts were true. The knowledge made her physically ill. Worse was realizing her mother considered her nothing but a pawn used for gain.

Violet expected Father would remain emotionally detached. He'd never shown any affection for his own daughter, but discovering both parents cared not one whit for her wellbeing was a shock.

Misplaced sentiments revolving around duty and loyalty to the family name had ensured Violet's cooperation for too long. Now, she would do as she pleased. And damn the consequences.

Steeling herself for an ugly confrontation, Violet watched Bridgette crack the door open. Murmuring around the door-jamb to the person seeking entry, the maid finally stepped back with a tiny curtsy.

Grace breezed into the room, clad in a shimmering gown of dark bronze silk. Gloves dyed a precise match completed the ensemble and, on her wrist, a gold bracelet crafted with tiny bees and sprigs of heather sparkled.

The duchess smiled at Violet, coming forward to take her hands.

"I've no wish to intrude but would it be possible that we speak privately?"

"Of course, Your Grace." Violet waited until Bridgette exited the room and motioned for Grace to join her near the fireplace.

Carrot emerged from his favorite hiding place behind the floor-length drapes. He streaked toward Grace, his funny, crooked tail held high, the end curled as tight as a question mark.

"Please, you know you may call me by my given name." Grace scooped the creature up and nuzzled him. "Even if it is not the proper thing."

Carrot meowed, butting his head against Grace's chin. Violet could not help but smile. Her standoffish kitten rarely showed affection to strangers.

Once they were perched upon a rose-hued settee, Grace set Carrot down between them, laughing softly when he began attacking the tassels of a small accent pillow. "I've heard the story of how you acquired this adorable creature."

"Longleigh remains unconvinced of Carrot's sweet nature. He encouraged me to leave him behind in the stables, so I imagine his view on the subject is hardly complimentary." A pang of jealousy nipped Violet as she wondered when Tristan and Grace found time to discuss her kitten.

"Celia's version was very amusing." Grace's tone was understanding. It was as though she knew Violet's terseness could be soothed once it was clarified she'd not engaged Tristan in a private conversation.

Ashamed of her own suspicious nature, Violet blushed. "Forgive me for the sharpness of my words. I'm afraid this afternoon has set me on edge just a bit."

"That is understandable," Grace sighed. "What a tangle that was! The duke is nursing a sore jaw, courtesy of a stray swing by Tristan. Oh, of course, it was not done purposefully, and Tristan apologized profusely. Were you aware Lord Gadley was forced to leave Darby Meadows? It's true. Before he and your father locked themselves away in the library, Tristan tasked Nicholas with making sure that man was escorted off the property."

Violet's lips tightened. "What could the viscount and my father have to discuss? I've not agreed to marry Longleigh."

"Which is why I've come to talk with you." Grace took Violet's hands. "It must seem awkward, my giving you advice, especially since everyone knows Tristan pursued me before my marriage. His interest was misplaced then, and I hope it's clear he has no romantic inclinations for me, or any other woman for that matter."

Violet's head tilted in confusion.

Grace giggled in her enchanting way. "My goodness, that certainly did not come out the way I intended. Obviously, he is interested in one woman. That man is completely entranced by you, Violet. I swear, when he speaks of you, or if your name is mentioned, his entire being lights up. It's the same adoration I see when I catch Nicholas staring at me." A dreamy expression drifted over her features.

"Richeforte loves you madly. It can't possibly be the same, Grace." Violet stroked Carrot's soft fur. She hoped Grace would not notice the sadness in her voice. "It isn't the same. I know it's not."

"Trust me, my dear. Tristan Buchanan loves you. Having experienced the fullest depths of that emotion with the duke, I recognize the signs. He adores you." Grace's caramel-hued eyes sparkled with kindness. "Do not throw away a lifetime of joy in sacrifice to your pride."

"Too many obstacles block a happy conclusion to our association. My parents and their debt, the extent of which I've only learned a few hours ago. There's Lord Gadley." Violet's voice turned bitter. "And Lady Fiona, of course."

Grace's laughter was sly, her eyes glinting mischievously. "There's no need to concern yourself over that one. Not only have I given Fiona the cut direct, but Richeforte informed Lady Blackerby that should her daughter even glance in Longleigh's direction, he would call in Lord Blackerby's gambling debts. No one dares question my husband when it comes to such matters. Indeed, even I've found it best not to pry."

"Perhaps if Tristan himself dissuaded Lady Fiona …" Violet started almost angrily before taking a deep breath. "Oh, what does it matter? Grace, I appreciate your kindness and that of the duke, but the fact remains Longleigh has no wish to marry. While I concede he may not want Fiona as his bride, he certainly does not want me, either. He has said as much several times. He will never sacrifice himself for me. Or for love. He only presses the matter now as a way of appeasing his father."

"You've much to learn of Tristan's nature, Violet." Grace's

head shook with exasperation for Violet's stubbornness. "There is not a soul alive capable of making that man do something against his wishes. Lord Darby will be very happy to see him wed, but Tristan follows his own course. *You*, Violet, you are his course."

Placing her arm around Violet's shoulders, Grace gave her a warm squeeze. "I suspect Tristan said some hurtful things to you. Unfortunately, men can be blind to what is in their hearts, and that makes them behave quite stupidly. I told him once he would find his own true love someday. Now, he just has to believe it. Please, Violet. I know it is difficult to see, but do not deny the love you share with him. You desperately need each other."

CHAPTER 32

$\mathcal{N}$erves jangling with anxiety, Violet entered the dining room once the majority of guests had already taken their seats.

Tristan and Lord Everstone were not in attendance. Lady Fiona and Violet's own mother were also conspicuously missing, although Lady Blackerby was there. The older woman gave Violet a tiny, apologetic nod before glancing away in quiet shame. No doubt her daughter's actions had caused much consternation.

Violet fully expected Fiona would be present. If nothing else, the other girl could gloat over Violet's disgrace.

The meal's seating arrangements would surely result in further gossip. It was certainly a dramatic statement, and with it, there could be no doubt as to Violet's acceptance into the Buchanan family.

"Here you are, my dear," Lord Darby said in a jovial manner over the chatter of guests. "Here is your seat."

It was one of honor, her placement to the right of Lord Darby's at the head of the table. Celia was seated beside her while Grace occupied the chair on Lord Darby's left.

Violet gave Lady Darby a tremulous smile. Gratitude filled her heart until it actually ached as she slid into the chair the elderly lord indicated.

From his own seat beside Lady Darby at the opposite end, Richeforte gave Violet a pleased nod of approval. For Grace, he had a wicked smile. A slight bruise shadowed the duke's jawline, but it did not detract from his darkly golden handsomeness.

Violet wondered if Tristan's own bruises might be oddly attractive. Not that she should care, but it remained a source of contemplation as the servants carried in the first course.

Between the two table ends, guests resumed conversations, and somehow, the atmosphere was both light and lively. Henry Bowman regarded her from where he sat across the table and a few seats away. The puppy-like sadness of his gaze was so pronounced, Violet squirmed in discomfort.

"Poor Lord Bowman," Celia said with a low laugh. "Someone should blot away the drool on his chin if he intends on staring at you like that all evening. He is elated over the news you are no longer marrying Lord Gadley but devastated you are also off the marriage mart. He won't dare approach you, though. Not with Tristan laying claim to you like a medieval warlord."

Violet speculated if avoidance of that afternoon's scandal resulted from Tristan's willingness to settle insults with his fists, Lady Darby's skill as a hostess, or Richeforte's incredible sphere of influence amongst the *ton*.

Perhaps it was a combination of all three.

Celia leaned closer, whispering from behind a glass of wine, "Your father is still making quite the fuss behind those library doors. I can't imagine Tristan will allow it to go on much longer. He is exhibiting an unusual amount of patience."

Violet's fingers tensed, gripping the stem of her goblet before relaxing. "It is of no concern to me."

The exasperated noise Celia made in the back of her throat was covered by a sip of wine. "We both know that's not true.

Grace told me you refused Tristan's proposal. Why, Violet? It's what you've wanted for so very long." The look she gave her friend was puzzled. "I'm afraid I don't understand."

"It is what I wanted," Violet admitted. Glancing around the table, she hoped others did not pay close attention to their conversation. "But it is not what Tristan wanted. And I'll not be bound for life to a man who—"

The doors to the dining room suddenly flew open as though buffeted by the winds of a cyclone.

A cacophony of voices lifted in excitement, and shock filled the room. All attention turned to the man who paused in the doorway. A stern, yet determined expression contorted his features as he sought Violet out amongst the dinner guests.

When he found her bracketed by Lord Darby and Celia, his dark eyes softened.

And Violet realized her earlier speculation was correct.

Sporting his own bruised jawline and a small cut above one eye, which had escaped her notice earlier that day, Tristan was rakishly, dangerously attractive. Donned in a suit coat the color of dark coal, and a snowy white shirt and cravat, he had obviously found time to clean himself up following their last, brief conversation

The entire room became glaringly silent as Tristan stalked toward Violet. He came to a halt, standing between her and Lord Darby.

"Father." Tristan's head bowed in respect. Bending slightly at the waist, he then acknowledged Lady Darby at the opposite end of the impossibly long table. "Mother. If you will pardon my intrusion, it is imperative I speak privately with Lady Violet."

Lord Darby harrumphed. Catching Violet's eye, he gave her a wink while still cutting through a slice of roasted pheasant. "Won't you have a bite of dinner first?"

Violet's hands twisted in her lap. Beneath the table's edge

where no one could see, she had practically destroyed a lovely, delicately embroidered napkin.

Forcing her hands to still themselves, she congratulated herself when she reached for her wine goblet and there was no sign of anxiety. Taking a deliberate sip, she did not look at him. How could she when his very presence was a manifestation of shattered hopes, romantic dreams, and unrequited love?

How she managed to appear so coolly unaffected was a mystery even to herself.

His cologne, subtle and yet so frankly masculine it could be an aphrodisiac, tickled Violet's nose. She remembered pressing her face against his bare chest and breathing deep of his scent only hours ago. Remembered despising the fact her skin smelled of him when she returned to her room earlier that very morning.

Setting the wine glass down, she was dismayed that her hand shook a little. When she quickly returned it to her lap, Celia reached over and gave Violet's fingers an encouraging squeeze.

"No, thank you, Father." Tristan shifted closer. "This conversation with Lady Violet cannot wait."

Before Violet could draw a steady breath, his large, warm hand cupped her elbow. The crackle of energy when he touched her was nearly palpable.

"My apologies, Your Grace. Ladies. Gentlemen. Mother." Then with the slightest amount of pressure, Tristan tugged Violet until she had little choice but to rise from her chair. It was either go willingly or be dragged.

"Come with me, Violet."

When Violet hesitated, prepared to dig in her heels, the only word Tristan uttered was almost contrite, although laced with a touch of steel.

"Please."

~

Tristan held Violet's hand as he led her down the corridor until they reached the library.

Ushered into the room first, Violet's body tightened with apprehension. Were her parents waiting there? Ready to force her into marriage against her will? Perhaps Tristan had reached an agreement with Father, one where restitution for taking her virginity was secondary to the money Gadley had already put forth.

It would make sense... Tristan may turn his back with a clear conscience while Gadley retains his right to our family name. And Father emerges with more funds than he dreamed possible.

"They are not here, Violet."

Tristan's quiet statement accompanied the door closing with the weight of his back leaning against it. In the most casual manner, he crossed his arms and watched her reaction.

"You reached an agreement with Father?" Damn her own trepidation and the way it made her voice tremble.

Tristan's eyes narrowed on her. "I have. It wasn't easily done."

Violet swallowed hard. "What I gave you freely last night must seem a terrible bargain today. I promised you no demands. No obligations. No responsibility. I never imagined our arrangement would come to light. Father has no right to make you pay for my stupidity."

"I agreed to his demands, Violet."

Her heart sank. *No. More than that.* It felt as though wolves were ripping her to pieces while her heart still beat inside her chest.

Violet briefly closed her eyes, praying she would not be ill.

"Oh? How much is a wallflower's virginity worth these days?" Her demeanor was one of resignation. With Tristan's payment to her father, she was well and truly trapped. "I ask out of simple curiosity."

"Violet." Tristan frowned at her question. "Seventy-five

thousand pounds, if you must know. And payment of the note Gadley currently holds against the London townhome."

Violet's laugh was bitter. "My father should have shown a bit of mercy, considering I threw myself at your feet. He took advantage of you. You see, only my marriage to Gadley will release the sizeable lien against Everstone Hall. It will take the devil himself to erase that." Squaring her shoulders as if preparing for battle, she said, "I should go now and pack my belongings. Father will want me delivered to Lord Gadley without delay."

In less than five strides, Tristan crossed the room. Taking Violet by the shoulders, he forced her to face him.

"Unless you indicate otherwise, I won't allow either of those two men anywhere near you. That goes for your mother, too, as much as I despise that being necessary," he said fiercely, giving her a little shake as though it would make his point more effective. "And if I must pay more so that you are released from their schemes, I will."

To Violet's shame, tears clouded her vision. "This is impossible. When I am handed over, my role in all of this will be complete."

"What the devil are you talking about? Hand you over—" Tristan swore beneath his breath. "I gave your father what he demanded. If the bastard wants more, I shall oblige him. Everstone will have no claim on you. Neither shall Gadley, even if he insists you still belong to him."

"I belong to no one," Violet said almost woodenly.

"Be that as it may, your parents will no longer control your future. Do you understand? You shall have your freedom."

"At what price, Tristan? What shall I give you because of my father's greed?"

Tristan's jaw ticked with frustration. "I do not want anything that you are unwilling to give. And what I want most of all, you cannot give me. *Will* not give me."

"What more do you want?" she cried.

"You. As my wife."

"You will emerge empty-handed from this bargain," Violet snapped.

"I would pay a thousand times more for the honor of untaming you, Violet. And I will pay any price to keep William Gadley from you."

She stared up at him. This generosity was not because Tristan loved her; it was simply an instrument to be used against another man.

Violet's knees wobbled with that realization. She sagged in his arms.

Tristan caught her easily, an arm snaking around her waist so she was kept aloft. He held her so tight Violet found it difficult to breathe.

But she didn't want to breathe. She wanted to crawl away and nurse her wounded heart. She wanted to cry. And fight. And rage.

And she wanted more than life itself to hear this man admit that he loved her.

CHAPTER 33

The restlessness Tristan could not shake sent him to his studio where he spent yet another sleepless night.

He worked until the early morning hours. The portrait of her kitten, of which he'd given the whimsical title *"Carrots and Roses"* was nearly complete. And *"A Feast of Violets"* was entering the secondary phase where he focused on intricate details, adding all the little touches that would make it come alive.

It was an hour or two before dawn when he finally laid his brushes aside, his thoughts consumed by Violet. He could not stop worrying about her when she appeared so despondent upon leaving him behind in the library. Her responses to his queries were dull. Listless. And each time he tried to touch her, she skillfully evaded the attempts until he finally gave up.

She is simply overwhelmed by the events of the past few days. It's been a total upheaval of her life after others directed her future for so long.

The niggling thought he might be guilty of controlling her as well was shoved aside.

He *was* doing what was best for Violet. And that meant eliminating Gadley. Already bleeding from a broken nose, the man's ranting that Violet would still be his only resulted in additional injury while being escorted off Darby Meadows property. Nicholas, with an examination of his own hand, had related the man's ribs were harder than they should be.

Doing what was best for Violet also involved cutting all ties binding her to her parasitic parents. Already, Tristan had made arrangements that any lien against the Everstone estate was fully paid. And if her father could not stand on his own two feet after having his debts covered, at the very least, Violet would no longer serve as a sacrifice to greed.

Tristan would soon give her a type of freedom unlike anything she'd ever known before. It was risky, however. There was a monstrous chance she would like flying on her own. Flying without him around to catch her.

Violet could have independence on her own.

Or she could have freedom and a life with him.

A life where he would adore, cosset, and spoil her until he took his last breath on earth.

Stepping into the corridor leading to his bedchamber, he was surprised when he encountered his sister.

Dressed in the same clothes she'd worn to dinner, Celia heaved a sigh of relief. She advanced toward him; her arms crossed in obvious frustration.

"There you are! I don't know why I didn't think to look in your studio."

"Celia, what the devil are you doing up at this hour of the morning? Have you even been to bed?"

"I've been with Violet, if you must know. And now, you must go to her as well," Celia said with narrowed eyes.

"Is she all right? She was rather… distant when I last saw her."

"No. She's not all right. Her mother… Well, I will let her explain it all. Just go to her, Tristan. She needs you. And for God's sake, *listen* to her."

Tristan was already brushing past Celia when she called out to his rapidly retreating form. He did not stop to consider what she meant by her instructions that he listen to Violet.

Celia's next words, floating down the hallway after him, made little sense either.

"She's your destiny, Tristan. *Your* destiny. And you are hers."

CHAPTER 34

Tristan tapped on Violet's door.

Would she answer?

He wasn't sure, but there was light emerging from the sliver of space between the bottom of the door and the floor.

His knuckles rapped on the wood again.

If she doesn't answer in a few seconds, I will go.

Violet's voice was low, muffled by the thickness of the oak between them. "Who is it?"

Tristan's heart pounded as though he'd raced to London and back on foot. "It is me, kitten. Will you open the door?"

Her hesitation broke his heart. When had the breach of trust occurred? When precisely had she begun distrusting him? Was it that moment in his studio? When he denied his feelings for her...

The lock rattled before the door cracked open a tiny bit. He could see she wore a gown of white cambric. It fluttered around her with a billowy softness, like a cloud of angel wings. She held Carrot to her chest, and the kitten regarded him with an imperialistic, yet sleepy air. At least the beast wasn't hissing at him.

"What do you want, Tristan?"

I want to tell you I love you. I want to tell you I need you. But I'm afraid, deathly afraid that you no longer love me. And while I deserve that, it will break me.

"I just encountered my sister roaming the halls at five o'clock in the morning, and she said you needed me. I thought you might be ill." Disappointment with his own lack of bravery had Tristan's jaw clenching tight

Violet tucked her chin closer to the top of Carrot's head. "Oh. Well, I'm fine. Really. Just fine. Goodnight, Tristan. Or is it good morning? I'm a little topsy-turvy at the moment, so you must choose the one that applies."

A funny hiccup escaped her as she went to close the door. But as light from the corridor lit her features, Tristan saw evidence of tears trailing down her pale cheeks.

"You're crying. Why are you crying? Are you hurt? In pain?" Firing questions quicker than she could possibly answer, Tristan laid a palm on the door, preventing its closure. "Celia said something about Lady Everstone..."

"It is nothing. Speaking with my mother was a mistake, as some conversations inevitably are meant to be. Do not concern yourself, Tristan."

"It is my concern," he breathed. "I swore you would not have to see them again if you did not wish it. Was she cruel to you? Abusive? I'll take a strap to her myself if she..."

"It was nothing I didn't expect from her." Violet sighed heavily, swinging the door open just a bit more. "You may as well come in before anyone sees you lurking in the corridor. And close the door."

A single lamp burned low beside her bed, and she turned toward it without sparing him another glance.

Tristan hesitated before entering her bedchamber. Violet's demeanor, one of distraction and heartache, concerned him a great deal.

She climbed into bed, still clutching Carrot, who purred so robustly the sound rumbled around the room.

"What did she say that upset you?" Damn her parents and their selfishness. A horsewhip applied with great enthusiasm would do the pair of them a world of good.

Violet sighed, waving a hand as if bruising the heart of their only child was a trivial matter. "That I am a horrible daughter. A weed that ultimately served no purpose. Mother says my lack of faithfulness and loyalty has doomed them, and I suppose it is true. I did not apply myself to finding a husband on the Marriage Mart. And when Lord Ghastly, I mean, Lord Gadley, presented a solution, I agreed; although, I resented them all for it. They placed our survival on my shoulders, but I am too weak. I couldn't save myself, much less rescue an earldom." The soft, golden light highlighted the confused anguish washing over her features. "But to be called those names, by my own mother. I wish it didn't hurt so much…"

Tristan crossed the room.

This gentle, ravishing creature was tearing him apart with her quiet sorrow. He wanted to scoop her up in his arms and soothe all the pain away.

But his own words had sliced and wounded her as well. Instead of reaching for her as he longed to do, Tristan stopped at the foot of the bed.

"You are not to blame for their shortcomings, nor their despicable character, kitten. They've done nothing to deserve a daughter such as you. You are a treasure that has been wasted on them."

"I don't know what to do, Tristan," she said simply. "Where I should go. Where I am to belong."

"You may stay here at Darby Meadows until you decide your course, Violet. As badly as I want you for my wife, I will not follow your parents' example and force you into it. My family all adore you. You know they welcome you staying here for the rest of your life."

Plucking at the bed's counterpane, a frown knitted Violet's brow. "I would be a burden."

"That's not true." Tristan could not help but come closer. She called to his soul, as deadly as a siren calling unwary sailors to a rocky shore.

"It's not a long-term solution though, is it?" Violet met his gaze, her dark amethyst-blue eyes piercing in their intensity. "Will you stay away from Darby Meadows if I remain here?"

Tristan's fists clenched. "Do not ask that of me, Violet."

"Would you do it if I begged?"

"No." The word burst out, frustration evident in the curtness of his tone.

"Then I will not stay. I cannot see you after everything that has passed between us and pretend none of it happened. Being Gadley's wife, anyone's wife, is preferable to that torment."

A roaring sound filled Tristan's head at the thought of another man touching her. "You forget the price I paid for your freedom."

Violet's head tilted. "My freedom or your accessibility, Tristan?"

Setting Carrot aside, she rose up on her knees, shaking her hair back until it tumbled like a waterfall of fire down her back. Her eyes glittered with something Tristan could not name. Resoluteness, perhaps. Angry determination. Something untamed.

She moved closer, reaching out to run a finger down the open vee of his shirt, skimming over the hollow of his throat. "How shall I begin my repayment?"

Tristan stiffened with the question. Her touch was akin to a burning flame licking across his skin, but he refused to give in to the compulsion to snatch her against him. "It is not repayment I want from you. It is that you choose what *you* want."

Celia's words echoed in his head. *She is your destiny. And you are hers.*

"What would you sacrifice for love, Tristan?" Violet whispered, moving closer still until, even on her knees, she was able to wrap her arms around his neck. "Mine is avoiding the very sight of you so my heart is not ripped to shreds again and again."

"Do not ask the same of me, Violet. I cannot fathom life without you."

Violet's eyes flared with his choice of words. "Then what are we to do? The freedom you bought me will not matter if I have it alone."

Am I listening to her? She is asking if I love her enough to keep her...

"Then I sacrifice my heart to you. You own it. You have for a long time now." Tristan's hand buried itself in her tumble of fire-sparked waves. Tugging her head back, he scrutinized the glow in her eyes. "I never realized until this moment, how your name truly suits you."

Violet caught her bottom lip in her teeth to still its trembling. "You also believe I am a weed?"

As if disturbed by the conversation, Carrot stretched like a lazy lion, gave them both a disgusted glare, and jumped from the bed to search for monsters behind the window drapes.

"Far from it, my love." Tristan pushed Violet back, following until they lay entwined on the bed.

It was then Tristan realized the truth of the matter. He loved Violet. Yes, loved her. With every fiber of his being, although he could not utter the words aloud. There was still that tiny, insecure portion of his heart demanding absolute certainty his love was returned before a declaration of such magnitude was pronounced to the world.

Looming over her, he brushed his nose against hers, breathing deeply of her delicate perfume. "You *are* a violet. Delicate and sweet, but stubborn and strong enough to withstand the storms. Spreading like an untamed wildfire into dark corners, blooming where you please. Only when it's too late does a man become aware you've invaded every nook and cranny he might possess."

Violet's eyes shimmered. Her fingers twined through his hair. "I've bloomed because of you, Tristan."

Tristan stroked Violet's cheek. "I never looked closely enough to notice your brilliant color and how you shine with such breathtaking light. You've invaded me, sweet Violet. Crept inside when I wasn't expecting it and unfurled your petals. You are the most beautiful thing I've ever seen, and I love you more than I do my own life." Taking a deep breath, he smiled at her. "That is what I should have said when you opened your door just now. It's what I should have said the night you gave your heart to me for safekeeping. Forgive me, kitten. Forgive me for not realizing sooner that I love you. I hope—I hope you will love me again someday."

Holding his breath, Tristan waited for her reaction. He'd poured his heart out and didn't know if she would mock his sentiments or...

Violet's arms wound tight around his neck. Sweet lavender and vanilla perfume teased him. The globes of her breasts pressed against his chest. She was crying, and oh, God, what should he do next? How could he fix what had hurt her so deeply?

"I love you now, Tristan. I've loved you forever. I will love you for an eternity."

His lips moved against her ear. "When you decide it's time, Violet, will you marry me?"

Tilting her head back, Violet's smile was one of sweet triumph. "I would marry you this instant if I could, Tristan Buchanan. I would give myself to you in every way you desired. I am yours."

"And my soul belongs to you, my wild Violet. Now, kiss me so I may live on it until you are completely mine in every way."

"A single kiss is not enough to survive on," Violet murmured, her lips pressing against his.

Her words penetrated the haze surrounding Tristan. She loved him. And she would become his wife as soon as he could arrange a ceremony.

Gathering Violet tight, he rocked against her, his need battering away at his common sense. He could restrain himself if he truly tried. Control his primal urges until she was legally his wife.

But Violet would not allow it.

Her hand crept into the space between their bodies. She twisted and squirmed until the buttons of his breeches were open and he throbbed in the palm of her hand.

His breath caught.

"Violet, my sweet, wild Violet. I have very little willpower when it comes to you, but I have enough to deny myself until you are legally mine."

"But I do not, Tristan. I want you now." She nipped at his throat like an untamed creature before kissing the sting away. "I want you to hold me. Kiss me. Remind me that our hearts beat together. Will you do this for me?"

And because he could deny her nothing, Tristan groaned in surrender. In a move that elicited a shocked laugh from Violet, he flipped her onto her stomach. He encouraged her to lay forward, her bottom lifted for his pleasure.

"I will do anything for you. But this, this will be done my way, Violet. Do you understand?"

Violet purred in response and arched against him, her beautifully plump rear rubbing against his groin. "Yes, Tristan. Yes. Only, do hurry. Morning will be here soon, and— *oh, God.*"

Her heated demand melted into a sigh of pleasure as Tristan's hand swept under her nightgown, smoothing over the rounded globes of her buttocks before breaching the space between her thighs. She was already wet for him, and the knowledge made him tremble with anticipation.

"First, we must rid you of this bothersome garment." Leaning back on his haunches, Tristan used both hands to rip the nightgown into two halves, the flimsy material separating like cobwebs.

Violet gasped in stunned delight, then moaned when Tristan's mouth touched her shoulder. In careful exploration, he moved slowly to the delicate length of her spine. He worshiped the satin skin until she was writhing beneath him before moving to her buttocks. He covered the pale flesh with a thousand kisses, nipping softly occasionally with his teeth and plunging a finger into the warmth of her vagina. A demanding rhythm soon had her crying for release, her flesh clenching around his fingers, begging to be filled.

Leaning back, Tristan enjoyed the view. Violet's bottom undulated before him, his fingers wedged into paradise, his thumb teasing the tiny bit of flesh in a way that would soon send her flying over the edge.

And then, because he knew from experience what it would do, he lightly slapped the pale flesh of one buttock, his hand leaving behind a pink imprint, his words a low growl.

"Come for me, Violet."

Violet choked on a sob, shattering so completely Tristan felt the shockwaves of her climax as it traveled from his hand, up his arm, and through his own body. The next instant, he guided himself into her sheath, groaning as the squeeze of her flesh nearly drove him insane.

He spanked her again, gratified when she rocked back against him with a cry of pleasure so pure and so sweet, he very nearly spilled himself inside her. Gripping her hips, he forced her movements to still, but inside her, where he was nestled so deep, he felt every quiver of her soul.

"Sweet, sweet love." He had a tenuous grip on his control, and he wanted to plunge over and over until his mind exploded in oblivion. "How have I existed without you?"

"Don't stop, Tristan," she panted, clutching handfuls of sheets and covers and even a pillow.

He wouldn't stop, but he also wouldn't take her this first time, this first time when they had declared their love for one another, without seeing her eyes.

Withdrawing from her, he turned her onto her back and sunk between her thighs once more. Yes, he still wore his shirt, his boots, even his trousers, which were currently hanging past his hips. None of that mattered as he buried himself. He could see her eyes now. See the love shining from them.

He could see her soul as surely as she could see his.

"I love you," he muttered, building her passion back up into a raging inferno in which he would happily burn for an eternity. "I will always love you."

"I know, Tristan." Lifting herself to meet him halfway, Violet kissed him. Her cheeks were wet with tears of happiness. "I love you, too."

His release was a combustible fire that swept her along with him. Violet cried out, clutching him tightly as he poured himself deep inside her.

"Thank God, you are mine, Violet." Tristan held her tight, absorbing and savoring every tremor as she surrendered every-thing to him. "Mine at last. And I'll never let you go."

EPILOGUE

*L*ongleigh Woods
  Three months later...

"UP YOU GO."

"Up?" Violet needlessly questioned. Her hands were damp, slick with nervousness. Quickly, she swiped her palms over the skirts of her riding habit.

"Yes." Tristan smiled. "Up." He bent over alongside the mare with hands cupped and ready for her booted foot.

"Up there?"

"You are repeating and stalling, love," he said with a patient sigh. "Place your foot here, and I will help you into the saddle."

Violet's face flushed pink. "What if you should put too much effort into lifting me, and I end up tossed too far? No doubt, I would land on the ground on the other side of Destiny."

Tristan straightened and took Violet's hand. He kissed it then chucked her under the chin. "Do you think I would toss my wife in such a manner? The one person in this world who means everything to me?" When she shook her head, he gave her a quick, intense kiss and bent over again. "Now, up you go. You can do it, darling. I know you can."

The mare shifted, turning her head to gaze at Violet with huge, liquid brown eyes. She really was a beautiful creature with a glossy coat the color of chocolate and a mane and tail of ebony black. And she was so very gentle, as if she understood Violet was unsure of her abilities and required a mount on her best behavior.

Celia, who had arrived a few days prior for a visit, proclaimed the mare as the very finest Willsdown Stables offered. Nicholas delivered the horse himself the week prior along with the news he was to be a father, and that his Grace, while stubbornly insisting on doing things that scared him half to death, was doing well in her first few months of pregnancy.

Swallowing past the lump of fear lodged in her throat, Violet nodded. Glancing over where Celia stood beside the paddock railing with Carrot in her arms, she called out to her new sister-in-law, "Hold that little beast carefully. He has become quite bold when I take him outside."

Carrot meowed as if in protest of being restrained, but Celia did not loosen her grip. "Do not worry. I'll hold Carrot's leash tight if I should place him on the ground."

Summoning her courage, Violet placed her foot in Tristan's palm. "Do not let me fall, Tristan."

"I will never let that happen, kitten," he replied solemnly.

The next instant, Violet was settled upon the mare's back. The ground was a staggering distance away; she held both reins and mane tightly as she gathered her bearings.

"There. You see? Not so hard, was it?" Tristan stepped away, holding the horse by the bit. "Now, I'm going to let go, and you are going to nudge Destiny with your heel. That's it, shorten your reins just a bit. Like this." He showed her what he meant, and Destiny began walking around the perimeter of the paddock.

Tristan smiled at Violet, encouragement and pride evident in his features. "You are doing so well, Violet."

Violet concentrated on the length of the reins in her hands while keeping her balance in the sidesaddle. Before she knew it, she had traveled around the paddock without having a panic attack or falling off.

A surge of confidence flooded her. She was actually riding. And she was only a little afraid of the horse Tristan had given her as a gift to celebrate their wedding just two months before. Another circle of the paddock, and she realized every time she nudged with a heel or tugged the reins, Destiny responded almost immediately.

This wasn't so difficult. And it felt almost… freeing.

She thought perhaps she liked it.

"I'm doing it, Tristan," she exclaimed in delight. "I'm riding a horse."

"Yes, you are. You look beautiful, too." Tristan watched her closely. When he thought she could handle it, he took the mare by the bit, breaking her into a slow trot by running alongside her. After a few minutes, Violet nodded that he could let go of the bridle. She and Destiny trotted several times around before Tristan had her stop.

With his hands around Violet's waist, he swung her down from the saddle, and because she was still in his arms, he whirled her in a circle until she was breathlessly laughing.

"You are a natural, Violet. A few more lessons and you'll be a better rider than me."

"I cannot wait to race you!" Celia chimed in with a giggle. "Mother and Father will be delighted to know Tristan kept his promise to teach you. They are so excited to see you ride in next year's May Day Chase."

"I really did it." Violet squeezed Tristan in a grateful embrace. "It was wonderful. I want to do it again."

"Remember, I told you once that certain activities become more enjoyable with repetition and a great deal of practice." Tristan's grin was boldly wicked as he murmured, "Perhaps we can recreate your lessons somewhere a bit more private."

"Are you still talking about riding, my lord?" Violet whispered back. "Because I'm eager to learn whatever you wish to teach me."

"Now that you are my wife, we can practice these lessons anytime we desire."

"I'd like that very much, Tristan." Her arms wrapped around his neck as she stood on tiptoes and kissed him. "I'll show you what I've learned while you tell me how incredibly brave I am and how proud you are that I did not fall."

Tristan tucked a stray curl behind her ear, his expression tender as he gazed at his new wife. "You are not just brave, kitten. You are my untamed, wild Violet. I love you to the depths of my soul, and my arms will always be here to catch you."

THE END

About April Moran

April enjoys writing both historical and new adult romance with a generous splash of heat. When not penning tales of passion, she enjoys traveling with her husband, attending rock concerts with friends, and time spent with family. Brainstorming new storylines is best done while riding her horse or during long walks with her German Shepherd. A tumbler of good whiskey helps tie all the details together and brings her characters to life.

BOOKS2READ.COM
https://books2read.com/author/april-moran/subscribe/33016

VISIT APRIL'S WEBSITE
www.aprilmoranbooks.com

SIGN UP FOR NEWSLETTER AND UPDATES
http://bit.ly/AprilMoran_BookUpdates
April Moran Book Updates

STALK APRIL EVERYWHERE

https://www.facebook.com/groups/aprilshoneybees/

https://www.bookbub.com/profile/april-moran

. . .

https://www.instagram.com/aprilmoranbooks

https://www.goodreads.com/Author-AprilMoran

https://www.pinterest.com/aprilmoranbooks

https://www.tiktok.com/authoraprilmoran

ACKNOWLEDGMENTS

It's *that* part of the book!

You know, the part where people are mentioned, readers are thanked, and professionals are praised for their hard work.

As always, I thank my readers. Especially the ones who have waited over two years for Tristan and Violet's story. There have been novels penned during this timeframe, but I've always come back to this special couple. I hope you enjoyed their sweet tale of finding true love.

Special thanks go out to my editor, Kendra G. This lady has taken my last four books and made them shine with her expertise. I am truly lucky to have her on my team. Thank you, Kendra!

Thank you to Cheryl for being the most awesome PA ever. Special thanks to Dakota at Dragonfly Ink Graphic Design for the beautiful cover.

I would never forget to thank my friends and family. Every single one of you contributes in some way to this writing career of mine. You guys make me laugh, and I cannot wait until we are having live book readings on our back porch again. James, Alyssa, Trey, Jodi, Danny, Chris, Ladyne, Gary, Karen, Dan, Deb, Lance, Winston, Cecil, and LeAnne—thanks for your support and love.

To my book world friends: I know I can always count on you to answer questions, give me a pep talk, solve a problem, or just offer sympathy when life gets in the way and gets me down. A special thank you to Michelle W. and Cindi M. Ladies, I love you.

And finally, it might be weird, but I must mention my sweet Edie girl. When our German Shepherd, Blue, passed away right before the publication of THE UNTAMED DUKE, James and I were devastated. I placed a special dedication to Blue in that book, and I still get teary-eyed when I read it. After swearing we would never get another dog because we would never love one like we loved Blue, we somehow ended up rescuing this skinny little German Shepherd. We named her Edie (after a fantastic song by The Cult.) She has brought us immeasurable joy and love and helped heal our hearts. We cannot imagine life without her now. Please remember, "Adopt. Don't Shop. Save a Rescue!"

ABOUT APRIL MORAN

April enjoys writing both historical and new adult romance with a generous splash of heat. When not penning tales of passion, she enjoys traveling with her husband, attending rock concerts with friends, and time spent with family. Brainstorming new storylines is best done while riding her horse or during long walks with her German Shepherd. A tumbler of good whiskey helps tie all the details together and brings her characters to life.

VISIT APRIL'S WEBSITE
http://www.aprilmoranbooks.com

SIGN UP FOR NEWSLETTER AND UPDATES
http://bit.ly/AprilMoran_BookUpdates

STALK APRIL EVERYWHERE
https://www.facebook.com/AuthorAprilMoran

https://www.facebook.com/groups/aprilshoneybees/

https://www.bookbub.com/profile/april-moran

https://www.instagram.com/aprilmoranbooks

https://www.goodreads.com/Author-AprilMoran

Https://www.tiktok.com/authoraprilmoran